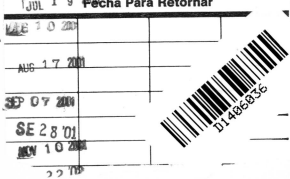

SOME DAY
TOMORROW

SOME DAY TOMORROW

NICOLAS FREELING

ST. MARTIN'S MINOTAUR NEW YORK

www.minotaurbooks.com

ISBN 0-312-26230-2

First published in Great Britain by Arcadia Books Ltd

First U.S. Edition: December 2000

10 9 8 7 6 5 4 3 2 1

'I REALLY MUST see about that one day quite soon.' People say this a lot, don't they. Everyone does, I suppose.

'I'll give you a ring to let you know, tomorrow absolutely definitely.' What you do know then is that he won't and probably never will.

There's of course a good English phrase to cover it, and that's 'Jam yesterday, and jam tomorrow.' And it never is 'Jam today'. Telephone to the doctor's office, or perhaps it should be the lawyer first, and say 'It's urgent'. Suppose then he were to say 'Come round straightaway; I can fit you in'? I'm trying to say that there has to come an end to this screwing oneself up.

Or a judge. I have a collection (I'll tell you more about this) of the old Penguin 'green jackets'. You know, the detective stories. Those were in the days when they used to hand out death penalties.

So that I know about the judge who used to put on a black cap and say 'You will be taken to the place from which you came, and from there –' He left it open, didn't say 'On Tuesday fortnight' because there were bureaucratic formalities, have to get things organized, write a letter to the hangman, Albert Pierrepoint, lived up in Yorkshire. And to be sure there was an appeal for clemency to the Home Secretary, nasty job he had.

So you said 'Tuesday fortnight, that's never.' But the only thing that's certain is that Tuesday fortnight always comes.

Perhaps, even then, the judge didn't like it. Had no choice, clear his throat, say 'I pass the only sentence the law allows'. Jam tomorrow, and this time it's for sure. Count on it. No death penalty in Holland, hasn't been for quite a time. We still have a lot of deaths, though. Everyone lives to be a hundred, thinks they'll live for ever. Tomorrow though, or Tuesday fortnight.

Make a start. I, Hubertus van Bijl, born the 20th April 1930 at Haarlem, Netherlands. Being of sound mind, isn't that what one's supposed to say? Or is it 'in full possession of my faculties' which isn't true either. Stilted rubbish. We used to have a schoolboy joke, that there was only one Haarlemse Wood but a great many Wooden Haarlemmers. We're a stiff formal people and our language is preposterous.

I've thought of a way to make this better. Put it in the third person; don't say 'I', say 'Bertus' and the narrative will be less stiff, less pompous. Less self-conscious? More human.

I'm not too sure I like it. Isn't that a way of saying 'It wasn't me; it was this other fellow.' Isn't that what they all do? Saying no, I never, it was the shadow, the Doppelgänger, the Other. The real I, the real Bertus, is a respectable, a responsible – oh this is hopeless, start again. It's all so banal and flat and dull and stupid.

Thought of something else: I'm going to do it in English. So often, even always, slightly astonished but invariably pleased – 'Bert, how come you speak English so well?' But we all do, though few as well as myself. Nothing weird about it, a Dutch businessman doesn't even think about it. Outside our own peculiar enclave nobody speaks Dutch, nobody'd want to try, it's an awkward language in the mouth and clumsy on paper, we've a great many talents but the 'taal' isn't one of them. Indeed it's widely agreed, overcoming this obstacle is a factor in our success. We're good at business, at the international dealing and handling. This, and being a small folk in this little corner jammed up between Germany and France and England. Julius Caesar remarked upon it: Batavii are awkward bastards to deal with.

Listen to the Queen – 'onze Trix' – we're proud of her. She speaks (to us) a lovely Dutch, elegant, musical. And in public as in private the easiest, natural English, or French, or

German. A shade of accent which gives a pretty colouring, but no stumble, fumble, or mumble.

I can't compare with that. Only in English. In our business, England was a speciality. I was always good at it, lived there many years, worked hard at it. I'm fairly bright. 'Our Trix' is quite a girl. Intelligent, educated, sophisticated, and so she should be. Considerable cow too on occasion but that's a Dutch remark. Born to the job and properly trained – law, economics, political science. The House of Orange hasn't always been conspicuous for grey matter, but she has it, and to spare. And *rich*, god-help-us. It was in Forbes. We always thought of the English Crown as rich. And the Oranges are ten times richer, dear-god. And she has considerable artistic talent too. I'm considerably royalist and our House was even more so.

I'm Son to Bijl en Zoon. Planten & Bloemen Handel. I've made my mind up, I'm talking about Bert. Bert was the junior, then the senior, and now the retired, 'Im Ruhestand' partner in and owner of a smallish but solid, respected house in the trade. And flowers, plants, this is as essentially Dutch as the Oranges are, and just as old and just as proud.

The original Hubertus van Bijl was this one's grandfather. Hubértus, the accent comes on the second syllable (in English, the first). Bijl, pronounce it Bile, subject of many an English joke. The 'van' is the hard bit, it's neither 'vann' nor 'von' nor 'vahn' – exactly the sort of thing which makes this language impossible.

But notice the over-meticulous fuss about exactitude. Bert is a banal and a boring type. Not though the priggish and constipated little accountant who is always the subject of crime stories.

Crime! That's a word like 'Love', so vague and loose in nature one can spend a lifetime trying to define it. My bookshelves of Penguin-crimes don't have much to do with the real thing. The newspapers are full of true-crimes right enough but they skip to something else, leave off just as it begins to be interesting. The public is thought, and taught, to have a short attention-span. There are the sensational movies and television series, filled with the most extreme violence, with all that in the human being is base, vile, evil. That is our entertainment industry.

We get, I suppose in consequence, a lot of talk about crime. It has to do with love, right enough, and when someone gets hauled into a law court, to answer for a criminal action, there will certainly be a cry set up about love withheld and love denied. True, and this becomes a whine of self-pity.

Just as much to do with too much love. Mostly a love of things, which is base, which we call greed. But short and simple words are out of fashion nowadays.

Responsibility is a longer word. We aren't taught, today, to answer for what we say and do. Self-control is thought to be bullshit. We give way, instead, to our 'pulsions'; all of which are base.

Bert attempts to be responsible. To answer. That's what all this is about. It's an answer. He isn't, I hope, quite as prissy as he appears. He was brought up at least to believe in honesty in his dealings. To be honest with oneself seems to me an essential part of this. The realities are a little harsher but a little less trite and glib than the explanations.

The old Hubertus was just a gardener, with green fingers and of course a shrewd Dutch peasant sense of business. His son Jan was still a good gardener but that much more of a businessman.

Bert, the third generation, was good enough at the business angle. Trained by Jan, who had rough-and-ready rules, but pretty good ones such as always to answer a query, or fill an order the same day. Never tomorrow, never a day too late. This made of him a hard, honest, independent, successful and even wealthy businessman. Work all day, if necessary far into the evening. He came home then, dirty and smelling of sweat, and before sitting down to a meal he washed from head to foot. Backbone, you see? One stooped all day in the plant houses. It was always humid there. Rheumatisms and lumbago were occupational hazards. The back, and the nape of the neck, had to be solid.

The green-fingers gene is still little understood. Yes, Bert went to the University to study biology. The ADN work was then in infancy but he knows a bit about genetics. The most unexpected men and women have the gift. It's quite common and it's quite often inherited but you can't breed to it. Like faith-healing or second-sight, or even water-divining. Heredity or not, Bert didn't have it. I'd almost think the seeds of the decline were sown there.

What everyone does know, and it's not just genetics, is the rise and fall of the bourgeois class. They climb the social pyramid, and often in the third generation they slip back again. In the Trade everyone knew this much too about genetics, long before Mr Crick and his spiral – you can breed for the decorative but you lose robustness. Roses are the simple example. The flashy, colourful hybrids are the ones who go and die on you. Word of common sense to any of you who happen to be suburban gardeners. Buy the old varieties, with as much as may be of the sturdy old stock in them. You can breed for colour, for shape, for the number of petals. For scent, for a longer stem, for less thorns, for resistance to disease or parasites. These will win prizes in shows. Sell well, make lots of money. Set a limit to your desire. That thorny old bugger in somebody's hedge which is always thick with buds and nobody knows what-the-hell it is – take a cutting from that. Holds good for everything, right down to vines. When I'm in France I like to talk to the vigneron who has understood that less means more, and traditional old methods – and no bloody chemicals – give him the good juice.

I beg your pardon for the heated parenthesis. This rambling, Jan would have said and did, is a bad sign.

Jan felt himself a coarse and ignorant man. So Bert had to be educated, go to the lycée, the Gymnasium in Haarlem, get his baccalaureate, go on to the University in Amsterdam (from us, a thirty-minute tram ride and fifteen more on the bus). A goodish degree, languages (whose genetics have always fascinated me) and Botany, Horticultural Sciences. Bert can defend himself in German and in French, has a good smattering of Spanish and Italian (South America is important to us growers). Dictionaries remain one of his foremost interests, won't say 'hobby'. Grandfather, whom he can recall, thought the boy not very bright. Useful in London, where he spent many years of his youth, as our agent on the spot, to buy and sell and exchange and learn. And then back in Holland...

We are three generations (before that it becomes vague) of Zandvoorters. Haarlem is close to the sea. Along and behind the coastline, protecting us from the storms and the high tides which used to invade us, lies a broad stretch of sand dunes. Behind this again, between Haarlem and Leiden, is a streak, quite short and narrow, of (for us, in the Trade) the most famous land in the world, whose geology of soil and sand and shell and turf – but you can read about this in any guidebook to the tulip-land. It is a great tourist attraction. On the coast are a few villages. Zandvoort is one, not quite at the centre of the world but for us who live there as near as makes no matter.

Willy came in. She wouldn't, while I am in here, unless she had a good reason – or one she's sure I'll listen to.

'Huub.' I do so wish she wouldn't call me that. She really doesn't want to irritate me, while knowing perfectly that I detest it. 'There are some policemen asking to see you, so I thought I'd better...' True that one is always curious even if it's the bicycle licence. As well always to be polite to them. Please-do–sit-down. Ho, something speedier than the local constabulary.

'Sergeant Bout from the Serious Crimes Bureau and this is Detective Dycksma.' Thinnish, smallish, ears which stick out, quick little greeny-snot eyes.

6

'We're making a house-to-house enquiry on account of a girl missing, I dare say you heard, she lived close by, I'm sorry to say we've found her, dead, and the findings point to homicide.' Willy, if one were suddenly to jump out at her, might utter a squawk. Not now. Looks disapproving.

'With your permission –' (or without, no doubt) 'I ask a few questions, brief, and Mr Dee here takes it down.' (Big smile, shorthand pad.) 'Routine, asking everyone in the street same thing. Not to be in the least bothered, apologize for disturbing you, and for any personal nature questioning might seem to have.' A practised patter. 'Is that clear? Do you have any objection?

'Very well then, need only say if you – we should be so lucky – turn-out-possess information relevant then Mr Dee types that up, comes round show-it-you, statement, you sign if you agree it's accurate, okay still so far?

'Right then, here's a photo supplied by her family, quite recent, name of Carla Zomerlust, lived along the road here, twenty years old, student at the university, d'you know her at all?'

'The face I think is familiar but I don't know her.'

'Lovely, perfect answer, short and lucid, easier for my friend here. Let's just check, de Heer van Bijl, given name Hubertus – age? Profession? Retirement, good, that, observant witnesses – now familiar how?' Snapshooting, he'll be good at that.

'Couldn't say. Like any neighbour I suppose, seen her in the street, shops maybe.'

'Caught your eye, like? How, would you suppose? Pretty girl?'

'Yes, perhaps, I don't recall in particular.'

'Appearance, manner? Attractive.'

'I doubt it. There are lots of young girls and they all look the same. You know – jeans, long hair.'

'Never spoke to her?'

'I don't think so . . . Did she have a dog?'

'Very good. That's her, took it out often.'

'Bouncy sort of woolly dog. I think I noticed that better than the girl.'

'Know the family at all – mother, father, little brother?'

'Means nothing I'm afraid. Should I?'

'Not particular, couldn't say when you-saw-her-last?' Blank. 'How about Wednesday evening?' Still blank.

'What else happened on Wednesday evening?' I wondered.

'It was raining.' Dutch giggles all round. 'Not hard, bit of a drizzle.'

'Quite right. I went out, I walk every day, rain doesn't bother me unless there's a lot of wind. Which hereabout there often is.'

'Great. So did she go out? – point is, she didn't come back. Did you perhaps see her then?'

'Not that I'd notice or remember.'

'Give me a rough idea of where you went, can you? Or even not so rough.'

'Much as usual, a routine with me. Round the outside of the village, Brederodestraat, along the dunes there –'

'Go into the dunes, at all?'

'No, skirting along, up to the Zuiderbad corner and back along the seafront.'

'Nobody walking a dog?'

'I wonder. There often is a young woman with a dog, there by the car-park, but I couldn't be sure.'

'Good because we've seen that young woman and she remembers you, sees you often.'

'I didn't know she found me memorable.'

'Point is, girl went out without the dog. Where'd she go then?'

'There, I'm afraid, I might have crossed her if that was her path, but it's left no memory.'

'Observant, ordinarily? In your own estimation? We feel pretty sure she did take that path.'

'Yes, I think. But I can be absent-minded too.'

'Would you have noticed, d'you think, if she'd been with somebody?'

'You mean, because she was usually alone? Maybe. A couple, it doesn't leave an impression, much.'

Suddenly aiming the eye at Willy – 'What about you, Mevrouw?'

'I think much the same,' timidly. 'As my man, I mean. I know her vaguely from the street. In the check-out at the supermarket? One gives a nod and a smile but I don't think we ever exchanged a word. I've a fair memory, for faces.'

'Right, right,' rather as though this confirmed something known or suspected. Typical police manner, thought Bert. 'Ever notice her in the company of other – boyfriend or – no? The point' (he was fond of this phrase) 'is that she was a shy, withdrawn sort. No known, ticketed –'

'Was she raped?' asked Willy. 'I don't recollect the paper saying.'

'Didn't say, didn't know. I'll tell you the truth. Doctor says no; intacta. Now I say, what's tacta? She'd been what the paper calls interfered with.'

'Oh dear.'

'You're sensible people. She was strangled, from the back and couldn't fight much. Clothing disarranged, as the paper calls it, what you or I call knickers pulled down. Next question, no, not menstruating.' Being brutal deliberately. 'Dirtied herself. What does that convey to you? Meneer?'

'I'd imagine a stranger accosted her.'

'What would she be doing in the dunes? Mevrouw?'

'I don't picture, I prefer not to think.'

'Quite so. Well that's it for now.'

'Now?' asked Bert mildly.

'We've only just begun. Other things may come to light, more to ask. For now, I've a hundred households, five minutes for each and makes a long day. Think of anything, here's the number to ring.'

*

These things happen. Even, no, also, in Zandvoort. I feel upset, as who wouldn't? The police don't perturb me; only doing their job. The citizen has to co-operate. A great many don't and won't. Here – still – most will. We share shock, and pain. For a family a tragic loss, and so brutal. For ourselves. The fabric of our being. Not much left of that, in a town. But in my village, virtually in our street, something like this tears the fabric. I feel shame and sorrow for that. I'm sorry for the girl too, of course. Along my route too. Since I take this path very often. For all I know, within my hours. Seems they found her only a day later, combing out the dunes.

Doesn't sound very competent? No, come on, they check the normal explanations first, and then accidents, and then an enormous number of these youngsters run away. Not for long maybe: while their money holds out. Start thinking about a crime next day, at best.

And then, I know how tricky that terrain is. Easy to lose and hard to find. Every sand dune looks just like the next. Take some time to mobilize a troop, to search. From what one hears she was some way inside. I don't know how sorry one should be for these girls. Shy and withdrawn? Brazen sluts most of them, ask for trouble. One presumes this is why they look near home. Someone she knew. Wouldn't talk to strangers. Well, I dare say I'm not adding anything to police thinking, suggesting that the close circle is likeliest. Family, friends, neighbours. She must have been confident. On a drizzly evening you don't take a walk in the dunes with just anyone.

That woman with the dog saw me, knows me. I wouldn't know where she lived, let alone her name. Zandvoort – irritating place and to anyone who's seen a bit of the world doubly, Dutchly so. Narrow, provincial – parochial and puffed with imagined importance. But I love it. Known and loved it all my life. Mine, me. I'm one of the few, the real natives, as Willy for instance isn't and couldn't be. A lot have left and a lot have died. In a township of ten thousand how many were born here? In the thirties one 'knew everybody'. One didn't of course but there were no big blocks then, and no creeping suburb. In winter the place was small, and highly self-contained. We still talk about 'the dorp' but it really was a village then.

Bert lives in one of the earliest apartment blocks built here. Back in the fifties, would have been. There was only the building along the seafront, and that only in the centre, where the north and south boulevards join, and what an architectural disaster that had been. This was a step inland, on an island site where three roads meet. Draughty it was thought, nobody wanted them. Got a good buy. Well built, solid, proper walls and insulation. Generously drawn, with plenty of space, roomy even to the balconies and one is never conscious of the neighbours. They don't build like that now! Plumbing which seems old-fashioned but was installed by real craftsmen and has never given trouble. Comfort. Bought on good, easy terms and long paid-for (think of mortgages now . . .) No regrets, none whatever. The 'quarter' is all small, family houses still: noise and traffic have never been problems. Along the street is the water-tower. Bert remembers the old one, dynamited like all the buildings here along, by the Germans in the war. This was part of their 'Westwall'. Emptied of all occupants and fortified. As though the Americans and the English would have crossed the North Sea, to invade. Such a pity. Our beautiful seafront, all destroyed.

A good-sized flat. Bert has a workroom, a 'den' Willy calls it. Used to be one of the girls' rooms. The other is now a spare, a guest-room which Willy keeps impeccable. 'Netjes' is the Dutch word. Net like a net price, clean, clear of all encumbrance. The girls are long grown up and gone. Here in his personal fortress Bert allows no more than Willy's vacuum cleaner and her endless complaining while pushing the thing. No tidying allowed. Here, also, Bert has (under glass) his collection of old green 'crime' Penguins.

Under glass, that's a trade word. Flowers are under, books are behind glass. Not often I make a mistake in English. One has to keep them carefully. Even so the cheap paper they were printed on goes the colour of a cheap cigar. Still a vivid, a living reminder of good days in England, in the fifties, thought of now with a warm, a happy feel. Prehistoric, when one was young and energy unbounded. Defunct now, Vaughns, big name then in the London flower markets, Ralph still the managing director and very much so. Good joke on the peculiarities, the Englishness, writing it so and saying 'Rafe Vawn', he'd thought he knew how to speak this language and had had to learn fast, keep your wits about you, a packer or a van-man speaking Cockney, that was like another and special 'trade' language. Ralph grinning and saying 'You're picking up the accent, you mustn't do that.'

Offices in Covent Garden. What they called the Shop out in Croxley Green and 'the Glass' in Rickmansworth. Boarding with Mrs Davis. The old brown 'Metropolitan' train, so flavourfully Sherlock-Holmes and not just because it ran in to 'Baker Street' (yes and went on to Aldgate; even now he could remember the names of all the stops and did it as a memory exercise, Finchley Road and Queens Park, Harrow-on-the-Hill and Neasden...)

The first months, lonely yes and homesick, it was then he'd started, 'Trents Last Case' and 'The Cask'. Freeman Wills Crofts, marvellously English (say the name now and would anyone know what you were talking about?).

I am perfectly aware that this is unforgivably self-indulgent, and don't care. Important to me. Bought two, sometimes three, in a week, to read in bed at Davises. The Dutch-laddy wasn't paid much, couldn't afford a night out in the West End often. Still rarer the train from Liverpool Street, the night ferry, the Welkom Thuis sign in Hoek van Holland and the streets of Maassluis saying yes, you're home. He'd gone on building up the bookshelf ('You're getting quite an expert' said kind Mrs Davis) and gone on for years, hunting in second-hand shops anywhere, everywhere; New York and Boston and San Francisco too, for the early ones, the pre-war. A pretty good collection it is now. No doubt *The Unpleasantness at the Bellona Club* or *The Rasp* would be un-readable now. There was no television then. England...

There was Verity. Fair-haired and very English, lived up Warwick Avenue way, an extraordinary dump. Poor, like him. Came out on the train one hot summer evening, a fantasy, went on, a stop to Watford-Met, she took his arm outside the station whispering 'I've no knickers on. Took them off in the Ladies-Only.' Whipped her into Cassiobury Park right opposite in the summer twilight to lift her skirt. Fair, marvellously soft fine pubic hair and 'doing a Watford' (even in Warwick Avenue) became a comic phrase. A beer in Swiss Cottage, a walk along the canal at Blomfield Road – I have good London memories. 'Chimes at midnight' Ralph called it; Justice Shallow; I used to go to theatres too. Don't tell me none of this is relevant.

Still, if one were to ... there have been more girls. Stick to essentials, because Willy – Bert married Willy; stick to that. This was – and is – the most important, the central, the absolute basic. Do justice here. Make no mistake. She was, is, his wife, an outstandingly good wife. An outstanding woman. Probably there are ten million Dutch women just like her. But not indistinguishable from this great mob, the monstrous regiment. She's unique. So are we all of course. No flower is quite like the next flower. Not when you know how to look.

This is my home, a North Sea village, smelling of sea and sand. Even our dust is half sand. Willy dusts, Bert sneezes and she says 'Bless You'. A perfectly conventional Dutch woman, of her generation and her impeccable bourgeois background.

A couple of important points to make, here. First is that Willy is my wife and entitled to my loyalty, her privacy, and the respect of all comers. A wife isn't just a woman you can scrub off. She's dyed in the wool. For instance she's constant, faithful, whatever it's called, could never be anything else and that's the most absolute of certainties, that she gives her word and keeps it. She can be the most awful liar; not in this. It could be thought ridiculous and it is thought laughable. Terribly old-fashioned to respect one's wife.

So – second point – I'm not talking about her the way I would about Verity (our affair lasted perhaps a twelvemonth). So that there was a difficult decision to make, here. If I am to talk about Bert, to try and understand, then I have also to talk about Willy as though she were someone else. I'm invading everyone's privacy, and my own to begin with. This – I hope – she will never know about and what she does not know cannot hurt her.

Or, in a plain simple phrase, one tries to keep faith.

This goes back a long way. We're of old stock, both, and it throws true. Calvinist Dutch puritanism? Some truth in that for it's strong, in us both, but 'virtue' isn't a birthright. There are uncomplicated beliefs like 'Honour your parents', and others are more complicated. In Bert and Willy's world they marry like the wild geese, who mate for life. Separations or desertions were not unheard-of but they were like dishonest business practise. Sand in the sugar, my grandfather would have called it. Letting us all down, a rip in the fabric. 'Fit only for grocers' – he was a narrow old man – 'fit only for the French.' Like Uncle Penstemon, whom he much resembled, he would say of a cheap wine 'Grocers' sherry I expect.' An adultery – which happened – would have to be patched, and however carefully fitted, sewn with the tiniest stitches, showed. The rip in the fabric was there.

Bert's grandfather, I have said, was 'only a gardener'. At home or at work he expected and endured only the best. A wheelbarrow would be hand-made by a craftsman who was also a crony of his. A knife or sickle that was not of the finest steel known would be thrown aside as worthless. His suits were made by the best tailor in Amsterdam and of the very best West-of-England cloths, and his boots ... If one bought a bottle of wine (for an anniversary) it followed that it came from the city's oldest-established wine merchant. He would eat dry bread rather than accept margarine. Jan, his son, was the same.

Willy came out of 'the interior', the villages between Haarlem and Leiden – Bennebroek or Lisse, 'growers' land' and a growers' family. Indeed they looked down rather on us Zandvoorters, but it was thought a good marriage. Her name of course is Wilhelmina, named for the old Queen, frightful old woman (word also meaning 'inspires fear'), upright, of immense character.

Do not think that England has the monopoly of pederasts, fly-by-nights, royal sluts, princes with their hand up the kitchen-maid's skirt. We have plenty. Indeed a journalist of long experience once said to me 'The House of Orange has a light thigh'. So it has and so has the entire country. Holland has changed, fundamentally over the fifty post-war years. The House of 'van Bijl and Son' no longer exists. This is one of Bert's greatest difficulties, that the world in which he was brought up has no meaning, no relevance, no purpose in today's Netherlands.

Willy is tall, she's one metre eighty, six-foot by English measure. Very slim, she always was and has never dried out. The Dutch women are big-boned, and many are this height and well over, basketball giantesses. 'The Grenadiers'. Willy has kept her figure, deep of breast and a boy's behind. Her long horsy face never pretty, but she had and has distinction of feature and carriage. She does not walk bent over with her arse stuck out, like so many English women. Her voice is not high and squeaky. She is not like the Zandvoorters. Living by the sea, in the sand, they are tanned like the Cheyennes, with the characteristic deep lines around the eye and the navy-blue eyes blaze brilliantly. Willy's skin is white, with blue veins showing on her breasts, inside her thighs. She will never tan, hates the sun, and her eyes are Dresden-blue.

(Any grower, however insensitive, can tell you that there are a thousand shades of blue, from the indigo and ultramarine through the endless variations, reddish, the greens, the yellows – let alone blacks and whites – down to the palest washed forget-not.) We growers are experts in blues. Petrol, peacock, turquoise. Breeding a blue rose, which would not disintegrate at the first shower of rain, was for long the growers' ruling fantasy. Never mind the ignorant tale of Monsieur Dumas, we got the black tulip a hundred years ago, but the truly green or genuine cobalt rose is an illusion. Stick, I repeat, to the old, pure, unadulterous stocks, and of these is Willy. It's nothing in the least extraordinary. Millions like her under every sky. And my respect, my admiration, don't have to mean that I would always agree, approve her beliefs. Less still echo them. What I like is that she has beliefs, holds them against all comers. To think it possible I may be wrong in some of my own, to suggest that the world changes, and we with it, over a hundred years, is simply to anger her. It would imply that she might be wrong, which wouldn't do.

Very Dutch. It makes her sound like the conventional 'silly woman' or stupid even. She's neither. But 'as the horse goes, so goes the wagon', which sounds like Father Cats, a Dutch worthy given to these sententious aphorisms. We also like clichés which rhyme, so that if you were to say 'Red sky in the morning' you could count on Willy to answer 'Shepherd take warning' instantly and unthinking.

This all must appear in contradiction to another convention now widely held, that Holland is a place of the most unbridled behaviour, swarming with brothels and marijuana on open sale in every café. Abortions and euthanasia raging unchecked. Rest assured that our reputation for tolerant laxism is as misleading as the extremes of conservative rigidity. Partly the fault of Amsterdam, which tourists think of as a raging Sodom. It's true that the Amsterdammers are a cross-grained folk who have always liked to think of themselves as being in contrast – and opposition – to the rest of Holland.

We are all of us a cross-grained folk. Our outstanding characteristic is to be forever and bitterly quarrelling among ourselves. Small as the place is, uniform though it appears. The differences between north and south are enormous. Between the sea-people and the inland river-people. Between old and young? – not as much as you might think. But we're all pigheaded and we all detest each other.

The differences between Willy and Bert. They came from a similar background. Physically too they seem well suited. Out of the same mould, pretty much. Tall, lanky. Or up to quite recently. I have said that Willy has not dried out, has not faded. This last year she begins to take on the looks of a flower pressed in an album. To some extent, it's her keep-fit mania, no fat and a lot of muscle. Womens' hormones, after sixty and she is well past that, get out of balance and they run either to fat or this extreme thinness. All that sport too. One remembers the fashion for exercising of a few years back; can you recall 'aerobics' and the ubiquitous Miss Fonda? Women in leotards, all sorts and ages, the beanpoles and the little Humpty-Dumpties, limbering and stretching. Up! – high – ever so high! Down again, ladies, keep the rhythm, stay with the music. At sixty-five Willy with the heart and lungs of a girl of twenty was still playing basketball. And for all I know still does. To the gym daily, bicycling in the track suit, comes home and has another long shower, turning it to cold at the end and leaping about with loud gasps. Oh well, does her a lot of good.

Bert isn't at all like this. God, Willy will even watch football on television, cheer for Ajax.

And yet Bert up to a year ago . . . was quite a good-looking chap. Distinguished at least, silver hair, a long tanned clean-shaven face – you know, standing on a yacht to advertise wristwatches? Some quite young girls are often attracted. All gone and inside a twelvemonth. Something went badly wrong with the hormones there. Bert has become *heavy*.

Even in the shoulders, the face. And that's not a spare tyre, a little pot. That's a *belly*. Says Willy unpleasantly, obsessed as she is with waistlines, that's beer, cigars, and no exercise. Rubbish, says Bert. Leads a healthy life, eats very moderately (likes his food, though), walks his five kilometres daily, since retirement no more than two to three beers of a morning, and has cut down on cigars; the way these doctors keep yacking, one starts feeling guilty. Damn it, themselves they're all smoking their heads off.

Hormones! Within this last year Bert has had a few more disagreeable shocks. But that was after – have patience please, I'm still trying to understand as well as to come to terms with it. 'Retirement' is notoriously a time of problems for a man accustomed to being active.

At home of course now are only the two of us. We have two daughters long since grown up. Married women with children. They are, conventionally enough, fond of their father. We live on good terms. I cannot say I am close to either. Nor to their husbands. We're polite to one another.

Nathalie and Stephanie, in Dutch (we have a habit of abbreviating names) Nat 'n' Steff. They went to the best schools to be found, pleasant and pretty girls, just that – to be bleak – they weren't bright enough for their own or my ambitions. Both wanted to read medicine at the university, qualify as doctors. The selection is quite rightly merciless, or the whole of Holland would be practising medicine. They slipped sideways into the numerous professions attractive to the rejects. Nat is a dispenser in pharmacy, I'm vague about what exactly her diploma entitles her to do. Works in Utrecht, behind the counter, in Dutch the word 'apothecary-assistant' has quite an important ring to it. Starched white coat, badge on the bos, but still spends most of the day dishing out contraceptives. Steff is a nurse, I think a good one, specialized. A calm, concentrated girl. Gynaecological unit, difficult deliveries and points-north, in the hospital in Amstelveen. Both have two children of their own. This is 'modern' Holland.

Useful and valuable, I mustn't sound for a moment diminishing, nor do I seek to denigrate.

Bert – it's perhaps odd? One can be a Hubert, a Herbert, an Albert. In England too one will be a Bert. But a Robert becomes a Rob or a Bob but never a – there was a Mr Brecht, name of Berthold, German playwright, poet – both maybe but I should like to know, was he also a Bert? Names are important and one fits into them, so that this horrible Dutch habit of mutilating them...

So that Lalage – her damned parents give her this name but Lallie or even Lal is what you are when you live in Zandvoort. One of the growers in the Club called his daughter Apollonia. He thought maybe that this had a suitably Linnaean flavour to it. (The Latin names Linnaeus gave to plants are universal still in the trade.) Good God, said Bert, it's a mineral water. Polly the girl became at once and has never been anything else.

But he liked this. La-la-jay – perhaps it's a good name for an obsession. Not altogether easy to understand Bert's telling of this story. Physiology at the bottom of it. Bert had a trouble brewing that he did not then know about, which would play jokes with his hormones.

The psychology, of the robust man (as he still was) in late middle life? We'll leave Willy out of this but they've slept apart for quite some time. Nathalie's doing; Willy always listens to what the girls choose to tell her about 'life' and ninety per cent of it is feminist bullshit. One can just about mention the fact that Bert was short on love, or anyhow on sex; they get confused. Fuck that Nathalie, only it would be incest, as well as vicious.

And the village plays a role. Like this girl Carla the police are asking about, Lalage is 'a neighbour'. Not strictly speaking since the village isn't that small. Now Lal's father is an Engineer-something, and the mother too works in some computer system thingy. It's of no real consequence to know. Well-paid and Lal is an only child. You'd expect them to live in bourgeois comfort, say in the Prinzessen quarter.

At least in their own estimation, they do better. In the oldest part of the village there are still a few of the fishers' cottages remaining. Primitively low and cramped, an outside tap and an earth toilet. The Ur-Zandvoort of my childhood. I felt some sentimental attachment, as one will to old photos of the 1900s, of fishwives in long skirts carrying their baskets to market, through the dunes to Haarlem. The dog carts were I think a feature of Scheveningen, just down the coast; the distance to The Hague is the same. When, after the war, so much had to be rebuilt, there was a move to get rid of these huddled little houses. The well-nourished Dutch of today could barely stand upright inside them. Bert's grandfather had built for himself a proper house, with two stories, on a foundation, and here on the Brederodestraat, facing the dunes on the inside edge of the village, Bert was born.

Belatedly, it was decided to keep what was left; nostalgia, and folklore, but I too approved. So little of the old dorp remains. Inevitably the cottages acquired a snobbish cachet. Knock two together, tart them up inside, bathrooms and a lantern over the entry, you've a fashionable residence. Low ceilings and no damp course, but it's our patrimony, a national heritage, and thereby Smart. To live in the Pakveldstraat is here grander than the Julianaweg. Exactly like the English buying, at a gigantic price, a shitty little cottage in a Cotswold village. This has to be mentioned since it throws light on Lalage's family background. Arriviste, show-off, exactly what you'd expect of the nouveaux-riches. Bert feels himself 'a cut above' and one can hardly blame him. These inverted snobberies are much akin to a few of the old roses we still keep on catalogues. 'Nevada' and 'Marguerite Hilling'; not much good and liable to the black spot, but still sold to people like Lalage's parents, who also buy old portrait photographs, have them framed in imitations of gilded Victorian stucco, hang them round a chimneypiece and tell people that these are their ancestors. Their daughters, as will be seen, react in turn, and violently, against such idiotic fantasies. Bert has never met the Engineer. The title, like Doctor, is much used in Holland as a prefix in formal address. You'll see letters addressed to 'Ir. Jansen' the way one would write to 'Dr. Simpson'. I have written such letters myself now and then. 'You say you've the honour to send me a note of your honorarium: I call it your bill, and tell you straightout it's inflated by at least fifty per cent. Please adjust this.' That would be – is – more characteristically Dutch behaviour. The only child, Lalage. In my memory, if pretty dim, is a song played on a lot of gramophones there around 1939.

'Mother, may I go out dancing?'

'Yes my darling daughter.' Only fair to say that Lally was not very heedful of these polite constraints and convictions.

Bert, one must say, doesn't always sleep well. Has discovered a well-known phenomenon: that the petty sayings and doings of one's childhood are vivid. What happened last week, which is probably last month already, is fast becoming a blur. If only one had diaries for those far-gone days, wouldn't it be interesting – but at night, in the dark, it's as though one pulled out a telescope which, magically reaching through wastes of time and space, sweeps one's own personal Milky Way. It will focus arbitrarily upon the haze and sudden stars appear, dancing and glittering. It has a nasty trick, of summoning disagreeable memories. Zooms, to a close-up. Time and space are gone altogether and one is reliving this very instant a moment of fear and joy. Or as now, a silly song, a tune played on a gramophone record; by who? Where? Lalage was not even born. Her parents weren't even born.

But if a young man were to start with things he-didn't-oughter, Mamma appears to believe that if you say No no no, the darling daughter would bear that in mind. Which goes to show that children haven't changed much. We weren't very impressed by stern injunctions of the sort, either.

Bert met Lalage where everyone in Zandvoort meets everyone else, in 'Albert Heijn'; in English it would be
Sainsbury's, a place where one falls into casual conversation
with strangers. Whether at the check-out, 'I'm sorry, I think
you're in front of me actually' – or while gazing at fruit,
'What are these West Indian things, have you tried them
out?' Bert, who shops often because he often cooks, is in fact
a better cook than Willy, is used to these housewifely ex-
changes, was not disconcerted. The schoolgirl, clutching a
piece of paper on which Ma had written it all down before
rushing to work, was hovering dubiously over the meat.

'It says steak but half these things say steak, and I don't
know one sort from another.' Bert amused, offered helpful
suggestions. 'What else have you got on your list? We might
be deduce from that.' Deep-freeze frites, from which yes, one
could conclude an unimaginative meal of steak and chips.
'How much do you think I should take?' Nice piece of rump.

Inside three minutes he knew a lot about her. Three persons, and a housewife in a hurry. They'd only had a sandwich at lunchtime. 'I've left it awfully late.' Green salad and
mayonnaise in a tube. 'It isn't the money that worries me.'
'Thanks very much – god, I must fly.' This is modern
Holland. The old family pattern is still strong in this country,
where fewer women go out to work, but there are still a lot,
and more and more they look for something fast and easy,
never mind the price, but we've had take-out three times
running and Dad complains he never gets a proper meal.
Not much to deduce from the girl's clothes, the jeans and
pullover of every teenager. Expensive though; people spend it
like water. She was getting on her bike when he came out,
gave him a friendly wave.

I suppose, thinks Bert, that I belong to a pattern of living
which didn't change much, traditional, would now appear
weirdly antiquated. To a girl like that I'd seem a hundred
years old. Willy, too: have we really stuck so fast, in our
accustomed tram lines? Shows up abruptly, in our eating

habits, amid much else. Even when by any standards comfortably off we held, hold even now, to the frugal ways of an earlier Holland; of our upbringing which really was 'pre-war'.

Asked what they had eaten, or were about to eat, we named the vegetable: spinach we'd say, beetroot. Meat was a sideline, one didn't have much, and then mostly stew, for the gravy to put on the potatoes. Our dessert was mostly milk-pudding, and we had two biscuits mid-morning with a cup of coffee. A bit of steak or chicken was for Sundays, and on somebody's birthday one went to the pâtisserie to buy cake. As a race we were very well nourished, healthy, good bones and teeth. The evening 'bread' meal was a slice or so of sausage, cut thin, the same of cheese, bit of jam to finish, and always margarine because butter was expensive. And the Queen ate no differently. Willy's family, wealthier than ours, was just the same.

Jan had aristocratic tastes. Saturdays, the glass of wine and the woman sent to the butcher for a hundred grams of larded liver or ham; boiled egg for breakfast and a better class of koekje (the American word is 'cookie' – but not in English). Yes, we were 'frugal'. Greed was punished – Calvinist they'd call it now.

What difference is there, today? Good ol' Albert Heijn is simply overflowing with the things we've learned to enjoy in other countries (Herrgott, the awful food I remember but Sainsbury too has got frightfully sophisticated). We like – Willy too – the bit of French cheese, the nice Italian rice or spaghetti dish, a wing of duck and yes a proper piece of steak if one can get it . . . We've got rather dainty as we grow older.

What we won't touch are the ready-mades, just warm it up in the microwave, the hamburgers from MacDo (yes, Bert does know how to make a real Hamburg-steak), the Quiksnaks, the never-ending fried whatnots that make the street stink so, the ghastly submarine sandwich dripping with aerosoled goo, the horrible dried out 'frites'. One of Bert's greatest prides is around once a month to make real

Belgian Pont-Neufs. Thick. Really crisp on the outside while juicy within. It takes every meticulous habit and organizational talent he has; the exact temperature for the initial cooking and the exact turn-high for 'the dip': nobody knows it but this is 'haute cuisine' as delicate as a soufflé. Impossible to buy them, any more than a genuine German curry-wurst which every filthy Imbiss sells and always vile ... We the Dutch get as fat and sloppy and disgustingly obese as everyone does – even in China now.

But Bert, I'm glad to say, has a figure as slim – well, nearly – as when he was twenty, and without those awful basketball games of Willy's (but her weight is hers at eighteen, and she's right to be proud of it).

Rather boastful, Bert? Oh yes, I've noticed. Not that I mind; it's legitimate, or anyhow harmless. Good amateur cooks aren't exactly a rarity, but are infrequent enough for this talent, for that I suppose it is, to be a source of pride. Like gardening? Need to have the feel for it.

He'd passed a test! One of his terrors is of getting old and smelling bad. There are too many old men with long brown teeth whose digestive processes are ill-managed. Suits overdue at the cleaners, a second-day shirt and socks. Even if they didn't breathe you'd be in bad company. There are also antique shibboleths inherited from Jan, who held that hair-oil or suede shoes were the sure sign of a sissy.

Now he'd been close-up, to a young girl who showed no aversion to the proximity. A clean and healthy, as well as pleasantly nubile young female. Strappingly Dutch. They scarcely exist now, the Zandvoort girls of his childhood, the red-brown tan of wind on them. Sun-puckered eyes, hard sand-scoured body. The bourgeois girls of today are a good imitation, because of spending so much time on the beach. This one had had the bleached hair, the long segments of shin and thigh. Muscular pectorals; he'd seen down her shirt. Well-spoken too, no hint of the dreadful nasal whine, common in Holland, jeered at by the Amsterdammers.

Pleasant manner, neither flirtatious nor touch-me-not. Today's girls are free of all that. It seemed such a long time since he'd spoken to one.

I don't think, to be fair, you could call Bert shy, prim, withdrawn. Certainly no provincial; the Trade is internationalized and extremely sophisticated. Simply, there are no girls of this age-group within his circle. His daughters are too old, his grandchildren too young. Willy's cronies are all women past fifty. Where would Bert exchange even a word with a young woman, outside waitresses or shop-girls? Now that he's retired he hasn't even a secretary. On the beach? Bert loathes the beach. Save on still days in winter, when the tide is out.

To my mind, it's that particular generation-gap one began to notice in the sixties, and Bert was already middle-aged by then, wrapped up in his work and starting a family. The beginnings of feminism, women's equality stuff, a lot we now take for granted. The pill, I suppose, largely. Which came too late for my age group; that is a fact in a sea of suppositions. One could plead some of these arguments in a court of law. But would it be a court of criminal law? Because that is also a court of moral law. I must not theorize, as Sherlock Holmes says, ahead of my data.

When we all smoked cigars; it's from then I date the big change. That was the old Holland, of certainties and securities. The greengrocer, even, served you with a cigar in his face: the hygiene rules applied – as I recall – only to those handling meat or fish. It's hard to be sure but I feel convinced that the man on the herring cart (that very Dutch phenomenon) or the cheese stall had also, permanently, a cigar going. In the tram, the train, was always that smell. We'd say now stale, acrid, horrible. It wouldn't have occurred then, to anyone, to notice. Let alone comment. They were dreadful cigars mostly; cheap Sumatras. 'Bourgeois' surroundings, the house of a doctor or lawyer, say, or an expensive restaurant, would be signalled by the better quality.

The grandest by Cubans. If I insist upon the details it is that you should realize. As with scented flowers, add a dimension to the picture. The picture for visitors (there were few tourists then) was then as now the crude cliché; windmills, tulips, and the Volendamse fisher in his traditional wide baggy trousers and wooden 'klompen' shoes. He had also a cigar in his mouth...

Try now to picture the interiors, of which traces will persist. Heavy, crowded rooms, with as now a great many lamps and potted plants; a lot of polished wood and brass; then a mass of curtains and cushions in heavy, hairy materials, plush and velvet. Now picture the busy energetic women, Mevrouw and her maid, forever dusting, shaking, airing with the windows wide open but never – even with the spring cleaning which lasted a week – getting the cigar smell out of the furniture.

To finish, a glimpse of Jan, my father. In a rare moment of leisure, so that there is the gold watch-chain across the waistcoat, the stiffish collar attached by brass studs, the seal ring on the powerful skilful hand which picks up a shallow, fragile coffee cup, the glasses on his nose with which he read the paper. And a cigar in a short amber holder; many men disliked the stub moistened by saliva, just as there were many who preferred it that way.

Now picture myself, Bert if you wish, for at this age there is little difference between us. I am the heir to a tidy, flourishing business, but (saving the years in England) treated as any other worker in the trade and given a small allowance instead of pay. Except on Sundays I am in corduroys, and when outside in wooden shoes. They were perfectly comfortable and going in to the house one left them on the doorstep. We all did, even women. Jan's leather boots were a symbol of ownership but even my mother, outside, slipped her feet into klompen.

I had of course no car. Even Jan used it only on special occasions and rode himself – upright, dignified – the solid, massive Dutch bicycle still sometimes to be seen, for they lasted for ever; well-engineered machines with the chain enclosed, a back-pedal brake, generous mudguards and a carrier fit to support a baby elephant, and when not on her own bike, which she mostly is, Willy is on the carrier, side-saddle of course. There was a guard to stop a girl's skirt getting into the wheel. She would never have sat on the bar in front of me. Uncomfortable and would have been thought indecent with her hair getting in my face.

Before the war, and after it too, the Amsterdammers liked to come to Zandvoort for the day, in summer. It's not much over twenty kilometres and they biked it, for they were poor, the tram or the train cost a lot for a family, and we spent our money on something better. It was a commonplace to see a man with a child in front (a child's saddle screwed to the bar) and a bigger one on the carrier. A woman's bicycle had often a baby-chair on the handlebars as well as a child behind. It was not thought dangerous. To this day the bike has precedence over cars, on any but an autobahn road and the Dutch driver has learned to respect this. And indeed, from this has grown the legend of the bicycling monarchs, which the English who do not understand make jokes about. Juliana's four girls, the princesses, biked to school like any other Dutch children, and quite rightly so. Trix as a student biked. And so did I. *Fietsen-maar*; wind or rain, pedal. The French call the bike *la petite reine*. Yes, with us the bike is queen. My mother, taking off her apron, putting on a hat, went shopping on foot, for the Brederodestraat is only a step from the village centre. But if, like most of us, she had lived in Bentveld or Aerdenhout, villa districts between Zandvoort and Haarlem, she'd have got on the bike. For anything more than the two-minutes-off, Willy, today, gets on her bike. The only difference between now and the far away fifties is that Willy nowadays is wearing trousers and doesn't think of her long 'new-look' skirt catching in the back wheel.

The schoolgirls out of Zandvoort who are in secondary

school, in Haarlem or Heemstede, eight kilometres along the Zandvoortselaan, they bike. As does Lalage. Bert saw her, learned to look for her in the morning going, afternoons coming home, with the crowd of her age-group, the Haarlemmerstraat and the Tramplein, 'on the fiets'. She has a modern, expensive sport-bike, the sort with twenty-one gears. It's flat of course, the road through the dunes, but 'coming home' you've mostly the westerly wind against you.

Bert was in the Public Library in Haarlem. Keeping-up, on paper so to speak, with his profession, is pretty well covered by our various trade journals, which are many and voluminous, but there is a flow of expensive coffee-table books on garden subjects and the section is well furnished here, as indeed you'd expect in a town like this. He is anyhow an assiduous library user. He likes to think that he keeps his wits sharpened. Intellectual curiosity. Fluency in English undiminished, German an easy read. He was on his way out when over by the reference section, brow a bit knotted over a catalogue, a handsome head of blonde hair. It was natural to cross over, to tap the shoulder, laughingly to say, 'Why the puzzled expression?'

'Oh, it's you. Hallo there,' distractedly enough. Adding a naïve proof that she hadn't really known who he was. 'Yes of course – the steak expert. Damn these things – chronology by author...'

'Perhaps I can help?'

'In the right place, again?' Producing a dirty, much-scribbled notebook. 'I have to do an essay. Professor gave a couple of standard texts to look up, hell I think I've the name spelt wrong.'

'What kind of professor?'

'Bio, it's a botany course.' Bert's ear pricked. Just think, if it had been somebody's learned tome on sine- and cosine-waves, then kindly-uncle couldn't possibly have made a show of effortless can-do.

'Let me see, if I may.' Conventional schoolgirl writing,

with nothing to set it apart from ten thousand others; a bit of dash, perhaps, or was that just haste?

'Wood, Woods, I can't even read it myself.'

'It's the learned and painstaking Dr Woodward.'

'Brilliant!' with open admiration.

'Not in the slightest and I'll tell you why. In the first place it's my subject, I'm a plantsman. In the second he's a standard authority ever since Queen Victoria and is probably in his thirty-fifth edition by now, and in the third it's always nice being able to show off. Find him for you, now, shall I? Here you are – excellent copperplate engravings, water-coloured and bloody well too. Instant recognition when you meet the real thing. Are you going back on the bus?'

'Thanks awfully. No, I've the bike.' He saw her slipping out of reach.

'In return for Professor Woodward, shining light of the University of Cambridge' – oh stop being pompous and heavily gallant – 'please tell me your name.'

'Lally, really it's Lalage, isn't that frightful.'

'No, it's pretty. Lalage Zandvoortinensis, just the name for a new and delightful variety.'

Laughing and flinging her hair about, the way young girls do. Better than a giggle. Settling herself on the bicycle saddle with an automatic hitch, known in Dutch as getting-my-pants-out-my-hole. Delicious bottom. 'Thanks again, a lot. Bye now.' Strong brown legs gathering speed. Bert, you are an old fool.

Boy meeting girl in pub-lib, god, that is the archetype commonplace banality. That is the cheapest, most magaziney ... Elderly party meets piece of fresh young crumpet in pub-lib, that's even worse. All the same – Qué, old? Not that bad, respectable waistline, still got most of my own teeth.

As in the supermarket, the smell of her hair stays with you all the way home. The heavy, clawky food smell, combated by a torrent of artificially cooled, cleansed, disinfected air-conditioning machine, the sharp chemical breath of refrigerated shelves. Different here, musty smell of the printed page in great quantity, billowing out at one when you take a tight-shut, seldom-disturbed volume off the shelf and turn a few pages. An intoxicating smell, where the supermarket is merely disturbing. Neither can compete with a young girl's newly-washed hair. They haven't managed that, yet, the advertising agencies. Show you always the same; girl coming out of the shower, quick shot of bare tits, same brushing it, tossing the fluid fall of hair from side to side, shot to finish of goddamn plastic flagon of shampoo with a monstrous scream of 'The new' goop. But you can't smell her hair. The way Bert could.

A third smell and the more prized however familiar. Every single day new, and they haven't been able to abolish this one yet.

The smell of the dunes. A delicate strong scent of the sand, of the growth, of sun on it, or rain, as the case may be; then entirely different but with sea in it here, for the coastline is near. Many of these growths have their own, powerful essences. Most of it is weed, coarse or fine, brambly or smooth. Children come here in late summer to pick blackberries. Until well inland there are few trees and those stunted, wind-twisted. But undergrowth aplenty with many interesting plants and unexpectedly many flowers, some rare. In the old days a great belt of this was verboten. For many reasons: catchment and water supply, to be kept free of pollution. Danger: there were many half-buried bunkers and pillboxes from the time of the German occupation and the 'Westwall' fortifications. Fragility: much of this growth is delicate, an ecological balance which must be left undisturbed, and hordes of trampling feet would be fatally destructive. Municipal hygiene: one cannot admit greasy plastic sandwich wrappings, beer cans, revolting debris of sun-tan oil or burst air-cushion. Or contraceptives; bah, it's all the police can do to stop couples fornicating on the beach. Most of it is still verboten – designated Nature Reserve.

It was our playground as children, the more exciting for being forbidden. Guarded too by the 'Boswachter' – now that I think of it, if translated literally that would be 'Woodward'! A sort of forester with an official uniform and limited police powers, including the right of verbal-process, an interrogation followed by a written report which went to the Burgomaster and if memory serves to the Commissariat, the police station in the Hogeweg, and constituted a Delict punishable by a more or less heavy fine. Like riding a bicycle without lights, or skipping through a red light.

I must have been a singularly law-abiding child. I know I was terrified of this figure, a sandy-haired and without his cap bullet-headed personage (a habit of carrying his head on one side as though it were stiff, and known to the village as 'Necky'). A disagreeable expression, a gruff voice, appearing old to a small boy but able as we knew to run fast enough to catch evil children and hold them painfully by the ear. I think he spent most of his time in the pub. Jan had threatened me with a tanning if detected in the Forbidden-Dunes. I had a wholesome dread, amounting to a nightmare, of being brought home in disgrace, Necky's grimy hand clamped to my ear.

You see? To this day there is a perfume of risk, of danger, of breaking-the-law. On one occasion we were, three or four of us, close to being caught, busied with some boys' game when a bellow went up of 'Come out of those bushes' and we bolted like rabbits, never identified though the heart thumped all evening at home with the dread of an official knock at the door; poor old Necky elevated to a dread Gestapo in a child's imagination.

We did to be sure what all small boys do; we built nests in the sand with bits of wood and branch, known at different times as 'the cave' or 'the fort'. Our gang was the Foreign Legion; we were at war with other parts of the village, the permanent hostility between Northside and Southside. We brought a bottle of beer to the fort and shared it out solemnly in tin mugs (flat, warm and tasting vile). Once a villain stole from his granny some brande-wijn, the dreadful Dutch 'cognac' coloured by caramel and blunted by syrup, which some old women preferred to gin, and brought it in a medicine bottle, and we had to pretend to like it. The two of us then masturbated one another; I think this might have happened twice, we were too young to enjoy it much. You see, we were still children when the Germans came in 1940, and Zandvoort was decreed a forbidden area, and we were all evacuated...

It is this pre-war time which is now so vivid. Those were the depression years, when little business was done and Zandvoort was 'poor' because so many men were out of a job. Even Jan did not find it easy to make ends meet, though we were 'rich' by contrast. On the edges of the dune bordering the village, not thus forbidden, men cultivated little plots of land, fertilizing the sand with chicken shit, better still pigeon droppings (how it did stink), seaweed, anything one could get. As for the forbidden dunes, they were full of rabbits, and many men went poaching at night with a noose of brass wire. The poor saw little meat. Off the beach here one can shrimp, but no more. Topping and tailing shrimps was a girl's job ... Herring, and the cheaper fish (meaning small, bony, dabs or whiting) from Ijmuiden was plentiful enough.

We talked a lot, boastfully, about bringing girls into the dunes and – in theory – fetching their knickers down free from observation and interference. As far as I know talk it remained. For a start no properly brought-up girl would have dreamed of going into the dunes with a boy. If they did so it was with the protection of their own groups. A girl from good family, like Willy, would to be sure never have gone tearing about with a gang. Played sedately with 'vicarage girls' thought to be suitable little friends.

Seen today, we were perfectly democratic. I was neatly dressed, in the Norfolk jacket and baggy breeches still familiar from Hergé's *Tintin* drawings, of good English tweed and remembered as the most comfortable, wearable clothes I have ever put on. The others of the gang were children of the poor, from the little low cottages of the old dorp (of which I have said, sadly, so few remain). Their trousers were not ragged, for these were self-respecting, proud, and fiercely independent people. But their shirts were much turned and their trousers much patched, and an old bicycle too big for them the most treasured of possessions. Girls darned, sewed, knitted night and day. Willy herself is an exact, scrupulous, painstaking needlewoman. It would never have occurred to Jan to think himself any 'better' than any other villager.

I want to make this point, I think, clear and unmistakeable. The Zandvoort of the pre-war years was a very happy place, and a children's paradise. I would have much to say of this, but it isn't relevant to the present purpose.

If the village is no longer magical the dunes still are. It does not have to be at night – though at night, and by starlight . . . I do not have to be knowledgeable about birds (there are many, and many unusual and interesting because here they are not harried) though I know a skylark when I see it. They are fewer: we cannot alas arrest the creeping pollution of air, of sea- and rainwater, even of our beautiful fine and fluid sand. Of the fascinating insect life I also know little enough. I am, I hope I have made it clear, a reader. Which Jan never was, but he was a sensible and even a wise man. One of my childhood presents was a fine edition of *Fabre's Book of Insects*. My entomology is the school stuff of anyone in the Trade, of the numerous bugs and larvae harmful to bulbs or flowers (anyone with a rosebush learns to combat blackfly and greenfly and carries on from there, trying to wage this war without the toxic chemicals and the filthy aerosol spray . . .). Fabre I read till the binding fell to pieces. La Religieuse, the praying mantis, has haunted my dreams from childhood up to the latest of my working days and nights.

This great French scientist, like all such a hermit, a saint, a profoundly good and holy man, pegged out a piece of

33

natural, arid, untouched and uncultivated Mediterranean ground and called it 'my workshop'. Bits of it were garden. He did sometimes plant things which his holy beasts might like or feel attracted to. For the most part untouched; bare limestone rock, sand, the thin meagre soil of the south, dry, sunbaked, to anyone but a pure saint utterly infertile, obstinate, useless save to the wonderful bees, wasps, beetles, their complex and skilful doings and creations. And overall, still, saying her prayers, utterly terrifying, La Religieuse. The illustrations, in finely detailed and delicate water-colour, are by Mr Detmold, an unjustly forgotten but in Victoria's day well-known illustrator of animal subjects. There must have been birds, interested in snapping up a juicy cricket. There were certainly snakes and lizards to whose flickering tongue a fat wasp is a banquet. Spiders are predators, and who preys upon the spiders? High in the then pure air are larks, and also hawks. The sudden terrifying pounce and the grip of talon from which none of us can count himself secure. We learned, it was the great slogan of the thirties, (*Guinness is good for you* did not make much impact upon Holland). 'That's Shell that Was'. To the kestrel, the sparrowhawk, a slogan fitting nicely: it's a mouse, it was. I am trying to say that in our own fashion, windscraped, rainscoured, we do understand. From the Nordsee to the Mare Nostrum is not in fact much of a distance. I have never found it that formidable.

The dune moves. It is a natural, also a magical barrier between sea and land. A shapely ecology, as self-contained as a flower's. It is man-controlled here, a pulsing impetus bridled by an ingenious people. For it can swarm all over you, breaking and burying houses, gardens. Often does, in the south. Somebody found a pretty piece of ground, with a lovely view of mountain and valley, overlooking the sea. There was bribery, dickery, people who knew kept quiet about the dune – until it swallowed that fine property.

It has happened to me. Tore me in half and buried me. I

speak of Bert because this is an agonizing tale. It sounds too as if I wished to blame Lalage, hiding behind her, finding some snivelling pretext. If blame there is it rests upon me, and myself only. But nobody, judge or advocate, psychiatrist nor parent, is going to tell me I harmed a child. Basta, to cant and to hypocrisy. Physically, and psychologically, these girls are hard-boiled. That fact may in itself be damaging but none of my doing. It is the climate which has changed.

The dune is fluid. It has waves like the sea. You can climb as though on a surfboard to a crest, but you will only see as far as the next hollow. Every wave is the same, and each one different. There are paths and there are fences. These would disappear but are tended, protected by windbreaks. Rather like those which criss-cross the lagoons, around Venice, familiar to those who understand them.

Bert walks these paths, often. He has a pass, to travel the dune and is accepted as a professional, by the warders.

There are never many people about. Even in early summer, June already and a fine day, for once. One can get a day pass. The price is high but not exorbitant. One is commanded in quite a blunt Dutch way to accept the rules about noise, or litter, or disturbing nesting birds, or picking flowers. There might be a few camera fiends. But in general people are uninterested. They whizz in cars along the Strandweg, past Bloemendaal and Overveen, or the direct Zandvoortselaan out of Haarlem and Heemstede, and these motor roads traverse the dunes, boringly. They are in a hurry to get to the beach, and the beach town. Only the older among us still call it 'the dorp'. Sand, they say, boring. Even among Zandvoorters there are those who have never had the curiosity to explore, here.

At this time of year there will be plants in bloom. They are mostly small and unspectacular. Not florists' flowers. It is natural that they are unnoticed. On a sunny day like this one they open. It can be very hot in the dunes. The soft fine sand bakes in the sun, reflects heat. It can be humidly hot but today is dry. Even so, floundering in this fluid slidy element which gives the feet no purchase is heating as well as tiring – the face of the dune is steep, as well as high. People stick to the marked, the labelled paths.

So that when he saw a bicycle flung by the side of the path ... the children don't bother to prop it on its stand. He knows at once that it is Lallie's bike. He has looked at it, at her riding on the bike-path bordering the Zandvoortselaan. He has almost 'lain in wait'. Dallying about. Here it is a surprise, but he doesn't feel surprised.

It is not likely that she will be far. As 'aforesaid', walking in the dunes takes patience and a certain technique. And the 'right shoes'. As said, it is a still, windless day. Bert went 'Coo-ee' as people did, or it's said they did, in the bush, in Australia. Dunes, in Europe, are about as close as you get, to 'bush'. There are no roos here, though there are peculiar beasts, and rumour (losing nothing in the telling) of more. 'Coo-ee. La-la-ge.' A faint scream answered. Not far but what's far? When you have to take a bearing on it. There was a sort of conversation as he ranged closer though she was no more than a hundred metres off. So that she knew it was him ... 'Give a call, again to steer by.' The dune can be an ocean. Need a helicopter or something really. Even with his ankle-height canvas boots and 'used to it' it is hard going.

'Oof,' Sitting down, to catch his breath.

Lallie was shiny, excited. Launched into a torrent of explanation.

'I've found one. It's in Woodward. I've taken a Polaroid. I'm going to make a drawing when I get home, from that. Pen, and water-colour it. Do field notes. This is going to get me a credit. Which I bloody need, I was nil in natural science and the coefficient is quite high, I've my finals next year and I have to have the minimum here to make sure I get a good mark. And it's thanks to you, telling me where to look. None of those other cows will have bothered, and the Pro-fess-or is going to be En-chan-ted with me, yippee.'

'Right. Good. Let me look, then. Some of these primula things are lookalike so we better make sure. Oh good, that's nicely done.'

What she has is pretty banal. *Lathyra tamariscifolia*, quite a boring little thing but she's quite right, it's 'in the book' and she's taken trouble. Quite surely, work this up into a neat drawing and add the notes – in flower so prettier – she'll get her 'good mark'.

Bert bent over it with her.

I don't think there's much to say, is there? She's too fair to tan, much. A bit downy, a bit sun-spotted and sun-flushed. Because it was such a good day – there is almost always a wind, here – she had put on a cotton frock. The smell of her hair. The world went upside down and he kissed her neck. In an unimpressed voice she said 'I owe you a favour, don't I.' His hand went to her breast and caressed. Both hands went to both breasts. She had hard sharp nipples. These girls see no need to wear bras. She's seventeen. Sixteen at the earliest, if she's doing her finals next year. A child. Nubile. This is a perfectly well-developed female, both physio- and psycho-balanced. The only emphasis needed, and this is quite frequent in young girls, not at all an oddity, is that she should be attracted to older men.

'Wait,' said Lalage. I'm prepared to swear, dispassionately. Bert is really no worse a judge of passion than most. Aware anyhow that Wait is better than Don't-wait, whatever the sidewalk sign says. A little taken aback at this great speed. She had undressed long before he had emptied his pockets. Dutch, that. Sand has an uncanny facility for swallowing small metal objects. Even the magnifying glass with which Bert looks at flowers.

'Put the rubbish in my bag,' indulgent. Her knickers have little forget-me-nots embroidered on them. No glass is needed and small opportunity given for this study. Sun, sand, Pirelli calendar. 'You are allowed to look.' Her body is unusually well modelled. If one looks at naked girls the way

Bert looks at flowers it implies criticism. Bad skin, spots, a badly-shaped bottom. Too much flesh when not too meagre. The horrible trick of shaving the corners. Bathing suits leave anyhow indecent white patches. How many have pretty feet? One could forgive Lalage being vain because she's impeccable down to her toenails.

('I wish to know' runs a French army song 'why the blondes are black lower down.' To turn the headlights on, do I pull or push?) Her nipples are prettily shaped, whether erect or not. Her bush is fair, fine, abundant. With her legs opened her flower is without vulgarity. To a man who has grown up with plants, desire should be a delight, unflawed.

'Oh, what a nice prick you've got,' said Lallie comfortably. 'No, stop, I don't want my cunt full of sand.' Very Dutch, that.

Bert will wonder at this casually worn experience, until he thinks about it, which is no impediment. She has had boys of her own age, and very unsatisfactory they were. Greedy and selfish but they know no better. He spread his shirt under her bottom. His return to the village bare-chested would not arouse much comment on a sunny June day. This after all is the seaside.

'No, don't dress, I want to play with you. And admire.' He doesn't feel his age. He is not astonished that she is plainly enjoying herself. Dances, jumps about, acts the fool. A very large, very good drink, at exactly the right temperature, and don't gulp even if there's plenty more in the bottle.

*

Bert sat on a café terrace, with a parasol over the table because any more sun and he'd be sorry for it that evening. No beer, certainly no gin. Holland is sophisticated these days. You can get a pastis and choose your make, and he knows the barman well enough to tell him what sort of glass, and don't put any ice cubes. He has already had such a colossal lift that the second and the third are just surfing. Pastis can give you a big drop afterwards if you're not used to it but he will feel no sadness. These intoxications, rare at his age and with a subject this disciplined, are plain miraculous. Willy was not home when he reached the house, put on a clean shirt, rinsed the other, 'which a stupid tourist spilt on; bumped into the barman's tray, lumping clown.' Three or four loutish teenagers have had Lallie's clothes off, but with such a self-satisfied ignorance that she could say quite truly that this was the first time.

'I can't come to your house. You can come to mine but only on Tuesday, I'm off early in the afternoon, then, and I've the place to myself.' After two socking Pernods (one can get better pastis but it is rare, and expensive; not to be found in Zandvoort) one has a Lalage-exhilaration owing nothing to alcohol. Bert didn't think at all about Afterwards.

Old men. He needs no reminding that he's closer to seventy than to sixty, but these thoughts come on every day but this one. He doesn't say he'll think about this tomorrow. He doesn't make faces although sleeping with schoolgirls is like telling the Pied Piper you aren't going to pay. A thousand guilders? Don't be silly – here's fifty.

She had, she said, the most fantastic climax. So did he. Jump on the table and go Woowoo, you're Tarzan. Childish but so's she. Don't tell Bert either that casual adventures are a Threat: that is a clean girl and needed no telling he was the same. On a pill-no-question; you need scruples about as much as you'd want advice from Mother Teresa.

There's this one fly in his eye. Its name is Wilhelmina. One will give thought to this. Of course. Not this minute. Bert paid the barman, took a little walk down the Zeestraat as far as the wine shop. It was nearly lunchtime. Whatever Willy had ready for lunch she wouldn't say no to a bottle of champagne. She thinks, it's true, that one ought to have a Reason. Saying 'I don't know, I just felt like it' will leave her unsatisfied. I hope she doesn't enjoy it less. And I hope I don't need to say what I feel, and I still don't intend to go into the matter. One doesn't need reasons. As for having a shower in the middle of the day it was hot in the dunes this morning. Are we having spinach, again? No, I like it, but give it a rest for a few days, shall we? A large number of things are moral questions. But not, I think, spinach.

*

A death of a thousand cuts. One wouldn't want to know how long it would take. Dr Fu Man Chu, an undoubted sadist, would regret that the walk to the Pakveldstraat on Tuesday afternoon, a hot sunny day again and disagreeably so, takes only five minutes. He would cheer up, knowing that each tiny nick is exquisitely painful. Suppose Lallie doesn't open the door. Suppose her father does, instead. Suppose Willy does. Supposing some nosy neighbour ... it is difficult to resist stopping for a quick drink.

It is an expensively furnished house, which doesn't necessarily mean comfortable, has little to do with good taste. Bert has good taste. He knows it, I know it, quite objectively. Everybody thinks they've taste. Very few people have. Largely because it has never been formed or trained, but as well because it's an inborn thing. Jan, for example, had never thought about it and quite probably would have said 'Am I some sort of pederast then?'. He had natural good instincts. Like hating double flowers (which one is obliged to deal in. Don't imagine that the Trade has good taste, because it hasn't, and a great many 'florist's' flowers are hideous. Jan dealt in them, hating them.) Bert has also a good training. Weeds and wildflowers have natural good taste. Nothing could be more beautiful than a thistle. The worst are the man-manipulated. Stupid as well as ugly, like a cactus dahlia.

Has Lallie any taste? She hasn't learned much from her surroundings. But she has a marvellous body and learns from that. Her clothes also are good. It would not I think enter her head to dress up in a black bra and suspender belt, though looking around I shouldn't be surprised if her mother did. What is the point of this interpolation? (Not an interpellation; I've looked up both words in the dictionary.)

It's that I'm not about to describe another sex scene. I'm aware that nowadays they seem to be thought essential, though I don't read a lot of modern fiction. In all simplicity (itself an essential, a basic element of this question) they are in bad taste. That's all.

So cataloguing the essential: – about a plant you want to know how tall it is, how broad it is likely to get. At what interval thus you should set more, for a grouping. You would like some notion of its port, like stiff, or droopy, bushy, or skinny. Technically you need to know the soil it likes and its preferences about exposure to sun, wind, rain. Is it hardy? What season does it flower in, and how large and numerous are its blooms? A good catalogue will give you this, in two lines of plantsman's abbreviations. To lay eyes on it in reality is not always possible.

He admired her drawing. As you would expect, stiffly self-conscious, laborious but not without merit. Certainly this would get her the good mark sought at school. Her shorts and top, which are in one piece and well cut. Buttons, two. Underclothes, a pale sort of orange today, tangerines and cream. Expensive dislike for what she calls 'childish cotton rags'. Her sex, described as her cunt; a crude lot, the Dutch. Warm and silky-furry, delicate and fragile, a little damp. Rather like a nest of small kittens. To play with, but be careful not to break.

How experienced is she? In a sense, considerably – and equally, not at all. What! – stupid boys.

Amanita phalloides: not a recommendable mushroom. Exceedingly toxic, mortal and unpleasantly so. Or there's the familiar woodland *impudicus*, well named the shameless one. Lallie likes playing with him. Adult, you see? The real thing.

Stupidly – bloodthirsty jealousies – Bert wanted to know about boys.

'Oh – boys ... stupid. So vain. And greedy. And then they go limp and get cross.' Bert was unused to this directness. A coarse vocabulary; she's highly pragmatic. 'I want more. I'm going to suck you until you're ready for me...'

'Will I make some coffee? You aren't in a hurry, are you?' Detumescence: another lesson in plant biology.

This male problem, which is that you might as well be staring at a plate of cold mashed potatoes, while furiously aware that by tomorrow you'll be crazy wanting her.

This awful niggling bargaining about next time. Why isn't there a cosy discreet house of assignation? Bert has no little furnished studio in Haarlem or anywhere else: the idea has never occurred to him. There are of course hotels. Lallie refuses point-blank. 'Somebody would be sure to see me, and I don't like...' Or the dunes, where privacy is not hard to come by. No: that once was fun but I'm not making a habit of that and it'll probably be raining anyhow.

There is no question of her coming to the flat. Not so much the neighbours but that is an insult to Willy which ... odd because where does mere dissimulation become an insupportable hypocrisy? Coming again – if only next week – to this house (as boys do, quite openly, damn the nasty little twits) is a risk he'd be ready to take but she's not. Bert won't quarrel with that. Supposing it had been his own teenage daughter.

Bert didn't know that this afternoon – that was all there was. He managed to get her one night to go out in the car. Parking in the silent shadowy corners of the Ijmuiden dockland. She was unwilling, sullen. Boys do that; borrow Dad's car. She didn't like it at all. First time I ever – I was fifteen. Hand up my skirt, sweaty eagerbeaver wanting me to masturbate him, I did but I never will again. No, I won't undress, I've the curse anyhow. (Is it their privilege to say so? Be it true or a lie?) Oh, all right then; I hope to god there are no Nosy Parkers but make it quick; I'll go down on you.

The age difference? One can't expect that a girl of seventeen – she's enjoyed fantasies, thinking of herself as 'the mistress' of an old man.

Be sensible, Bert. You had better see this in a natural-science context. Leave a hornet alone or it will sting you. Herpetology. The Mexican Indian meets a rattlesnake he keeps himself quiet. Go your way in peace, brother. Do not frighten or fluster him. Do not push him in a corner. Respect him.

There were painful torments because in a village like Zandvoort one sees people. When he didn't see her, and thought at any moment she might be there, in the frame of his vision – then the sting is as keen. The painful inflamed swelling lasts as long. She's obeying – he said – a good healthy instinct. Get involved with a married man, there's no end to that. Plenty, rather, and all of them bad. She knows she has to grow up.

What, an old man? Pushing seventy. What importance has age? Be bloody grateful, man. Your beloved wife leads an active, hard, highly physical life. Nor is she in the least averse to – just be patient. Don't take her by surprise.

Everybody says that, to be sure, until it catches up with them.

*

October is my favourite time of year. Nowadays, in the Trade, there are no seasons. They (it's only force of habit that I still say 'We') have no winter. There's less 'outside' work, that's all. The young plants are all reared under glass, and that's another old-fashioned expression. Since there are hundreds of acres with automated temperature and humidity control, and electricity can make us a thousand suns, and the investments are huge, the word 'glass' would give any insurance company a falling-sickness. A hundred kinds of plastic go into as many kinds of sandwich. Some are rigid, some are supple, and they'll answer any specification called for. You needn't think about wind any more, or snow, or hail, once the worst of our hazards. Nor of small boys throwing stones. Think instead of the plants we rear from the southern hemisphere, at home in New Zealand or a jungle in Borneo, and whose winter is our summer. Indeed we can bring a plant into bloom, and put it on the market, at virtually any moment to suit us.

When I grew up, in Jan's day, there was the rush for the winter markets, the St Nicholas and Christmas, and then one looked forward to the daffodil, the iris and the tulip in their seasons. We were outside still, working at jobs to finish before the early frosts, and could snuff at the air, and the colours of October. I am a creature of habit, still.

Habit brings us still to this pub, which is an unofficial sort of club and clearing house for the Trade. We have our grand palaces (containing a lot of glass), in Aalsmeer where the auctions are held and they load the planes at Schiphol with cut flowers for the markets. We have the 'Castle' in Lisse, still called after the Princess, Jacoba van Beieren, where they bed out the millions of particoloured jester tulips for the tourists to Ooh at. Habit is strong, and the continuity of centuries. That princess belongs to the time when Holland and Zealand, yes and Brabant, were provinces belonging to the Duke of Burgundy. I have already spoken of our magic streak of tulip-land south of Haarlem, could mention the Westland, where they grow on the silt brought down by the rivers, to the Rijn and Maas estuaries.

It is a café such as hardly exists now in Holland, in the lavish old style and scarcely changed since Jan's day. This too is the force of habit. We like it as it always was, with a great deal of polished brass, and the shaggy oriental runners on the tables giving that dim, rich, Ali-Baba look. Newspapers in wooden racks, old (good) Delft tiling, while the beer engine or the taps in the lavatories would command a fortune from antique dealers. And another thing – the cigar smoke. A great deal of it Cuban, for the men of the Trade, who are the Stamm-customers here, look like anyone else but are among the weightiest and wealthiest businessmen of this land of businessmen. They are mostly elderly; the young think the place a joke, and you won't see many women here except the waitresses who know where to bring a Pils or a gin without being asked. Jan drank a deal of both, under this roof.

We don't talk much, but we keep up with the news. This is why I come. The international news comes here as fresh as the cut flowers, and quicker. It isn't all the Bourse columns in the daily paper, by any manner of means, whether electronic or 'Do you know who I saw, just last week?' In the village of Bennebroek as likely as in Moscow or Washington. The beer is just the right temperature, and the gin famous for purity and age.

In here, we're very Dutch. Huge windows, two walls full of them in big semicircular arches and kept, moreover, shining bright. We have a fondness for these floods of light. But the lower halves are in little mosaics of stained glass (in flower patterns of course) designed to block the indiscreet gaze of the vulgar, outside. And there are heavy curtains tied back with loops, as in 1900, while the deep sills are crammed with pots of fleshy, invasive plants, much cherished. To ensure a great deal of light and take it all away again is one of our talents.

No one wants to look at flowers here so there aren't any, save a vase of huge dreadful gladioli back of the bar. On the terrace outside are banks of geraniums, good enough for tourists.

Who should I lay eyes on but Henk van der Scheur, known in the USA as Hank and given to pale silver-grey silk suits cut sharp to a massive figure; a massive pale face with white eyebrows, and a lot of gold teeth, and a gold underwater watch, probably Jaeger-le-Coultre. He sounds awful and is, but a good friend for all that. He has always the newest jokes, is offensively jolly, enjoys farting and then making jokes about that, which is also very Dutch. Even if not a contemporary – we were boys together at the Lycée – he'd still be a good friend.

'Bert! Haven't seen you this long long while.'

'No, I've been ill. Don't want to talk about it, in here.'

'No. But tell you what – Irene was asking after you. Why don't we have dinner? Say out in Ijmuiden where the fish is good, the three of us quietly.' He knows Willy doesn't like him.

'Good scheme.' Irene is his wife, it annoys Willy that I'm fond of them both. He's looking in his little book, morocco of course, with a gold pencil. There's no room in his pockets, which bulge with telephones and sixshooters.

'Tomorrow okay? Deal – I'll fix that with the thief, out there. You could do with a shot of the good juice. Pale – what's this walking with a stick? You'll tell us then – Irene will be mighty pleased.' Henk even talks Dutch with an American accent. 'Who's that over there staring at us?'

'I've met him, he's a police officer.'

'Police in here, what next?'

'Some girl in Zandvoort got killed last week. I might have a word with him at that, see if he's getting anywhere with it.'

'Right, right. See you out at the harbour.' I moved across, trying to remember the man's name. Alone today, or possibly his dogsbody is off duty. Off-duty himself maybe but as Henk says what's he doing here? It's open to all but we still look down our nose at tourists. However, this is no tourist, propped on a stool with a beer, little peeky eyes everywhere. A large jacket of rather loud check. They always wear one because of the big gun in the small of the back. We never used to have that but they're omnipresent nowadays. Holland fills up with crime.

'Mr van Bijl, howdy. Bout's the name, Bout like Hout,' grinning, knowing I'd forgotten. 'Think of Hout.' Which is 'wood', no doubt a familiar joke because he isn't wooden. Eel-like slippy little man. 'Get you a drink?'

'Got one, thanks.' I'd left it on a window sill, chatting to Henk, had an idea he had noticed this. 'Bit out of your road, here, no?'

'Ach, we get around, know all the nice places, huh? Few enough good points to this damn job.'

'How's your investigation going, or is it finished?'

'That girl? Far from finished. Just begun.'

'I hadn't seen anything more, in the paper.'

'Public would be bored,' stubbing out a fag and unwrapping a stick of chewing-gum, I loathe people who chew. 'Smoking too much,' instantly aware of distaste. 'Roll-my-own, shaggies, they wouldn't like that in here. No Agatha-Christie about this job. Me Hawkeye – Gotcha, little enough of that. 'Less we see someone, running up an alley, bicycle under his arm, where you going with that then? No no, homicide squad, this is Holland. Permanently in the pub, no screaming sirens.'

'Yes yes,' getting impatient with this bar humour, 'but aren't you getting anywhere with this?' Familiar public reaction: what are we paying monstrous taxes for?

'We move around. Buzz-buzz, like the flies, never welcome. Zing about in irregular circles, gather honey, mix my metaphors. Try to get the circles concentric, spiders now, is it?'

'Look, I'm a businessman, not the concierge looking for a gossip. Keep the chat-up for the waitress.'

'Sorry. You're an intelligent man, so am I though I don't look it. Great advantage not to look it. Seriously, most police work is an endless accumulation and sorting-out of bits of paper. Compare this one with that, maybe you get to fit two together. I'm just having a quiet beer, why pounce on me this way?'

'Quite right, and I beg your pardon. Local thing, and you came to see me, it's normal I should be interested.'

'No offence. Got to be patient. These things when they aren't quick and obvious can take months. We're beginning to be sure of one thing. Local man, we're pretty confident about that.'

'Well I mustn't disturb you. Forgive me, I'm going to circulate awhile.'

'That's what it's all about,' grinning with those snot-green eyes. Observing us is he, in our native habitat?

I haven't been speaking about 'Bert'. I've had to be concerned with myself, and since a corner of this slipped out, I had better make some explanation. There isn't any secret, but I am a secretive man and I don't discuss my personal affairs in public. With an old friend like Henk I can say what's on my mind and make no drama of it. He'd be interested if only as a man of exactly my age. As for Irene – Henk would tell her anyhow. Better that she hears it ungarbled.

And Bert, in all of this? – of course, and much so. The whole object is to determine where our paths cross, join, entwine – like a rope? Or are we just hopelessly entangled? Put it that this word 'concern' is with responsibilities.

Bert has been worrying about making a fool of himself over Lalage. Taking the clothes off schoolgirls – well, really! Was he prey to a kind of senile satyriasis? He has been going on about not feeling all that old, actually. Hm. He hadn't much wanted to think about this matter now afoot. I hadn't mentioned it before, as the sort of detail one keeps to oneself. Now, it has to come out anyhow. I didn't mention it to Willy either, at first. Not to frighten her with false fire.

Earlier this year ... I'd gone to our house doctor. Fellow who deals in colds and coughs, but he's good, and he's good at listening – no fool either. A man gets bothered, about a bit of bleeding; nothing much but noticeable. 'Is that something you ought to know?' They can laugh, ask if you've been eating beetroot. But – 'Need a blood test. When was the last, let's see. Come back when you've got it.' And then – 'Your PSA has taken rather a jump.' One is alert to any change in the tone of voice. 'Think it would be nice to have a second opinion. 'One was alert, even to the laboratory jargon, so one wants it put then in plain words. Talk to a man about his prostate and he'll be amused, irritated, bored, in roughly equal proportion. Or so I'd have thought.

Professor Heinrich in Amsterdam is rather grand; the sort of doctor who's always away at international congresses, which are invariably held in pleasant surroundings. I liked him. Young, makes jokes, and here's another good listener. The brilliant eye rests on one, thoughtfully. It's unmistakeable, that eye. One doesn't meet it often. I have met it in scientists as often I suppose as in artists. Seldom, either way. 'I think we'll run a few tests.' This idiotic prostate is acquiring importance.

University hospitals have sophisticated procedures: yes, to be sure, of course – they scan you in tunnels which make odd star-war noises, make movies of you, float lasers at you. A pile of nice girls saying don't-move-till-I-tell-you. Boring but not nasty. Not until you get the special treat. Biopsies *are* nasty.

I've never been sodomized, never having been gay. Or imprisoned. Being arse-bandited by girls – jolly, laughing girls – is a further reaching experience, not in the least funny. Even Heinrich doesn't make jokes about this one.

'The girls have taken ten bore samples of your geology and nine of them show cancer cells present.' I have never sodomized a girl, either. I cannot conceive that either of us would enjoy it. I am pleased that Heinrich is businesslike because that I can understand. 'We can handle it two ways, medical or surgical, which would you like?' 'Which would you say?' He took his time thinking. I like him for this. 'Surgery is what I'd suggest to my own father.' I liked that too. I should put him in the mid-forties. 'You've a deal.'

We've thought about it. I find it difficult to imagine. I'm not a brilliant imaginer. Difficult to picture – envisage. It goes too deep. It is rooted in childhood. Goes back, I could almost say, to the moment a baby struggles out of the birth canal. They hold it up and make it yell, to get air into the lungs while taking a quick look to tell the mother – 'Boy'. Good news in exalted circles. Or among Chinese peasants. You start being male before you have any clue about this world.

Man says, he's not going to snatch my balls (his language is technical but blunt. We have neither of us a need of elegant euphemism.) He'll snip the wiring, though. No more girls. No more erections (one instantly feels 'I haven't had my share').

Trying to be dispassionate, if that's the word. Little boys fiddle with their dicky. He'll be shoving a catheter into mine. I've a month or so to get used to – come to terms with? – the idea. His fat, comfortable secretary has to fit me into the schedule. 'He's away for a few weeks.' She introduced me to the anaesthetist, delightful woman, tiny, thin, hair in a knot and granny glasses. She is just out of the theatre, still gowned, her mask round her neck, bringing with her the smell of outer space. She annotates her formidable checklist. Neat tiny writing like herself.

'It is profound. It lies deep, your prostate. You can rely upon him. He's slow, and he's very precise.' She is gentle, with a surprising, innocent smile. I am in good hands. But when I come out of them I will no longer be a man. There are many in my situation, at my age a banality. This though is me.

In July. I won't miss Zandvoort much. In high summer beach and village are aswarm with tourists. But I am going to miss...

Willy has taken this well. It might surprise those who don't know her but – no, I won't discuss her personal affairs. Her private life is my affair still but nobody is going to pry. I'll say this much – I can see her puzzling, trying to put herself in 'the man's place'. Very disagreeable things – as radical – are done to women. Hysterectomy, there were appalling butchers who talked about a clean sweep. 'Better off without'. Who took everything, ovaries, all that makes a woman female. Horrible to think of these men. Tying Fallopians as though a woman were no more than a cat. Willy, I'm thankful, is in excellent health. The house doctor – had I sounded dismissive? – understands her very well, and she has an admirable gynaecologist; a woman, young, and pretty, says Willy with approval.

It's that pest of a Nathalie who worries me. Women like

this are always full of medical talky-talky. When like both girls they've had some paramedical formation – I am sure that they're both competent and meticulous – they become self-important and fussy. Quite capable of saying 'Oh, Heinrich ... the Chef de Clinique in Utrecht is much better'; forever laying down the law over matters they know nothing of. The way they bring up their children, with that bright certainty of being forever in the right, infuriating me more than I can say. I know they'll worm it all out of Willy and lecture her interminably on all I should be thinking, doing. It is my permanent weak point, vulnerable area. Unhappiness. Jan, though he never showed it, was far from content with me. But I was his son. A son is a good thing to have, and the more as you get older.

Bert reappears upon the scene. I am, tiresome, whimsical about this? It's something I try to handle.

I have been faithful to Willy. Technically, it is true, there have been moments, across the years, when I have flounced off to Amsterdam in a pet, found myself a girl more or less obviously a prostitute, and found much relief and comfort in screwing the behind off her. On the numerous business trips or visits to garden exhibitions, of course you know the old joke about the Japanese laying on hot-&-cold running girls in every room (we did a lot of business with Japan and in the Trade they keep us on our toes). The point – is there a point? – is that they are professional. Our Amsterdamse gei-shas have quite a reputation. There is no emotional or psy-chological charge, the physical – metabolic – involvement lasts an hour and is equivalent to the big cold daiquiri after a grinding hard day. Whereas Willy is my wife. Rijst-tafel, and plenty of it, hot with the eastern chili we call in Dutch sam-bal, is a major delight on occasion, but one is longing to get back to Dutch boiled potatoes. Pick them up and peel them yourself, dropping them now and then to blow on your fin-gers before reaching for the butter. Sprinkle a little salt. In our world, potatoes count for more than tulips.

I've never had a 'mistress'. The thought amazes me. Bert worries me. Taking the knickers off a schoolgirl. One can say, to them it is as devoid of meaning as to the geisha – and a lot less satisfying. I don't pretend to understand these children. The girls seem to undress on command and even before. Neither boy nor girl can grasp, apparently, that if you make sex as cheap as cornflakes, 'we'd rather read a book and that was that'. (Noël Coward's 'Señorita Nina' is one of my English memories, along with *Kiss Me Kate*, the Cole Porter musical at the Coliseum in London – I've never seen anything more fun than that evening.)

I can find excuses for Bert. I could have told him that the girl Lalage was pleased at this kind man's helping her so handily to a good school mark. She found it pathetically easy to give him a good reward. She felt an obscure sexual attraction towards an older – just say *old* – man. She had a young, we may call it a healthy curiosity about the old man's penis, which was more stimulating, more civilized, less greedy – and bigger – than the stringy objects she'd had as playthings. Enjoyable to find it unexpectedly vigorous. Modern young girl, normal healthy reactions. And for poor old Bert I have the warmest fellow-feelings. Our generation, we managed to unhook some girl's bra it was with the sensation that you were the first to reach the South Pole. This was untrodden snow. Nobody had even seen or touched it. As for her cutting him off so abruptly, I don't think one can blame her all that much. Inexperienced surely, rather than heartless. She didn't know how else to handle it. A social rather than a moral problem. Not a sin but a solecism. Arguments in youth are simple and it's as we get older that we find situations a mosaic of clashing attitudes, conflicting motives, and we're slower to come to judgement. I think Bert choked suddenly on the idea of this being a last fling before the packing of the little bag, unpacking it in the bleak little room at the clinic.

It was Willy who suggested 'a holiday'. Humbly hinting that he might like a few days 'on his own'. Glowing with pleasure, which she thinks doesn't show, at a brisk reaction, which is indeed spontaneous; that he wouldn't dream of going anywhere without her. Does she know anything, has she guessed anything, has she been told any damaging little insinuation, about Lallie? Willy has the shrewdness of the experienced wife – and he, perhaps, the transparency of the inexperienced adulterer. But no, it's just the understanding that Zandvoort is too small, now and then.

'You hate it anyhow at holiday time.' Yes, and a possible glimpse of a girl on a bicycle is intolerable.

'There's that. Time we had a break ourselves.'

'I didn't know whether you might not prefer after the –' By suppressing words like 'clinic' or 'operation' she thinks she's being tactful.

'No reason why one shouldn't make it both.' Visible relief and the production of a lot of travel-agency junk from a shop-ping bag. Bless the girl.

'I'm in no mood for anything southern. Far too hot and too many people.' Humbly, she will be swayed by his every caprice. Most unusual, but this plainly is a 'treat' before a nasty moment.

'There's a Gartenschau in Köln I'd like, anyhow. Why not then up and along the Baltic coast? We've never been further than Lübeck.' Because it all used to be Communist and forbidden.

This is a seductive idea. Willy has rushed to get the atlas. And that bottle of champagne the other day had been so nice that she produces another. O, a telling stroke. I found myself swept away. Hanseatic cities. This coastline will be changing so fast one had better go now – this minute! Stralsund. Danzig. Tallinn and Riga...

'But if it's pouring rain?'

'Then we'll be like brave Germans, rushing up and down the beach in raincoats pretending it's warm.'

'Oh Yes!' shouted Willy, entranced.

Women cannot of course ever, 'this minute'. Have to have

their hair done, lots of things to buy, oh dear. I was ruthless about the new bathing-suit and the cotton frock – you pick all that up in Germany. While for instance I am looking at the flower show.

'Oh but I want to see the flower show too.'

'So you shall, my love,' and don't think I don't mean that. Girls, even Lallies, are two for sixpence and five for a bob, as the barrow boys shout, in London. Bert, you idiot, you ought to know that Willy is unique. So that flinging everything in the back of the car – I do that, but she insists on having everything proper.

This car is like me, hard-wearing and reliable, doesn't show its age much. Say this for Daimler-Benz, they don't let one down. Change the models little, reluctantly, and this ten-year-old 'taxi' looks as good as new. These make light of the autobahn, a stinker like all such, or the distance from Köln to Lübeck. Willy who used to be forever squeaking that I drive too fast, now – I notice – drives faster than I ever did. And safer. She never rides on top of others, and always gives way to the pushful. Since the women are as bad as the men and often worse, this sheds some light on her character, which is as obstinate and obstructive as any one has met. We're on the coast and it's not even suppertime.

This interlude isn't relevant, much, to the tale. I am not going to dwell. The weather was rather good. The Hanseatic buildings are a joy, an immense expression of faith and love, as distinct from the confidence, the commercial hard heads, the civilized serenity. I have heard the Palace of the Doges in Venice described as the summit of secular Gothic building. I wouldn't be at all sure that I agree.

Germans like to be naked. Nature is a great shibboleth of theirs. Baltic beaches are a good place for the study of this phenomenon. Many are shockingly overweight? There are plenty of Utes and Elkes lissom enough to enjoy, for Bert and me both. This overripely erotic display – not quite up to Lalage standard – gives one a few shrewd pinches. For the days of majestic lechery thus to be numbering off until the inevitable Tuesday fortnight is a melancholy thought. So perhaps would a sailor in a lifeboat watch, from a little distance, his torpedoed steamer. Head down, and sinking, but still gallant.

Willy's muscular, tanned open-air-ness is at its best here. These Baltic beaches, almost tideless, are gentler than our violent North-Sea coast. A large obstinate anticyclone, sunny and windless, has warmed this water to August levels. We swim a great deal. The crowd of white-winged little sailing-craft, numberless and greedy as the seagulls, tacks about whistling for a breeze. The prim row of pale green dustbins marked 'glass' and 'metal' must be emptied daily of their freight of beer and cola cans. In the evening we sit over drinks and the local choir sings, splendidly, the 'Nancy Lee'. These rousingly capstan-turning shanties, a Liverpool leave-taking, move me. What songs invigorated the oarsmen of a Venetian galley, outward to Crete and Cyprus?

Serenissima Stralsund. I wish I had some knowledge of history. Or failing that, imagination. These two landlocked seas, the Baltic in the north and the Med in the south, have surely been the shapers and civilizers of this pissy little European peninsula, the so-small which is bigger than all the other continents together. We gave birth to and nourished the Americas. We gave them the men. They gave us trees, plants, flowers. Their other contributions have not equalled their promise. Who has paid back the debt they owe us? George Marshall, and Ernesto Guevara. History, I think, will not be moved – nor Venice preserved – by Disney.

Willy does not act Aphrodite-naked upon northern strands. I do, to unyielding disapproval. Perish-the-thought is a guiding light to every breath taken. The bathing suit cut high on the hips was dismissed with ignominy. Quite right, it would even on Lalage be sniggeringly prurient. Focusing a spotlight upon a little fig-leaf cache-sexe is no way to look at women. Walking, and all too conscious of what Lallie (and Willy) calls

'my broek in my hole' they drag uncomfortably at the inade-
quate scrap. One's behind if not Aphrodite-bare should be
modestly obscured. Willy, in hotel rooms, fiercely draws the
curtains. 'There's a Bauer out there with Binoculars.'

I am perfectly aware that Mr van Bijl's blameless seaside
holiday is a bore. Bert is a stiffish, dried-out, uninteresting
man. As it were, a pensioned head-of-section, the sort of man
who has spent a lifetime checking household accounts for
the North Thames Gas Board. Now the computer does it.
One might regret Bert, who made few mistakes, but there's
no place for him in the modern world. He's another of the
great army of oldies who are no longer productive, who do
not contribute, who are a drag upon society. A worry because
there are far too many of them. Advances in medical research
mean they all live for ever, costing the young and active
much trouble and expense. If only they could be made pain-
lessly to disappear without tweaking the body-politic with a
bad conscience.

Damn it, they even go on holiday. Another car clogging up
the roads. More bodies polluting the beach. Primitive socie-
ties did it better. Leave them behind in the desert or wherever, they'll hygienically be eaten by hyenas. Now this chap –
a cancer, good. Arrange a nice painless overdose of morphia.
Surgical clinic, University Hospital, hours and days of extremely expensive skills and resources, what, to give a fellow
like that a few more months of his utterly useless existence.
This is a *crime*, I tell you. The very most that should be
allowed is if he can pay for it himself out of his savings, and
if he can't, too bad.

Bert has been reflecting upon *crime*. Lot of it about. He
has never done anything really criminal, perhaps. Dirty old
man corrupting young girls? He doesn't think she was much
corrupted. He hadn't done her any harm. No violence and
she was asking for it anyhow. Now all these people driving
recklessly and too fast, convinced that a large, shiny and
powerful (preferably new) automobile is their own personal

indispensable morsel of Liberty (the State has taken away all remaining freedoms and speeding on the Autobahn is all we have left) these people are not criminals and only cranks pretend they are. Bert is a criminal for taking up good space. Breathing our air. Using our water.

'And what's more, the Unfit ought to be sterilized! Eugenics got a bad name because of Hitler, but in the 1930s, I tell you, all civilized countries had programmes for preventing degenerates from reproducing. That's what we want, a firm line taken.' In club and in pub, you can hear this talk.

Sea, sand, sun, sex. Willy, amazingly youthful. Bert monstrously active. Must be something psychological, also. Knowing you're about to be – now come on, not castrated, only sterilized really and what d'you need erections for at your time of life? – creates (but that's not the right word) lots of *ardour*. He is preternaturally pleased with the naked women on the beach. Doughy lot for the most part, too much fast-food. One would rather look at Willy, who has kept a remarkably good figure, but men want refreshment through novelties. Bert dislikes porn, the Dutch are even worse than the Germans, nobody can ever make out whether these are lingering traces of the puritan-tradition, but loiters after erotic stimulus, there's plenty of it about and Willy of an evening is healthily tired and would be greatly bored. A bit of chocolate and a nice book helps her sleep soundly. If pushed she would say – but she prefers not to be pushed. Has nothing to do with material considerations of hygiene: Bert is sensible enough, he's not going to pick up a hepatitis or any of these horrible things; Nathalie has fearful stories ... to her it's rooted in a *moral* framework. But she doesn't want to quarrel, on what may prove their last real holiday. Impatient and inconsiderate these forty years but he's been a true *Mann* to her, and few people can say that.

Tuesday fortnight always comes. Bert packs his little bag, and Willy repacks it for him. She drives him to Amsterdam, with much careful planning about where to park the car for visits, and where to shop for delicious-small-things-to-eat. Flower shops in Holland are never lacking. Remember, says Bert, I'll likely be a day or so in the Reanimation unit.

A room, to oneself of course, worth the extra money even if they do stroll in and out like this was a railway station, at least you have quiet at night and your windows open. A lot of nurses being cheerful and comfortable, 'nice girls', and Willy goes off to be brave by herself. He is hardly left to himself a second, there are so many damned details.

I don't think we'll spend any time on this. People are far too fond of telling these tales, convinced that it has never happened to anyone else. A pleasant, serious but humour-tinged visit from Professor Heinrich who is never in a hurry. The same, gentle, from the anaesthetist whose name, delightfully, is Gertrude. A continual flow of good-hearted girls, a few of whom are pretty. A journey. Many hours of oblivion. Reanimation. This is the painful part, the misery and the journey back to living. The girls here have a higher level of training and of education, and of patient kindliness. Morphia is the kindliest of all. I am in love with these girls, I kiss them with the affection which comes with being helpless. A baby would do the same, if it knew how. They are accustomed to love, and wear it lightly. Back at last in one's own room, entangled in tubes and drains and perfusions – the girls here (welcome back) seem negligent and careless. One's life is no longer in danger. Willy comes, gentle, sweet, even a bit asphyxiating. One begins to concentrate on getting up on one's feet.

I can go home. I'm still trailing clouds-of-glory. Heinrich smiles tolerantly. It's the policy now to push them out early. Saving money, too, which I'm Dutch enough to applaud.

'Ambulant surgery' says the delightful Argentine intern, winking at me. 'I can get you an ambulance,' says kind Erika (notable for her sexy eyes enhanced by skilful make-up). No, I'd rather the faithful Mercedes. A fearful job climbing in, and I'd no idea the springing was so hard.

Sitting down is anguish. I spend the entire day walking about, instead, which I'm sure is good for me. Willy's nursing is technically clumsy. An awkward, pain-nourished love. Nathalie appears, with adverse comment upon the entire medical profession. We loathe each other. She loves me, and I love her, and we know it, however determined not to admit it. The house doctor comes, to take out a staggering number of those abominable little wire clips.

Soon another lovely day – the weather is magnificent and the beaches are full. Bared bellies which no more invite exposure than my own. I have to go back to Amsterdam for an elaborate photo session but it culminates in Heinrich looking pleased. The final blessing is Erika taking out the infernal catheter. Her white trousers tighten when she bends over. Worn thin, these display her elegant behind and blue Prisunic knickers. This certainly modest sight is sadly academic. I am grateful but I must accustom myself to remembering her lovely eyes. Not her bottom. Handling my penis, which is a little sore and swollen, her phrase was: 'I've seen lots worse than that one.' Also lots better, I hope.

*

How am I to know that I am programming myself towards crime?

*

I'm getting better. A bit tender round the crutch, and everyone's present is a new walking-stick. I can manage the flat hard sand of low tide very well now. It yields just enough to the foot, gentler, as it were springier than the vile concrete slabs which replace, all over Zandvoort, the friendly zigzag courses of brick which used to pave Dutch streets. So much more sensible, needing no road drills when there was cable to lay or repair. The hardest sand shifts. When they got too uneven there was the paviour with rubber pads strapped to his knees, clinking with his hammer. A gentle, a human sight.

I cannot of course manage the soft, fluid sand of above the

high-water mark. Or of the dunes. Will I recover that pleasure?

Two months later and you'd scarcely notice. I walk, dressed-up in the jersey track suits Willy affects and now buys for me (very comfortable). I need the stick, but for reassurance as much as for support. She buys me these canvas basketball boots with thick rubber soles which all the younger generation wear. She's expert in such things. I walk along the seafront, what we old-Zandvoorters called the Boulevard. There were two, the North and the South, meeting at a point called the Rotonde (police post, place for lost children, weather forecast as well as café, originally a coastguard lookout and imperceptibly the beach centre). It is now a pedestrian walk. The municipality – pretentious imbeciles – laid down patterns of coloured tiles in a crude and gaudy imitation of the Piazzetta in Venice. On a North Sea coast there is nothing you can do about seagull shit. Nowadays, I suppose, there is precious little you can do to stop dogs (dog shit is not a peculiarly Parisian problem), nor can you do much about the Volk, which flings fast-food debris everywhere save in the baskets. We are now quite as filthy, as noisy and as undisciplined as the English. What revolts me more are the black stains on the tiles where they spit out and tread in their repulsive chewing-gum. These are nigh-indelible.

I walk down, through the dorp-centre, of little attraction nowadays though I might still sometimes stop for a beer, what the Germans call the Frühschoppen, at ten in the morning, at 'Arie Koper' though this is now unrecognizable (Arie is in his grave).

I cut on down to the familiar still-dear Brederodestraat and angle on – along the line of the dunes, it has been forbidden to encroach further upon them – to the old 'Zuiderbad', now a rigmarole of hideously expensive 'condominium' building. I turn along the seafront and work my way back to the northern limit of the dorp, where these cold, bleak, draught-inducing apartment blocks peter out at last and one looks over scrubby stunted pines to the suburban housing estates of 'Plan Noord'.

Often I am tired before getting this far. At the limit of the old, the true dorp (the pompous little station, the humble little railway line to Haarlem mark the original limits), I often turn down the Zeestraat, which has still most of the beautiful real Zandvoort house-architecture, always a joy to rest the eye upon, and so along the Haltestraat full of shops, up the Pakveldstraat, where I am no longer frightened of seeing Lalage, and so home.

I stride out pretty well. Heinrich and our house-doctor agree. 'Therapy' is not found in pills, though I have a tedious morning-and-night sequence. It is in a minimum of an hour-and-a-half of daily walk. I am good about this. The children roller-skating on the Boulevard (illegal but they cannot be stopped) frighten me the most. I cannot dodge out of their way. So I don't, but they don't yield either, and I'm always nervous of being knocked right off my feet. I am now *un petit vieux*, a little old man, and fragile. That wouldn't worry these healthy, brutal boys and girls for one solitary second.

In passing – I don't smoke much any more. Little titchy cigars and in my own room because of Willy making faces. I should like a *proper* cigar here in the open. I'd rather forty-a-day than chew gum. Something else – as a boy in England – I asked 'What's Titch?' An old man in the office said he was a music-hall comic, he was a dwarf, fifty years ago it must be. A hundred, now. I am persuaded (the place swarms with people giving English lessons) that it's futile trying to learn a language without living there. I remember the market men in Covent Garden.

'We're just going up the boozer.'

'We were just getting in in the boozer when –'

'They were saying down the boozer, fags were going up again.' I suppose it's the same in every language.

On the way home, you might buy a titchy bunch of

chrysanths. They're just coming into season. I like the smell.

We've had summer storms of rare violence. In the Baltic the traditional autumn anticyclone – but there's nearly always a wind, here. This is a rarity – a real 'Indian Summer'.

Beyond 'Zuiderbad' the village comes to an abrupt end. There is a path for walkers, through the dunes, to Noordwijk, the next beach settlement, ten kilometres along the coast. Down the road. Up the coast. Holland is obstinately flat. To the north, beyond 'Noorderbad', a wide motor road, the Zeeweg, curves inland a kilometre further, towards Bloemendaal and populous parts. Saving this, and the Zandvoortselaan in the village centre (and of course the little railway line to Haarlem) we would be utterly isolated, an odd, meaningless settlement in the middle of nowhere between the dunes and the sea.

On the Boulevard are the high flat-blocks and hotels. From here you go down ramps or steps to the beach eight metres below you. This is the 'reep', not so much a seawall as a bank of sand long settled and consolidated and fortified, Holland's centuries-old defence against the North Sea. In memory it has not been breached. A long way south, in Zealand, in 1953, it was breached, and the memory of a terrible flood is very much alive.

Nestling under the reep, well above high-water-mark, each with its hundred-metre stretch of sand carefully demarcated and numbered, are the twenty-eight beach 'tents'. We call them tents still, for in my childhood they were flimsy structures. Come a summer storm and the owners would quail. It is much like our 'glass' in the Trade, come to think. Modern materials have changed the tents into imposing, comfortable pavilions where not only can you drink on the terrace but order quite an elaborate meal. The old slatted boardwalks are long gone. Nowadays the bulldozer comes, clears a large level space, and they put down cement paving, line the limits with steel-and-glass windbreaks, and the tourists lie baking in rows on long padded chairs. You'd think yourself in Cannes.

The pavilion is walled, roofed, solid, with a kitchen and lavatories and potted plants, like any inland café.

But the municipal regulation is still that they must be impermanent. They go up in prefab sections well before Easter, and stay until the equinox, when there are no more tourists. They are gay with flags and bunting, welcoming – and dear ... We, the few remaining 'echt-Zandvoorters' (we'd say *Ur* in German) don't bother with them much. An ice-cream perhaps of a fine evening, and once or twice in the season the sacred tradition of eating fish on the beach. We are conservative, and drink a beer in the village, 'by' Bluys, the famous old Zandvoort granny known as 'Jans-de-Kraii' – or by Arie Koper. They're all dead and gone, but to us alive. Now, I allow myself to ramble. I am old, now.

If we were to 'eat out' we would never go to the hotels, nor the fly-by-night tourist traps. We, 'the bourgeois', would drive to Haarlem, to Brinkman opposite the Great-Church, to the lovely old Heerenhek in the Tempelierstraat, or to Willy's Heimat – Treslong in Hillegom. All, too, long gone ... But if the spirit moved us to stroll 'up the road' (down, if anything) then a decidedly homely-meal 'bij Annie-Appeltje' – there's another famous old village character. I think it's her granddaughter now, and the food is revolting. Dutch applesauce (eaten with absolutely anything, together with 'frites') is now a bland oversweetened purée out of a tin. Perish the thought ... and Willy makes her own, when she can get proper sour apples, with plenty of salt and pepper, and cinnamon ...

You might well ask the purpose of this nostalgia, this long ramble through les-beaux-jours. There were famous summers in the thirties. A little patience, please.

North of the dorp the buildings peter out. By the point where the Zeeweg turns inland – you could, if you wished, walk in nigh solitude along the beach, right over to Ijmuiden whose jetties and lighthouse can be seen there in the distance, it is quite a trek – there is a little café-restaurant perched at the top of the reep, and a draughty, dismal bus-stop. A couple of hundred metres short of this, and below, like the tents on the beach, is an old Zandvoort landmark, Café Riche, rather forlorn nowadays. A permanent structure. I haven't been there for ages. It isn't really off the beaten track. Plenty of space at the top, to park cars. But coming in, from the Amsterdam direction, one sees the lights and the fleshpots of Zandvoort barely a kilometre in front, and one isn't inclined to stop before reaching them. Perhaps the place *looks* forlorn. Even a little furtive.

Bert made his way through afternoon sunshine, still and autumny. Hazy over Ijmuiden, out there to the north of him, or was that a bit of industrial smog from the cement works? There would be mist later. The sea was placid, shiny with the oily look of low tide. The sun was very hot. No longer the August fire but quite enough to burn asparagus-white tourists who had only now got away on holiday but could enjoy Zandvoort at its best. Thinned crowds and an unstressed waitress. In the village the smell of diesel exhaust and frying oil had lessened noticeably. This far out, there was hardly anybody. A few boys trying to keep surf-sailers upright, but there is not enough wind. The usual sturdy woman striding, not even trying to control the usual bouncy smelly Labrador. The usual long, thin, pink man in a baseball cap, jogging on his enormous shoes which left a vast complicated imprint of the beige and mauve-grey plastic sand, above low-water-mark. A little boy trying to fly a kite but there isn't wind enough even for that.

Bert had walked from the Zeestraat, just clear of lazy wave-lets, the rubber tip of his stick keeping pace with his boots. Now he had to cross the soft sand, so fine as to appear liquid, even in September burning like embers. Here neither stick nor foot leaves trace and he floundered in it like a large stupid fish that has got itself into a shallow. This element, neither earth nor water swallows things, and since quicksand it isn't, and a slowsand we can't call it, we need a new name.

To Bert an element familiar since all time, and only since acquiring his big surgical sabre-scar does it appear this hostile.

The café, huddled under the ramp of the seawall, had an unused look. A few chairs and tables left over from outdoor lunchers, which the waitress had not yet cleared. Two belated businessmen being earnest over a pile of papers and empty coffee cups, and a girl with half a glass of tea gone cold, reading a book. Bert sat down gratefully, to get his breath before climbing the steps to the roadway, and to empty his shoes. All other sand is coarser and less obstinate than ours, which gets in over the tops and even through the eyelets.

As often happens, the how and the why are never quite clear. The tiny initial mechanism, yes, one can remember that. Bert propped his stick against a chair and it instantly fell down. On the principle that a piece of bread and butter always falls butterside-down it fell away from him. Bert's big cut is now painful only when he has to bend double. He may have muttered a half-deleted expletive. Politely, the girl leaned over, picked up the stick for him and held it out at arm's length with a shy smile. But where does an exchange of conventional polite manners – Oh that was kind of you – become something more? Not a conversation. Too disjointed for that. A flicker, first. Sometimes after a thunderstorm, when lightning has knocked out a little local transformer which modifies high tension into domestic current, the lights in the house have gone out. They come on again once or twice in little jolts or trickles, before steadying in reassurance.

There were birds, he remembers that. No nasty seagull, which perches and looks at you with that amazingly disagreeable knowing eye (you are as cold, as greedy, as egoistic and as downright vicious as I am; you're just too much of a hypocrite to admit it.) They don't come within arms' length; you might take a sudden swipe with that nasty-looking stick of yours. The little birds, which the Italians call *uccelli*, the millions of Roman starlings. In Dutch we say *mussies*. They're sparrows, I suppose. Here they potter about, more or less unnoticed unless you're sitting on a terrace. Where someone has eaten a sandwich they land unconcerned on the table at your elbow to pick up crumbs, neat, agile, anonymous as the hovering waiters in expensive restaurants, silently filling your glass and changing the ashtrays. Something of this he said, and she contributed to.

Then he looked with some distaste towards the steep uneven steps, reached for the stick. 'I must be getting along.' She looked at her watch, something like 'Time for me too.' Shyly – 'You find it difficult to walk?' 'Not really but I overdid it a bit, came a thought too far, down on the firm sand where it's cooler.' Timidly – 'Would you like a hand, up the ramp?' He accepted gratefully.

'Think I might wait for the bus back into the village.'

'I've got my bike.' Leaning against the railings. She gave him a steadying, patient arm. Like Erika, the first time he'd got out of bed. She climbed on her bike, gave a cheerful little wave, rode off. It was extraordinary how vivid, how exact – as though she were imprinted on eye and ear. As though there were a tape he has only to rewind and play back. Extraordinary how consoled and comforted ... he was no longer tired, but the bus came and he got in and said 'Hogeweg' – took the short cut home but took pains to play the tape.

Student – nineteen, twenty? Tall girl, not particularly pretty. Well made, good figure. Reddish, brownish cotton skirt and top, neat and cool. Bare arms and legs, tanned, tiny shadow of fine silky hairs. Dark, good skin to tan, apricots. Been a lot on the beach, almost 'olive' ripened, some dash of southern blood. Wide, pale pink, unlipsticked mouth, well cut. Marvellous natural eyebrows, fine and dark and not plucked, a beautiful arch. Couldn't remember the colour of the eyes.

One would know this face again. Plain isn't the word, he

thought. Broad, yes, even heavy, but fine shallow modelling. So that the features are both striking and delicate. He knows that he's floundering. There are roses with this broad flat structure, this multiplicity of close-fitting petals; camellias of this delicate precision, but he hasn't got it right yet. He knows very little about painting. More's the pity as he has often thought, but pictures, somehow ... Still, one hasn't studied old flower books to no purpose at all. And museums, and in Italy – there is some memory eluding him, just there on the periphery of his sight, he'll get it in a moment. A bas-relief, or perhaps a cameo.

*

Stupid Bert. Susceptible Bert. I made it into a comic story for Henk. Something amusing since at a dinner-table one doesn't want a depressing tale. An occasion for robust Dutch humour. And there was Irene. She'd understood, earlier, on an occasion we're not going to mention to Henk. That he wouldn't understand. Old friend of mine he may be but he'd have thought it overstepping friendship. So it was too. Irene handled it better than I did.

That harbour restaurant is a good place. The cook there, he's not just the chef-cook but the owner. Ambitious fellow, in the style of good – and fashionable – restaurants in France or Belgium. A Michelin star or two is what he's after, and from what I hear he's getting it. He had a place in Amsterdam, and had built up a nice reputation for his cooking, but the house was too small for his customers, cramped and awkward. A listed house which it's not allowed to alter, structurally. Endless trouble with the city authority. Ministry too; fine-arts people, architecture. One could find a solution there, but then one's stuck with the Sanitation people, fussy, rightly so, about restaurants. Washbasins, lavatories, I don't know what else – the kitchen itself of course, rules about ventilation and how many cubic metres of fresh air you have to allow. He got fed up and made a deal (as omniscient Henk tells me) with the bank, for this place, which was just a fish-fry joint until he took it over but it's big, and has a good view over the harbour – we have a table on the window side. I remembered a syrupy line from a sentimental old ballad and quoted it to them. 'I saw those harbour lights – that once brought you to me-e.' I'm fond of them both.

Fellow must be carrying a load of debt. Making money, though now. That was always my problem, in business. Like my father, didn't want the bank owning me, telling me what to do. So that like Jan, we stayed small. A good little business but cramped, like the restaurant in Amsterdam. I could have been as rich as Henk is now if I'd been able to take a few risks.

Henk isn't mean. Sure, he throws money around to impress the customers; that's business. He has no need to impress me, but he's generous to a friend, and generous towards his wife. They make a good couple.

Fish of course. What else, in Ijmuiden? And it's the chap's speciality, he's famous for it. Damned expensive place, so we take our time choosing. Henk being Expansive orders a bottle straight off of extremely good wine, and the moment he's tasted it – a Corton Charlemagne no less – and the waiter's filling glasses says 'You better bring us another of these and that'll give us time to think further.' Good, Irene is another hearty swigger.

We live in sad times. My mother, who was German, had a fondness for fish, and so did Jan. Piet Paap the Zandvoort fishmonger had anything you want, in those days. And now you have to come to a house like this, to get anything worth the name. The few and undersized little things left in the North Sea ... So that's why we come here, says Henk, grinning. And we'll have some more nice juice too to go with it.

They've sole of course and turbot and bass. And some real deep water splendours. We can tell ourselves we're in Spain. As well as plenty of the spiny shelly things some people are allergic to. Not us though. This all takes a lot of time, so that we're well into the second bottle and finishing the cunning little goodies to give one an appetite, before we're free at last of the damned head-waiter and Henk wipes his mouth to say 'Come on then Bert, tell all about it.' So now it's my turn to make jokes, but I want to say a word about Irene, sitting there 'being discreet' and has hardly opened her mouth. She has heard most of this already...

She must be pushing sixty but she's a very good-looking woman. As banal a phrase as that might imply a suspicion that describing her is not quite that simple. Seeing people, as I often do, in terms of flowers is not much help because the best, no, the closest I find would be sweet-peas. These are nice little things on a table, in a small pretty jug. Yes but their growth is fussy, untidy, takes up too much space. They need strong supports. This won't do for Irene. It is true that she smells nice and is given to wearing sugary pastel colours.

A smallish woman, trim and neat; a light elegant figure and a light dancer's step. She'd be pretty if her eyes weren't too close together; this with a sharp enquiring nose is foxy. Beady eyes and overquick, as though she were turning everything over wondering whether it was good to eat. This isn't really fair. Nearly everyone thinks her pretty. She is always carefully and skilfully made up, her hair nicely done. Lots of jewellery which she likes and Henk can afford. What is it that sets one's teeth on edge? The eating, in ways indefinable furtive, secretive? No, neither is right. Frightened that someone might come and take the plate away? Better. Perhaps *daring* them to come. Some self-satisfaction, the young vixen who has seen the children well provided-for and is now having a good tuck-in herself. Being also impossibly dainty with the knife and fork; enjoying this mouse (one can't expect rabbit every day) and cleaning the bones, so ladylike.

'So this young girl, really pretty young girl, the loveliest eyes, tells me she's going to shave my bush, can't bring her name to mind, Eva? Edith? – it'll come back to me.'

'Elfi,' suggested Henk with enjoyment.

'There's me, thinking this is the very last train because tomorrow morning is the long-goodbye, but have you ever tried getting it up when she has your dick in one hand and the razor in the other? Even worse is her hand's so light it's like being shaved – your jaw shaved – by a professional with a cutthroat. Whip, he goes with the elegant gesture wiping the razor on the towel while you're wondering is your nose still there, you never felt it gone. So you take a look at dick because it's damn draughty down there, like a poor plucked chicken, without any bush just pathetic. Too late, too late, he cried in grief, across the stormy water.' Henk is guffawing roundly, peeping to see how his wife is taking this. Looking haughty before but now the face is well-brought-up blank.

Holland is a country – England or North America are the exceptions here – where even at a dinner-table a poop joke will not cause consternation. Oddly enough for the original puritan country but Dutch like Spanish lends itself well.

'More lovely girls in Reanimation. You're thinking about taking a crap but down in the mouth because it's all far too much trouble to think about. Two of them have this hideously brilliant scheme for propping you up on the pot, a beauty each side for support, just like two lions on a coat of arms.' Yes, very Dutch, and Henk guffawing is the same man I saw once with a flowering lily.

'It's the same one as in the Grünwald picture, with the Madonna holding out the baby to enjoy it, and the child is laughing – the very same one.'

A funny business, flowers. The debate has always gone on. Aesthetics; beauty? There are those who say that's nonsense, it's merely molecular engineering. Biochemicals, pharmacy. To raise a new hybrid is the same as a new antibiotic. The beauty is irrelevant. What's beauty anyhow? – a feel-good mechanism.

Henk is not like this and neither was I. In the air, the water here, there's more than genetic modification of molecules. There is passion.

Candle-light and wonderful fish. Coarse humour and wonderful wine. Three of us, sharing friendship. Irene is a woman of quality.

She's always a bit overdressed. Odd that Henk, whose taste is good, doesn't see this. Or does he choose not to notice it? Fussy, too elaborate, a flower over-crammed with petals. Her figure and features, her port, her carriage, are good enough to suppose a simpler florescence. Her skin is not very good, and her neckline always too low; overmuch display of bosom and shoulder. Perhaps, Henk might say, this is a natural expression of her personality. That one shouldn't try to alter it. Here, by candle-light, and looking out over the candle-lit harbour, she looks perfectly splendid.

*

I came into Amsterdam by the Amstelveen road. I'd been to 'the office'. I said, I remember, that 'Van Bijl & Zoon' still existed but gave, I think, no other detail beyond saying I sold out when I retired. No need for any detail now except to remark that I'm a partner still, appear as a director and have something more than a life-interest. This only because I was boiling. Word unsuited to the old, or the crippled; I was extremely upset.

Adriaan is a cousin of Willy's, so we've known him all our lives. He grew up too in the Trade: I couldn't and wouldn't deny that he knows it like the inside of his trouser pocket. Good businessman, better than I was: if I'm going to be honest I may as well be clear-sighted. We were showing signs of decline when I left, and now we're on the way up again. Not 'we'. He. Family-arranged affair as well as a sensible business deal; he'd inherited a piece of another smallish firm and a fusion, regrouping, the current phrase is 'restructuring' (typically soapy lawyers' expression) was a natural sort of move when I reached sixty-five years.

I remember that when I was a young chap, working in England for Ralph Vaughan, one heard it sometimes said of him that he was too much of a gentleman to be really good in the 'business' sense. Excellent horticulture technician, good botanist, taught me a very great deal. The sort of man who knew the family circumstances and children's names of every packer; sneered at now as 'paternalistic'. A nephew of his is still around, works at Kew; happier there no doubt. 'Too much of a gentleman'; they won't say that of Adriaan.

'Why – good morning Bert. Glad to see you about again. Heard you'd had a brush with the knife-and-scissor man. Fit again, I hope? Good, good, soon be rid of the stick. Plain exercise and fresh air, that's the thing. Was there some particular question?'

'No no,' said Bert (the damned fool). 'Cast an eye. Needed after being away a while. One gets out of touch so quickly.' I'm not spelling all this out. If I've wounds, no need to rub salt in them. There are more ways than one, too, of being impotent. Anyhow it's obvious, isn't it? He'd been irritated this longish while at my liking to see for myself. No more than every month or so. Nobody's going to say I made a pest of myself. But now the illness gave him just the argument he needed to dislodge me – we've never seen really eye-to-eye. Eject me, that's plain English for you. Statement of accounts from the auditors, for my 'approval', needing my formal signature as a director, that's good enough for me. There's a thing too about a cancer; you've everybody being tactful, wondering how long it will be before the damn thing recurs. Counting the months.

The Dutch! Not conspicuous for tact. Make a virtue of being blunt. We've a phrase for this. *Kat uit de boom zien komen*, we like to see the cat come out of the tree. Don't like messing about. Don't like the English habit of wrapping it up in polite euphemisms. No tangents. We go head-on at things. As I'm about to relate, of silly Bert.

Who says Bert's wrong, come to that? Who says he's silly? Could be I'm the one. Think myself tough?

Our generation's heyday was I suppose the immediate post-war, late forties, fifties. Trying to reshape, rebuild, but it wasn't easy because we had still so much of the old world obscuring and blinding us. We were trying to work with the old tools, unable to break old habits – like poor Ralph, being gentlemanly? It's in parenthesis but this time was also an old-Hollywood heyday. We admired the movies of this period and Bogart was one of our favourite actors. I have always treasured a joke current at the time.

'Bogart? Oh yes, tough. Very tough. Not perhaps quite as tough as Shirley Temple.' I should maybe apply this to myself?

Now good, one is in a rage. First thing one thinks of in a situation like this is reach for your lawyers. In lieu of the gun. This simmers down fairly fast. All that would happen is he'd listen, let me spit it out, get it off the chest, before telling his secretary to fetch a copy of the contract, read it, before saying gently, 'Well, he's got a controlling interest, hasn't he'. It's not like a big company with shareholders. Talk about a blocking-minority is bullshit. Operative word is 'block'. Who's blocking who, and what, and why? I'd only end up blocking myself, blocking Willy, blocking whatever future I still have in the way of prospects of peace.

All I want is quiet. Yes and a regular, reliable, undisputed income is part of that. All a good lawyer does really is to say 'Avoid litigation'. The rest's verbiage.

I walked about. I've known these pavements since earliest childhood. There's a great deal in Amsterdam which changes while you're putting on a clean shirt. There are a few unchanging things left. Among these are a couple of the old stamping-grounds. A lot are swept away. Some of the old hotels keep the style and décor of the past because Victorian luxury is still wanted, still needed. It's in their interest to stay unchanged. Old brass fittings and mahogany furniture never wear out, and were so well made they need no modernizing. A slab of marble can only be replaced by another slab of marble. If some illiterate lout of a footballer or pop singer tears the place up – they've so much money they

think everything is permitted them – it's replaced; it just
goes on the bill. There are places where for a hundred years
the ashtrays have been stolen, and not only by Marlene
Dietrich. They've a contract with suppliers; just go on turning them out the way you've made them since the original
specification. We've lost some treasures. One or two are recognized monuments and it's forbidden to demolish an old
art nouveau interior.

It's the mentality which has changed, the character.
Schiller in the Rembrandtplein; I can recall so well old Frits
Schiller pottering about in his woolly bedroom slippers with
an eye on everything which was his. Nobody left like that
now. Managers are all cheese-rind and candle-end types worrying about the dividend. Nobody now like Ralph Vaughan.

I dug myself in to a place where they keep up the pre-
tences. Much like our 'pub' in the country, the interior is
dusty and they don't wipe the tables down – marble, marble
– the way they used. Along the panelled walls, the stuffed
heads of African beasts. God only knows what – impala and
gemsbok, species probably now extinct in the wild and only
existing in the zoo, and here amazingly antlered if moth-
eaten. A place for cocufied husbands and out-of-date bug-
gered-old-imbeciles like me. Hang your hat and stick up on
the Victorian-mahogany. Say hallo to the giraffes and the
wonderful faded old mirrors. Pee on the yellowed marble
saying 'S$_r$hinx in Maastricht' (Shanks in Barrhead). The
newspapers have all changed, and the *Nieuwe Rotterdamse
Courant* is now part of the Allgemeine-something-else, but it
still comes in the wooden frame to prop up in front of you
while eating. Here came the old boys retired from the
Military-and-Civil in the Dutch East Indies, to drink gin and
pick at the *bitterballen* (tiny meatballs, breadcrumbed and
deep-fried). Served in a starched folded napkin with parsley;
they're still there but now they throw them at you, grease,
crumbs and all ...

The gin had to be very cold, practically deep-freeze, the

way you still get schnapps in a few of the old cafés of Hamburg. The herring was famous and so was the beer. Now it's all like anywhere else. Dearer, that's all; we're paying for the giraffes and for our memories. The menu likewise was very Dutch; the twenty-five varieties of beans (side dishes of gherkins, of chopped onion, of crisp fried bacon). Now it'll just drive home how old I am – Luchow in New York used to be like this. Thick, Dutch pea soup in a silver bowl, the spoon standing upright in it, as one wanted it coming in from skating on the frozen canal. A pork chop *Jagerschotel* in a casserole with onions and apples and plenty of potatoes. Asparagus in season with a hard-boiled egg and lots of nutmeg. The fish was always halibut or turbot; big battered silver sauceboat of *tartare*. Gulls' eggs. The waiters were hobbly old boys who always forgot things but always ran at once to repair matters.

What the hell am I going on about?

Upset. I was feeling pain. I was in pain too, physically. My belly is not that well healed yet. Walk, for any small length of time – Damrak, Kalverstraat, Spui, Singel – from my navel down to my balls there's a message saying Stop. So here I am combating a few kinds of pain. With alcohol. I've never been a gin-drinker. Nor a real beer-drinker. They've a hundred brands of whisky here, Scotch and Irish, bourbon and rye. I don't metabolize the way I used and Willy would have fifty fits. I don't care, I only want to kill the bacteria. I don't want to know. I want only a solid meal to take the edge off and this afternoon I'll be able to drive home and tell Willy it was a boring day really; nothing much happened.

'Why Hal-Lo.' A soft voice penetrating stupor. So I look up and that's Irene. Can't remember when I saw her last, but glamorous as always. Too much so, as usual; her overelaborate dresses and movie-star entrances have always made me laugh. An old friend. I'm fond of her and she knows it. Indeed a pleasant fiction has always existed between us, that I find her attractive and would make efforts to seduce her given the opportunity and acquiescence. On her side a mildly flirtatious manner towards me (and others too, it's part of her style) might lead the onlooker to suppose more than in fact exists. For those who do know her, which would include Willy, a woman with an acid eye upon her own sex, there isn't any question. Irene takes a severely upright view of her married state. These equations are always interesting. Thus, Henk adopts a dashingly gallant approach to any woman he meets, which probably – it is none of my business – masks a few skids out of the path of virtue. Short if sharp, I'd guess. I've seen her smile indulgently, with a pretence of being deceived while making it very clear to Henk (he has some-times dropped a rueful hint) that she knows perfectly what is going on. A good horsewoman. Light rein but the steely hand. Spurs and whip too, I suspect, if the steed is skittish. I've always thought it a pity that they are childless.

I got up and we exchanged the chaste but cosy kisses one has for the wives of old friends. Henk enjoys the pretence that we're really secret lovers. 'Go on,' guffawing, 'take her in your arms.' There may have been moments when he really believed it. We've been friends all our life – she's ten years and more younger than we are – and friendships this old are loose and flexible, well-worn, like a good, comfortable old car all of whose corners have long worn smooth and easy. You can put a strain on it without it complaining.

'What are you doing in this male-chauvinist dump?'

'Taking the weight off my feet. I've been shopping and it came handy.' She is clutching two or three of those huge gaudy plastic carriers, now discarded happily on a spare chair. She loves shopping and spends a great deal of time and trouble on it; agreeably feminine. Willy hates clothes and goes out to buy them groaning as though condemned to stonebreaking in a quarry. 'Look after those, I must pee. What's that you're drinking, pastis, order one for me, back in a sec.'

'Let's have lunch together. Will here be all right?'

'Yes of course. You're looking rather down in the mouth. Come on then, unburden.'

I'll have to watch my step, here. I was indeed down and depressed and that as often happens meant that Bert's features showed more than my own.

One wasn't going to talk about the little business squabble. That would get straight back to Henk, and friends or not – and in the Trade there's no real rivalry between us; our specialities do not overlap; one will still keep quiet about such things. I'd talk this over with Willy, since Adriaan, damn him, is her cousin.

But Bert is still full of his accident. This is perfectly understandable. One had a cancer, all right, there are worse places to get it than in this stupid prostate. No regrets, or no really serious regrets, for being radical; surgery, what the hell. Not like getting the bullet in wartime and knowing that a field hospital would only make the going slower and more painful. Surgery is nowadays bourgeois comfort, and one hasn't the right to complain. There is, though, the psychological shock. One had this crab in the gut, pretty deep in and passably advanced from what one had learned of the biopsy and Heinrich's fairly laconic view of the matter. Right, Professor Heinrich, seen as a first-class knife-artist by all save that abominable Nathalie, went ein-zwei-drei, if you can call it that, over four hours of careful patient carpentry, counting the stops for running pathology tests to be sure the crab has metastasized no further than was foreseen. Afterwards, he was admirably honest. One can be pretty sure, but one can't quantify. Percentages of risk mean nothing in this game; no such thing as a one, a two, a three percent chance of a recurrence with an ein-zwei-drei of months or years. It's the some-day-tomorrow, and it's Tuesday fortnight, and live forever, Jo, because that's just as likely.

This still takes a bit of getting used to. He isn't totally carapaced, ol' Bert. (If we're going to speak of crabs. Bert is fond of them: a crab salad, what the pub calls a 'dressed

77

crab', is one of his favourite meals. In the States they have exotics. Soft-shell crabs. 'Porcelain' or stone crabs. Maryland crabcakes – hard to get nowadays. And right here in Europe many's the happy moment spent in Brittany swimming in bits of shell and overdoing the mayonnaise – and in London: pint of Guinness and don't hurry in the pulling it.)

Hell, it's only three weeks ago. He gets very tired still after a bit of walking. Big slash down the belly like cutting a goddam melon in half. One can't disguise from someone as sharpeye as Irene; she'll see the stick anyhow, and the way Bert walks.

Last, and this is a painful twinge, only yesterday making the small therapeutic stroll through Zandvoort, who should he see but Lalage riding her bike, carelessly muscular those lovely silky brown legs turning so effortlessly. It's all still a bit raw, a bit harsh, gripes one in the balls.

Is this some kind of 'diary'? People do keep diaries. I never have, but have sometimes wondered 'what are they for?' I'm not talking about a business record of meetings and such: Jan kept a daybook of work done, taught me to do the same. No, but the Got up, washed, went to bed sort (the old schoolboy joke of 'Day Three – didn't wash') – what are they for? Is one going to put 'To Whom It May Concern'? If one were some kind of historic personage; Queen Victoria writing 'Dear Mr Disraeli came to tea and we had such an interesting talk about China'; somebody in later years might think it pointed to a moment – if he were writing the history, say, of the Opium War. But Jan Jansen in Purmurend. Are his grandchildren supposed to read it and think 'What an interesting life old Dadda had; just think; the day Kennedy was shot he was on the bus from Bussum to Naarden, and he's not going to let you forget it.'

I have found out this much: something happens to make you suffer a moment of horror, humiliation, fear – terror. Write that down. It helps, in getting a grip on that, learning to live with it. So that now I'm going to write about that fool

Bert. I've got him in the pincers. Shine a light and hold the glass on him. Let him wriggle. Too bad. This way, I get the better of the pain.

He can talk to Irene. She is a good listener. She's experienced and has some sophistication. She is kind. He can feel free of social inhibitions. There've been years of Dutch humour about this fictional supposition, that in her company he was excited. Get a pleasantly teasing erection from imagining himself in bed with her. And now the poor old boy 'can't get it up'. 'A banal, a boring, quite likely a commonplace subject of remark among elderly men. With a woman liked, even trusted, will it be in such bad taste?

Between a man – oldish man – and his wife of many years there is a good deal that goes unsaid, but is well understood. That's as it should be. This is more than that good old comfortable car with which I compared a friendship of years.

So that after coming to an understanding with Professor Heinrich (there is also a special relationship with the man in whose hands you put your life) there wasn't a lot Bert needed to talk over with Willy. If there's a moment when courage is needed, and one might feel that the reserves are running short, the other will supply without thinking about it. So do friends; it's what friends are for. So can complete strangers when they're in the same boat – or the same wartime cattle-car headed for the unknown destination – herded together with people one didn't know and had perhaps never before seen, but friendship comes quickly when you've barely enough to shift your feet and there's not much air, either.

A few technical details to discuss (she'll get it all from the girls within an hour or two, anyhow). Like the risk – there is a risk – of incontinence; one's wife may find herself with a bit of home nursing to do, once he gets home. But the castration thing one doesn't need to talk about; that's the modesty of people who have shared the same bed these forty years. Is it surprising at all, that in a café, over drinks, over a meal...?

No; I don't find it in the least strange. Bert gave it no thought, felt no constraint, where with another man – however old a friend spontaneity would give way to an act, a comedy. Pride to protect, and maleness. He could tell Irene, in simplicity, that feeling oneself no longer a man is a bitter thing to go through. She listened quietly, her face gentle, no inclination to fidget. Nothing more asked of her.

Not that one would sentimentalize: there are plenty of women whose purposes and enjoyments appear to be talking about castration – really one does have to laugh at Bert, whose view of women as devoted wife, helpmeet and friend is as Victorian as the Albert Memorial.

I couldn't claim to be an expert on the subject. Men among themselves put on the knowing face, let fall truisms in the world-weary voice of those who've been around and could tell a tale if so inclined. 'You know how it is in Havana in the early morning.'

As far as I know then, the hardest women can show kindness. There are badhearted men, but most evil is born of suffering. That ballbreaker is trying to live with her own unhappiness.

There's an old Hollywood joke. The actress playing a fearful nymphomaniac was coming across flat. Said the director, 'Try to look as though you'd just had an orgasm.' To which the girl is said to have replied 'What's an orgasm?'

Bert was a bit shaky leaving the café, from a good deal to drink as much as anything. Putting weight on the stick. Most of Amsterdam – in the old town – is still paved with brick. They jump and they settle; this old ground is unstable. Tourists like to photograph the picturesque waterways, the dear-little-bridge. Underneath your feet it's full of sewers and cables. The Amsterdamse workman, not in the least Dutch, leaves bricks lying about where he digs holes. Ralph Vaughan used to say that since as far as he knew there was no subsoil at all he could never understand why all the buildings didn't fall down. Bert isn't drunk, but footline and skyline alike are a bit crooked. Kind Irene is helpful: here, take my arm. All the ensuing dialogue had a surreal quality. Of innocence, as in a children's book.

'But I can drive you home.'

'No, dammit, I've the car here. Can't leave it. Bit pissed, too. It's only fatigue really. This morning, walked too far. Hurts now. Abdo. Had a Caesarian, right down the middle.'

'If you could have a rest. A sleep, perhaps.' This awful street. 'Why not, oh hell, book a hotel room for you? In a couple of hours you'd be —'

'Be all Stunden-hotels, around here.'

'Who cares? In a way, so much the better. What's wrong with this?' To a practised eye, of course a hotel-by-the-hour. It was a bit early in the afternoon, business still slack.

'I'm ready to sit down on the bloody step.'

'Don't be so silly, I'm going in to ask.'

'No, you better leave me here, could be embarrassing for you.'

'Nonsense, I'm coming in to see that you're all right.' The desk, naturally, made no difficulties.

'Can you manage the stairs?' These are all steep, narrow old houses. Surprisingly clean and unsmelly, which perhaps is Dutch. Irene took a sharp, Dutch look around. Bert let himself flop on the bed, glad of it.

'I'll just have a quick pee, profit by the opportunity.' Bert horizontal, shut his eyes, breathed deeply.

'Irene.' She was arranging her hair in front of the glass.

'Yes dear. Is that better?'

'No. Take your clothes off.'

'Oh.' Thunderstruck.

'Don't haver.'

'Oh dear. I don't think I can.'

'Of course you can.'

'But that's . . .'

'No it isn't. I'm helpless as a bloody baby, couldn't lay a finger on you.'

'It's still adultery.'

'No it isn't. Not even here.'

'Oh dear. You don't really think that would help you.'

'Irene, you're an old friend. Do as I ask.'

'Isn't it hideously cold-blooded?'

'Believe me – it isn't.' She stands unhappy, irresolute.

'I want to do anything for you I can, if it would help quieten you.'

'Yes but stop talking.'

'Oh – dear – this is voyeur, isn't it. If it will unwind you – you mustn't touch me.'

'Don't worry because I couldn't.'

'Oh Mummy, if you could see me now.'

'Darling Irene.'

'Don't talk to me or I'll scream, and what would they think here then?'

Not, I'm afraid, at all enthusiastically, she took off her jacket and began unbuttoning her blouse, banana-fingered.

Skin; bra. Bert who is trying hard to be thrilled pulled the pillow under his head to stop his neck from hurting. From a curtained window comes a cold grey afternoon Amsterdamse light upon the Voorburgwal. Seagreen bra. Seagreen skin.

'Take the bra off.' I do not intend to be crude, nor offensive to Irene. I have wondered about her mind here, plainly a mass of confusions. A good and a kind woman. There wasn't any thinking. People spout a lot of silly cliché about dreamlike states, acting 'somnambulistically' – what a grand word. I don't know what she thought she was doing but I'm sure that neither did she.

Poetry hasn't entered much into my scheme of things. Not predominant, you might say, in the lives of Dutch flower growers, though I wouldn't want you to think we were totally insensible to beauty. I've seen some hardhanded and hardheaded characters stand staring at a plant as though mesmerized, and stock still. There are lines, possibly I'll call them back to mind, in Spanish. No; gone – but they concerned 'my Andean and sweet Rita' and began 'I wonder what she is doing at this hour'. She is standing outside her door looking at distances, hearing harmonies. She shivers then, in the cold. She is wearing her skirt with lace; she smells of sugar-cane. Why this should have struck a note which moved me I have no idea.

The bra might have been a bit tight, because she massaged for a moment her ribcage, under the arms. It wasn't cold in that room but her nipples came up as though snow was fall-ing on them. There must have been a mechanism which took over, an automatic pilot of sorts. Sounds cold, that. Speaking for Bert this pleasure has to be called erotic since I know of no other word. There might have been impotent poets who could describe it better. Dutchly speaking he ought to have been getting a lashing great hard on. He hasn't and doesn't; his dick is just sore and feels bruised, like the legendary lady who caught her tit in the wringer.

About Irene I've no notion whatever. Erotic or auto-, she was under strain. If the word 'erect' can apply, that was her. A very good figure for her age; no way could you call her limp-breasted. Odd thoughts fleet by one. 'Limp' reminded him of the charming old drunk on the Bogart-island who asks 'was you ever stung by a dead bee?' – Bert would say he knows now all about stings from dead bees.

Her eyes had gone glassy. She was staring hard at the picture they'd slapped on the wall above the bed, to make you feel at home, like. A cheap flower-print; van Huysum, good still-life man if a bit florid for our tastes today. Cut it off a calendar, likely; the sort of thing one does have on calendars. I've sent them out myself, to customers. Compli-ments of the season, lady and gentleman, from your friendly neighbourhood suppliers. She undid her skirt.

The sea-green knickers match the bra. In the bygone, lecherous Hong-Kong years we used to call these 'French'; they're cut with a flare instead of tight and clinging. One knew to be sure that her taste in underclothes was like this,

83

grand and expensive, not what we'd have called tarty but certainly flashy like everything else of hers. Crêpe de Chine. A cunning detail, the lace edging is 'to contrast', a warm orangey pink. Bert admires. Splendiferous. A floriferous composition. Mister van Huysum, specialist in peonies, would appreciate.

I don't know what instinct made her turn round to undo her placket. A pathetic bottom, white and vulnerable, but intensely, plastically female and quite lovely. One can see also that she's never had children. She made up her mind then to turn around. I think that instinct, again, brought her arms up to cross her wrists over her head, the pose of caryatids, of dance-trained Russian gymnasts about to flip. Women have these three enchanting patches of hair; a great mistake to shave them.

Now I am really sorry, to make vulgar comparisons. One can if one so wishes observe the difference on television. There's porn, which leaves much less to the imagination than you'd like, and there is 'erotic', which isn't, and is indeed so prudish you're bored stiff. (No, not stiff.) Both are sad. Irene was neither, and she'd stopped being sad.

Laboriously, Bert had managed also to get undressed. I am safe in saying that she was filled with pity. I think that the wretched sight determined her to show what she could do if she tried. With maybe fury? No, now I've got detachment back I think the word would have to be 'frantic'. She reached for the room's one chair (What is it for? One must suppose, to hang clothes on.) She sat on this, spread her thighs, gasped out 'Will this be better?' This – by the way – is a well-known flower of the lily family. I don't care for amaryllis and the kindred, but the curves of a girl's opened thighs and the lips of her vulva are the lily's petals. The biological details of corolla, stamens, need not concern us. Remember, you have been stung by a *dead* bee, and need not thus envy bees, so buzzingly self-satisfied as they burrow into these opened, ready, sugar-cane-perfumed delights. The growth, the disposition, and the display of pubic hair is identical to flower configurations.

This is 'to have and have not' with a vengeance, if I may reach for a cliché, unable to unsheathe the sword. I am horribly sorry for them both. She took the only way open to her, and poor Bert tried hard, to no end. She didn't make a lot of noise.

'My poor dear. Is there nothing at all I can do?' Bert had – one had better not say himself in hand – under, eventually, some sort of command.

'It would appear not.'

'Will I dress? No, my poor lamb, get into bed and I'll come and cuddle.' Two poor wretches.

Warmth, moisture, it's better than nothing. She loosened, tightened, made her best effort. Better than Carmen Sternwood. She came under his hand, even if he felt nothing at all: well now, isn't that just lovely. Mark, that horrible Carmen, all she did was lie on the bed with no clothes on and giggle. Irene no doubt has her selfish side, but here she was so unselfish it hurts. She thinks of herself as experienced, and tries what she knows which isn't very courtesanely. She 'had plenty of time but oh dear, now we both have to cope with the rush hour'. So that the desk wasn't sorry to see them go, if saddened at not selling them drinks: these bourgeois adulterers are always so bloody penny-pinching.

One last word and it's about flower painters, since a flower trader ought to know something about them and I've looked at a few good ones. You can tell because the good ones can draw. Thus Klimt, great calendar-man that, isn't very good, but to go no further than Vienna, where they've whores as well as flowers, Schiele is. So I think of Irene, and then I think about those poor starveling skinny street girls (but he drew them well) who took their clothes off for a penny bun and masturbated for another threeha'pence. She just for love.

*

Now I wonder; would I have spelt all that out, going into fine detail, if it wasn't for the wound deeper than I could have known or guessed at. Professor Heinrich would be interested to hear of this? Or merely irritated (doctors are never 'upset' for they always think they know it all, and if they find they don't, then keep quiet about that.) 'I can assure you that there's no reason medically speaking why you should feel suffering. The photos would serve as a textbook illustration of a lovely clean job.' Of course he never said anything of the sort. 'The psychology of this is something else; I'm only a surgeon.' It should be obvious that I'd never dream of going back to utter anguished yelps at the good man. This isn't a story for doctors.

Oh all right then, I suppose it is. Lawyers would cringe, and hide behind their psychiatric experts...

Holland really is a ridiculous country. Before the war we were among the most backward-looking corners of Europe. Largely I suppose because in the '14–'18 war we maintained our fiction of neutrality. That time the Germans took the quick way through Belgium. We wrapped up inside our frontiers and had a fit of the dignities (a good deal of trafficking no doubt with both sides). In 1940 we got awakened rather brutally. (It is famous that the prime minister of the time addressed us on the wireless, the day before they marched in. His words are less notorious than 'Peace in our Time' but are remembered in Holland. He said, 'Go peacefully to sleep, good people'.)

I'm sorry; I'm getting old. My mother never wore lipstick in her life. In the moral sense also we were extremely hidebound. The Calvinist (Reformed) church was still a great power in the land. Whores painted their faces. There were a good many in Amsterdam, that sinful city. What I mean, look at us now. Economically, socially, 'scientifically', we are the sharp edge of progress, at the forefront of the European Community, held up as an example by all shambling old-fashioned places like Germany and France – and of course

England. We're the shining light of everything modern.

Down in the south we've a loony-bin – I must apologize again; this calls for two immediate modifying comments. First is that of course we mustn't call it that; it's a *psychiatric hospital*. I'm afraid that in the club, the pub – we are disgracefully racist. We still say 'Oh – women!', we still say 'the niggers'. Second is that even within our own minuscule bog (Holland, historically the Pays Bas built upon the silt of the Rhine and Maas estuaries, today contains the fleabite of some fifteen million souls, which is about the size of Mexico City) we still manage to be racist. Here in the province of Noord-Holland we view the south as inferior. 'Belgians' down there; 'Flamands'. There'd still be a few of my age who'd say 'Catholics'.

'Afijn' as Jan used to say (a Dutch version of 'Enfin' or 'Anyhow'), the psychs down there thought it would be a good idea to bring a few of the less disturbed patients (under careful supervision) to the local bordel now and then. This would appeal to one's sense of humour; if any. Picture the fearful outcry from the Tory Party! What – Mentals brought to a house of prostitution and that on public funds ... a very Dutch detail is that Social Security gets a forty per cent discount from the bordel.

I think it hilarious. Can – never mind the ethics – a public prostitute be called a therapist, to be reimbursed from state insurance funds?

In Denmark nobody would turn a hair, while in France a good half of the Judges would still get a sharp go of the falling-sickness, rolling about in their ermine: take care he doesn't swallow his tongue. Still, nearly half of them are now women, and the proportion is rising. The women seem somehow less stuck inside the McNaghten Rules governing insanity. Perhaps it is reassuring to think that a good half of the prostitutes are women, still.

A customer of Jan's was a judge, in Haarlem; a famous and sinister old reactionary (but he had a loved, fine and cherished garden; will we ever know upon what grounds we may seek acquitment?). He would have swallowed his cigar, mightily multiplying in impassioned advocacy: Bring back the Cat. I am not going to give his name. He might have had children, conceivably still alive, and who could be bitterly embarrassed since ashamed of him. Or, which would be worse, proud of him.

Not a 'sitting' judge. The French call these ones 'standing' to make a distinction, since they have all the same formation and could at some stage transfer to 'the bench'. Of course they don't stand; they occupy the curule chair of the Public Prosecutor. Here in Holland they are called the Officers of Justice. This one was notorious, among the public; among the lawyers who plead in the criminal courts; among other judges – even, which is to say it all, among the police. He shouted, he bullied. In his office, preparing ferocious requisitions, he always had a cigar going. Not Cuban, one is glad to say, but a good, thick, massive Dutch cigar. And he had a profound sense of sin.

Sin. Very serious affair in Holland, that, even today. We had much too much of it. Though today, I wonder, now and then, whether the world wouldn't be better off with a bit more of it. Since the only tenet nowadays applicable is that money is a good thing and we ought to make more of it. I know a lot about sin, was brought up amidst a great deal of it. My mother, God-fearing North-German woman, even when Catholic they are very protestant, had a powerful consciousness of it. If she picked up a cent dropped on the pavement the fact would worry her.

In England too I have found remarkable traces of the puritan, image-breaking, Papist-burning tradition. Astonishment; there is also in the traditionally Catholic countries (it's in Spain, as in Holland, that harlotry is the most virulently religious observance). It is I suppose the same everywhere. Travels in Bayern or Poland showed me nothing different: where Jesuit architecture is at its most extravagant, whoredom follows suit. Henk knows Japan better than I do (he has made rather a corner in maples); I must ask him whether the same applies. Of the incestuous relation between Sex and the Law I have a pretty example found in Ireland; a fair treat, squire, my old market porter would have called it. I'm telling this because I've *time*; though I don't know how much.

Monks; I was making a garden for them. A liking for plainchant led me to their church at Compline time. They have a very beautiful evening hymn; 'Te lucis ante terminum'. Two or three onlookers in the nave, and an elderly congested gentleman taking it very seriously and bawling the responses in Latin. I am moved when the tenor voice breaks so abruptly into the surging rhythm of the 'Salve Regina'. Those gruff celibate voices (celibacy is apparent, it has a very strong smell) hailing the Queen, it is brought mightily home to one that she's a *woman*.

But this red-faced chap shouting about love and mercy, it was a Tory Party delegate on about his Land of hope-and-glory. So at supper I asked the Father-Guestmaster who that might be. He was illuminating. That is the Attorney-General, a gentleman who often comes here for Refreshment. A cleansing, and the restatement of principles. Like for instance the death penalty for wilful homicide. Right now he has to prosecute a dreadful case of – the holy man seemed well briefed.

We did slip into a, I won't say debate. Intelligent man if a bit greasily tactful with the Guests. I mustn't be tactless – Dutch businessman, sound on oh, cypresses, and the like. Not my role to say the Salve-Regina is about hope, gentleness, patience, fortitude, and being a mother. Was it Bernard of Clairvaux who composed this? What's this death-penalty-man, veins swelling in his forehead, bellowing about? Suddenly that got right up my nose. Heilige Maria, she's the mother of mercy and I could do with a word from her. A fine invocation for the government's Attorney-General. Mercy, that's for us bourgeois. For the Lumpenproletariat, put a stop to these infamies. Man there killed his wife, up the chimney with him. Monks and Judges, great experts on women.

My trouble is, I belong on both sides.

*

Even now, when we're on top of the Alle-Heiligen, this weather ... I'm groping for the English word. Easy (as often, when you look for something, cannot find it) – All Hallows. Tomorrow the Eve of the – that's right, Halloween. We don't really set much store by it here in this traditionally Protestant country. It's more a southern, Catholic thing – the 'Toussaint'. But I've always liked it, and not just for professional reasons. You have to recall that this is florists' heaven. Bigger than Mother's Day because that's only a commercial fake, whereas this is rooted in the peoples' hearts. Everyone, and I mean that, brings the pot of chrysanthemums to the family graves. Heather: florists have often invented modes but these two are constant. And in the churchyards that evening is a very pretty sight. The graves have been weeded, the stones cleaned, the flowers lovingly – and reverently – placed. And at twilight on every tomb burns a nightlight in its glass bowl – even a jam jar will do. Be it only this one day, it is good to remember our dead. On this one day we call them all Holy. How many American children, one wonders, know the meaning of the word? Dressing up, and Trick-or-Treat, I suppose it still goes on. In our villages too the gangs go from house to house looking for sweets, and singing songs whose meaning they've forgotten.

It was only to be expected that people would cash in. The supermarkets are full of pumpkins, ready hollowed out to save you the trouble; Dracula masks and witch outfits. Plastic fangs – plastic pumpkins too. Children love the delicious shiver of pretending to be frightened.

The day belongs to women. The guardians of the past, of memory; it is they who hallow. In Paris they have set out before dawn, in the mist, on a journey of maybe many hundred kilometres, to the village of their origins. And here they come marching, set of face, cradling the chrysanths in their arms, and with a shopping bag for the little fork and trowel, and a Scotchbrite to clean the stains and lichen off their stone. When the housekeeping is done they will kneel, for a prayer, a *memento mori*. It isn't merely pious. They are good women. The men trail behind, self-conscious, wearing their faces of solemnity, clasping their hands and bowing the neck for Granny and Grandpa. Do the English, too? Some few, at least. A thought for Uncle Jim lost in Burma. Hurry up though; it's beginning to rain.

There are women who stop for a second at the abandoned, neglected stone where nobody ever comes, and some think to carry a spare flower, to lay on it.

Willy has had her pious face these last two days; she has graves in two or three of the villages. I will go with her, and we'll finish here on the edge of this village – at the edge of the dunes. In this churchyard there is also a fresh grave. Luckily it is a municipal cemetery, a large one. It is probable that I would not recognize 'Carla's parents' even if our paths should cross. We have several pots to deliver. Willy likes the small-flowered, domed plants. We get these of course at cost price. Willy kneels. Not in her eternal trousers; this day she'll have a suit on, with a skirt. She always manages to ladder her stockings but this once she won't care. Our children will not be visible. Perhaps they go to their husbands' families. There are many choices. In Germany there are those who go to the sites of the death camps. Or to where the Wall used to stand. To throw a flower into the Elbe would be as good a way as any.

My own turn will come soon enough. In some ways I'm 'quite well again' but I catch Willy looking at me now and then. A lot of people now have themselves cremated. It doesn't worry me much.

This weather! Disconcerting is the word and we ought to be grateful: does one remember it going on and on like this?

– the subject of conversation, with everyone I meet. It does of course, if rarely. Jan, who marked it all down on his desk calendar (and seldom kept those), could have told you; seldom, but not extremely so. Myself, sitting here, I could tell you and have, boringly, to anyone who'll listen, of a year some twenty years back when we sat like this in the blazing sunshine till almost the end of November. But we are so conditioned to it being bad when not vile ('Toussaint weather') that we're quicker to remember the years when it was already snowing on this day. The year the car skidded on dead leaves and hit two more; there was a considerable fuss which I turned round by threatening to sue the municipality for not having swept the street. Here there are leaves which haven't even begun to fall; some scarcely beginning to turn, in this long and placid series of windless days ... a sky so blue and untroubled. The sun has that heavy, oily quality, yellow as boxwood, soaking in to one like varnish. The table is hot to the touch. Here on the terrace outside 'Arie Koper' they've left the parasols up, the late tourists are shirtsleeved and summer-frocked, sit down and fan themselves, and order ices. One or two old-Zandvoorters (counting myself, known here these fifty years) sit like lizards with unmoving eye. Not everything has changed. The pub isn't what it was in Arie's time.

This is the centre of the dorp, between the 'Hervormde' church and the town hall, the Raadhuis, pompous name for a fairly unpretentious building. But I can remember when the Kerkstraat was lined with trees, and over the way was 'Rinkel' where they had the best cakes and the female bourgeoisdom sat to drink coffee. Where now are the old-Zandvoorters? – in the churchyard.

Stretch the legs well out, for a slight alteration in posture still eases the sitting. And to feel the sun go in. I am healed? That fearsome slash down the centre of my belly; that, yes. Deeper in, I'm none too sure. The walking strengthens one. There isn't the total exhaustion of the day with Irene. Down there in the centre of – gravity is it? – the brutality, perceptible. Nice to imagine that this therapy-sunlight could get that far.

Damn. Damn. I was wondering why that face seemed familiar. Worse, my eye strayed there while wondering. Catching the eye, fellow feels encouraged to cross the terrace, all smiles and bonhomie, to go howdy.

'Meneer van Bijl. Top of the morning, lovely one it is.' Deep-breathing muscle-stretching idiot.

'Mr Dijkstra isn't it?'

'Dijks – ma. Lots of people' – grinning – 'make that little mistake.' I have him pegged, he's that plainclothes dogsbody from the police, writer-down of heaven knows what in his little shorthand booky, it's sticking out of his pocket. 'Mind if I join you?' I do mind. As usual, got pinned down; it's too obvious I'm in no hurry to get away. Even if I could spring to my feet. My stockbroker waiting there on the corner.

'Where's your friend then? Bout, right?'

'Oh he'll be along. Any moment.' And right on cue another one that's so terribly pleased to see me, shaking my hand like I was four years lost in the jungle, Dr Livingstone, odd name that; this of the flap ears and the little greeny eyes would be the sleuth from the *New York Herald*.

'We're only having coffee but what can we get you?'

'Thanks, one is all, this early anyhow.'

'True enough,' looking unnecessarily at his watch, 'roll on apéro time, work work work,' theatrically. 'We envy you.'

'What is it this time?'

'No different.'

'Never cleared that up? Newspapers are always the same, lose interest and rush on to the next thing thought interesting. Sorry, confidential is it? Just being curious, I've the time for it.' What are they both grinning at? Fellow with his 'little error' grinning all the time.

'Ah yes, these big walks along the beach.' I looked astonished, maybe I was, too, at that. 'No need to be surprised.

The whole of Zandvoort wends its way, under our weary but paternal eye. Nothing we miss.'

'It doesn't sound very interesting.'

'No but it's our job. The net is paid out – miles long, those horrible Japanese trawlers – and what do we bring in? Man defaulting on alimony payments to his divorced wife in Almelo. Dog licenses, three joints of mary-jane, very poor haul for the Murder Commission. We better start catching fish or they'll begin that nattering over our expenses – what, all that petrol just to go to Zandvoort? Mean, you know. But we will, we will. Ol' Dave here, plodding round Plan Noord; she lived out there, you know.'

'No I didn't know.' I don't think it makes the faintest odds what you tell them. They expect everyone to tell lies, whether or not there's any need to, whether or not about something trivial. They're the police and everyone lies to the police automatically. 'I must be on my way,' getting my arse upright, which still doesn't come easy. 'Your coffee's getting cold.' As good an exit line as any.

Am I Pitiable? Did Irene find me merely pitiable?

Along the beach. When the tide is out, and the sand is firm, without being sticky. Tide in, along the Boulevard; no way can one walk in soft sand; as well wade in knee-high water. The same keeps me out of the dunes, these days ... Of course there are paths too, stretches packed hard, trodden by many, and whom might you meet? Grassy bits, and the sand firmly anchored. Watery bits and even canals, paths along them. Even paved bits and nigh-roadways, for the cars and little vans where agents of the different administrations keep an eye on affairs – others again would need a four-wheel-drive, bogs where it would be easy to get stuck. There was once a well-established track along the shortest line from here to Haarlem, called the Fishers Path since along here the bonneted fishwives carried their creels and baskets, for sale on the market – many years ago. There are old postcards showing them, barefoot and sturdy; they had need to be.

Low tide is wonderful; at night too. These still sunny days – the nights are frosty, and the sky full of stars. You'll meet nobody, and there might be a moonpath along the water. An elderly romantic is indistinguishable from an elderly Tory: we are both rigidly, fanatically con-ser-va-tive in our ways. Reactionary would be the accepted term. I do not like the village as it is today.

Along the Boulevard – even at night – there are too many damned cars. Few people walk, then, or bicycle. One won't maybe say dangerous but there is the risk. Robbery for any motive, not just to buy drugs. Other peoples' money is nice to have when you can pick it up easily. Assault; there've been people beaten up badly, you'd almost say for fun, and not only frustration because they'd nothing in their pockets. And there's the stink, our ever-present reek of frying oil and diesel exhaust and the filthy chemical scents manufacturers now shove in anything even to clean the drains out and which are so nauseatingly lingering. I avoid the streets at night. By day it's evident that the smells are worse, but you notice them less. I dislike the dust, and these days I dislike the heat, which bounces off the concrete. The bricks of my youth seemed to absorb both. Or was it that I was young, and altogether without thought?

So now I'm an old dog, taking the same walk every day, stopping at each lamppost to check the smells, irritated by anything new or unexpected. Then one goes back home; glad to be home; pleasantly fatigued and aware of having done one's duty. Willy has opened the windows; shaken and hung out the smelly blanket from my basket. I climb into my basket, after a lot of turning round to make myself comfortable. I might well go into the kitchen, pour myself a drink. Shortly, Willy will open a can of dog food. I am a creature of routine, like the same thing at the same time. Willy gets old too. With her it takes the form of saying the same thing upon the same occasion, which is very Dutch and one has learned to dread it. It is in contrast to the body she keeps so limber. I realize that this sounds denigrating, and it is quite unfair.

No, I do not take the same walk every day: I may as well be fair to both of us. The dorp is small and one does have the feeling of being wrapped up in tissue paper and laid in a nice clear florist's cardboard box (the name embossed in copy-book gold lettering.) West is the sea and that puts the lid on us. North is Ijmuiden and south is Noordwijk and east are the dunes. So that I do quite often take the car, park it in Vogelsang or – the restriction is that one has to walk in a loop back to the car, which I dislike.

I was in the car. She was on her bike. Close to where I first saw her; just where the Sea-road curves inland, back towards Haarlem. I slowed and said awkwardly 'Hallo'. Awkward because Bert, because of sitting in a stupid car, because 'Hallo' is a stupid thing to say.

She recognized him. Smiled – stopped. Her foot down; on the old high bikes one had to jump off. It's a modern bike, like Lalage's – cheaper. She could sit on her saddle and talk, to him stuck behind the controls.

But what is there to talk about? Amazing how this weather keeps up. No I'm not going anywhere particular. Bert gets a dashing, a brilliantly original idea.

'Lets go eat a bite somewhere.' Super-quick planning, yes. 'I'll drive slow and you follow. There's quite a good spaghetti joint in Overveen.' She thought about it. Had been thinking of buying a sandwich. Well okay; why not?

As far as the next village; drifting along; watching her in the mirror; sagely bicycling.

'I don't even know your name.'

'Carla.'

'A bit early for eating. Sit in the sun, have a beer, shall we? Better idea – an Italian apéro. I just have to make a phone call.'

'And I have to wash my hands.' Bert can be awkward; she is not. Self-possessed, modest but not primly so.

'Willy – don't wait lunch, I met a friend, I'll have a sandwich in the pub. No, out in Bloemendaal. All right; see you...'

'So now we've time to think of the next step; spaghetti maybe but which one?'

'Oh what a pretty colour.' It's only Campari.

'Gets better still when you put orange juice in it.'

'What's funghi?' A pretentious menu and a simple girl. 'I know bolognese and carbonara – these things intimidate me.' Bert paternalistic; try not to be pompous. The simplicity goes with a natural poise. She is open – a sense of fun; she is plainly enjoying herself. This is a treat. She is not guarded. A student. Must work at it; she is not rich. A straitened background. She's never been in Italy; never been anywhere ... By next year, she hopes ... a solitary girl; doesn't fit much into the band. Withdrawn; not a lot of friends; boyfriends you know – not a lot of time. There'll be time, she's at the very beginning and there's a long way to go. A long path to trudge; be serious about it. Likes raw things, likes salad; yes please, I'd love a glass of – I like the straw-covered flask. 'And I was going to eat a bread-with-ham...' But where have I been all my life, wondered Bert. Willy – forty years ago – strictly-brought-up, stiffly-mannered dancing-class young bourgeois girl, but the stamp of money on her. Narrow convent education. Been to Paris or Florence, look at the pictures, without understanding a damn thing about them. A few months ago, Lalage; the new young, used her body as something to have fun with. Ambitious and shortly-to-be-wealthy background: what the hell, eat and drink everything, take huge bites. That's what it's about. Have Fun. Don't look back. History is all balls. It's happened, you can't change it, so what importance has it? Don't look forward: the world is probably coming to an end: make sure you enjoy it.

But in between – where has he been, all his life?

'I enjoyed that,' said Bert pouring out the last of the

wine: she put her hand over her glass, no more.

'It was delicious.' A conventional phrase, in a conventional voice as though having said too much, no doubt drunk too much, she was signalling, like at a level-crossing: do not attempt to cross after the gates have closed. But there is a little pause before the light begins to wink and the bell starts ringing. Boys duck under the barrier and it has been known that they got killed doing so.

'We could do it again,' keeping the voice light.

'Wouldn't that be very boring for you?'

'Then I wouldn't ask, would I?'

'I'd think – but tomorrow I'm back at work. Students' canteen.'

'What time do you finish?'

'Late maybe, six or after – bureaucratic kerfuffle.'

'I'll pick you up. We could drive out along the riverside.'

'They'll expect me at home ... I can say I had a students' meeting or something.'

'No, don't tell stories on my account.'

'You don't understand. There probably is a meeting, since we're never short of things to protest about. I can cut that ... Fusspotting rather ... tend to cling. I try to be tactful. I don't call that telling lies ... Listen, I have to buzz. Thank you ... uh, all right, pick me up outside the Fac – you know where that is? There's a pub at the corner.'

*

I should be laughing. Student-time again – what, after half a century? Hanging about, eaten by nerves, will she come? – it's getting later and later. Didn't have a car, of course. Had the bike; she'd get on the back carrier. There weren't many girl students. There weren't many of us – the University wasn't a quarter of the present size. Students were still an 'élite'; we wore special scarves, had funny hats, eccentric affectations of appearance and manner. The 'Lawyers' in Leiden, the 'Engineers' from Delft or Wageningen. Confidence, arrogance; we had an assured future. I was worse

98

than most because I hadn't the polish of the bourgeois background, didn't know which knife-and-fork to use.

Then there was the great expansion, bringing with it the Great Illusion; that the Schools existed only to provide children with bigger and better-paid jobs. Education? – the enormous Ministry no longer called itself Public Instruction and became simply the diploma-mill.

My own daughters, 'Nat-&-Steff', got caught in that trap. Rosy dreams about their blessed careers. The medical and pharmacy faculties bulged with mediocre students, had to slim, through ever more severe selection along the road. Poor girls – they weren't good enough. It explains a great deal about them now; the acridity, the snobberies. They picked up Diplomas, with their knowing voices and the high-sounding technical jargon.

Then the trap closed. There aren't enough jobs outside and they stay on as students, to get a better-sounding qualification. Small wonder they aren't happy. Reception-girl with a degree in Accountancy. Boy checking inventories, says he's a Master in Business Administration.

Carla? The best sort. Arts Faculty; work hard, keep your sights fairly low. A degree in history, languages, something old-fashioned and unpretentious. A bright intelligence, plenty of common sense. You'll be a teacher and may be a good one: this country can use you. Her parents will be proud of her then: well they may be.

Jan, my father, was sensible in this way. I had my degree, in the natural sciences; thought myself a hell of a chap. Jan sent me as an apprentice to Covent Garden. I learned to get my arse kicked. Only one thing counts here. These flowers are perishable; learn to shift them. You are perishable. So learn not to perish.

It's the same now, Bert. You are old, disappointed, see yourself as a failure. Hardly even a man, now. See to it that you don't perish.

Bert going home whistled a little song. Between the teeth,

as though wheeling a barrow, heavy with rotted leaf-mould. Get on with your work; let the dollies dance.

> 'Hop, Marianneke,
> Stroop in 't kannetje,
> Laat de poppetjes dansen'

– it's centuries old; from the time of the French overlordship. Subversive – to whistle in the hearing of occupying soldiery. Let the dollies dance; we'll survive.

Now to concoct a cover for the following evening. Like Carla. It isn't some slimy little lie: it's tact. To save pain, anxiety.

Willy cross-examines him nowadays, over a half-hour of delay. She feels obliged to be watchful, for old men have had a heart failure before now, out on the road, or under the shower.

No 'cover story' had been needed for going out to Ijmuiden, a solid evening of bouffe-and-booze with Henk and Irene. Willy had never been more than moderately fond of either of them. It had anyhow been one of her club-nights; she has many, devoted to exercises physical or spiritual, good works of whatever sort; she has several. These are for her more real, more actual, than old-pals-night in the harbour restaurant.

So it's neither a suppression of truth nor a suggestion of falsehood. To avoid mention of meeting Irene in Amsterdam and ending – astonishingly when one thinks of it – in bed with her in a Stundenhotel. What good could it possibly do to blurt that out?

In case anyone would wonder, for this idea of captive wives ('Monday is always our night for the choir') is a bit over-facile, Bert, and Henk too, would agree unhesitatingly that when the wife comes pelting in rather late towards suppertime you do not cross-question where she's been. You trust people or you don't, but don't haver with in-betweens.

'Fell asleep in the deck-chair, did you? Lovely sunlight,

does one good. Sinister only the wondering when it'll stop. I keep saying tomorrow and catching myself hoping 'not quite yet, please'.

'Reminds me, ran into a group in the club, kindly asked me over for a pot and a bite to eat tomorrow night, I really don't know why, somebody retiring.'

'Who can that be?' She knows of course most of the growers in the broad sense of 'one's always known so-and-so.'

'I've no very clear idea, conceivably Arthur Harteveld.' With which she was perfectly satisfied, never having liked the man. A dry stick, indeed rather an old priss, but given to smelling faintly of gin and salt-herring by lunchtime; that long lawyerly nose has hung over a good few quick-ones along the arches of the years.

Visitors to Amsterdam see the Amstel River along the Dam, south probably as far as the Stadthouders' Kade because this is the central waterway of the old town – historic Blue Bridge and Skinny Bridge, all the waterbuses take this route. The canals of the seventeenth-century spiderweb all empty into this stretch; noble, but don't fall in the water: only the born-Amsterdammers have the necessary immunizations from tetanus, cholera, sleeping-sickness, bilharzia or mad-cow-disease. The plummy, rich, wedding-cake texture of the old 'Centrum' is all within this antique frontier-post. Cross, for instance, the Blue Bridge and you'd pass from the tourist outpost of the whores' quarter to the old Jewish area of the Waterlooplein; walk on, it's no distance to the Czar Peter straat and the docks, for ours is a remarkably compact city. The next concentric belt is the Old-South, the pits I call it because nineteenth-century Amsterdam was cramped and crowded, mean-featured and dirty-minded in a prim secretive way, while the New South a stage further is a little better, though not much. But here our little Amstel river – it's of no size – takes a kink, potters out through Buitenveldert; you're in what we have the cheek to call countryside. No more than a pleasant canal really, with towing paths and weeping willows, pompous 'country' villas with really hideous gardens, and a great many blue herons, protected but much detested for shitting on parked cars.

All this detail? Everything that evening was full of sharp-cut detail, while the background is all misty pearly and opaline lustres.

He picked up Carla as agreed, a little downcast at her dishevelled look and grimy shirt while he had taken the trouble of looking a little less workworn. But the freshness of her eye, which had so, the day before delighted – the simple tongue: – 'Golly' (driving through Old West) 'it's like wading through cheese. Admittedly, I always take the tram ... Oh, isn't this lovely. I've never been here. God,' when I stopped, 'may I just stand and breathe, and then perhaps gaze?' Yes it is pretty. Night falling on the autumn evening, the bronze leaves falling upon suburban pretensions to grandeur, the chemical tubes of angular street lanterns haloed and fuzzed. I don't think I'm particularly romantic. Not about to get lyrical about a gas-lit, Bois-de-Boulogne, Belle-Epoque Paris. But I can see the point; wouldn't have blamed her if she had. I'm only a flower man. I do love the Third-Empire flowering bushes though – the hortensias, the camellias, the magnolias.

Carla grabbed her great horrible student tote-bag off the back seat.

'I'm going to ask forgiveness – maybe ten minutes? I can see you're ashamed of me. I'm ashamed of myself. So I'm going to rush into the ladies' lavatory, please.'

They'd cleared the riverside tables of course. On the terrace they'd a marquee, and under it heat-radiant lamps for a few people like me enjoying the end-of-the-evening. Bert went to check on his table inside, give the head-thief a bribe and say yes he'd have a 'perroquet' outside and give the young lady a steer when she comes out of the lav. He enjoys rituals. Like the Thurber bear, who said 'See what the Bears in the back room will have'. He likes head waiters who put their fingertips together and bow. He likes them to wear narrow elegant

black-and-white evening clothes which are Eugénie, or
Proust, or La Belle Otéro, or whoever the hell. He wouldn't
want any scruffy student heaving in sight saying 'Hi, I'm
Wally, I'm your Waitperson tonight.' He doesn't know about
poor Proust, who booked a table on the island, Château de
Madrid, for Mademoiselle de Stermaria, because Robert de
Saint Loup has told him that after a lavish meal she'll be
only too delighted to have all her clothes taken off, very very
slowly. She cuts him at the last moment, the bitch; poor
Marcel.

In a style of simplicity (thank god) she has done much
better than that revolting Stermaria (the pretty name reminding us of Joyce, and the Star of the Sea in Sandymount, and
Limping Gertie MacDowell.) Gratuitous insert, Hillyards
Catalogue being closer up the van Bijl street than Joust and
Proyce. No literature needed to see a springy young figure in
a pullover plain-knit, high-necked shortsleeved, a pretty colour. Bit of a flush on her face instead of make-up; nothing
but a bit of lipstick on a wide pink mouth. No jewellery
either; she'd decided that everything she had looked cheap.

No literature needed for the dinner. The sort of place
which is ... agreeable. Neither oppressive with heat nor
chilly; neither madly full nor depressively empty. A nicely
square and solid table a man can put his elbows on, nothing
tipping over edges; plenty of bread, a tiny bunch of flowers
and no damned candles. Friendly girl to take the orders. A
menu one can understand, free of pederast nomenclature.
You'll get enough on your plate and it'll taste of what it says.
A few expensive items and some homely. So foie gras for her
because she's never had it; a real one and so simple he
wished he'd taken it too. After that you don't want to upset
her stomach. So veal piccatas, alla marsala. Bert had a cup of
consommé. It has become almost impossible to get it since it
takes time and trouble to make: when really strong and very
hot and plainly home-made you do not care how many mad
cows have fallen by the wayside. One will be allowed then to

have something creamy. A sweetbread with morels, which are probably radioactive but one isn't going to worry, a lot of cream, for this is Holland, and the whole disinfected by the lovely yellow wine from the Jura.

If you can get a good meal hereabouts it's very good, because of getting lots of fresh vegetables.

Just as important is to get drinks in large, plain, well shaped glasses. Defend us from those terrible Bordeaux which charge you a thousand francs for instant diabetes. It's not the moment to boast of the wonderful Lafite (a case of it, for the good job on the garden). This isn't a place for Henk.

An honest place. Bert finds it so – I believe – because of his own honesty, because at this moment there is no pretence in him; nothing faked. The girl is happy because simple; enjoying herself. Her eyes get bigger, the tips of her ears pinker. Yes, she'd like cheese, if he'll tell her which is which.

The two of them sound too good to be true? I won't agree. If one is enjoying an expensive pretentious restaurant it's probably because one is in that frame of mind – showing off.

In here, you see everything you'd expect. Men who've brought cordless telephones in with them. Women who stub a cigarette out in a bread roll. Spoilt children and over-indulgent grandparents. Secretaries trying hard not to be discarded mistresses, and wives with unhappy mouths constantly repainted. Bert's not the kindly uncle giving the pretty niece a treat, for doing well in her exam. And neither is he a seducer, softening a young female up with plenty to drink.

A whole evening in front of one. He has been here before but never was the food so good. They have both an excellent appetite. Salad; cheese. Pudding which a girl enjoys. An Alsace 'pinot gris'. The bourgogne. Glass of bordeaux with the cheese. Nobody's going to get tipsy.

'I was a boy. Not long after the war. Sent to London to learn. The first day, in a huge hotel – Bloomsbury, that sort. Breakfast in the basement, very dark, smells of boiled kippers. The English eating stacks of compressed straw.' It's conversation, to make her laugh. 'The bacon-and-egg which has been slowly stewed, now vitrified.' The girl is laughing because she has been there. The bus tour, from school. And the 'cultural' trip to Paris...

'Right, let us never forget, the limp croissant like a thing to stick on when you've a period. The one minibutter. The dolls' tea-party jam. The black-black stuff which went grey when you put the milk in.'

'Stop, stop, it's too horrible.'

'That day in London, there was a man, god I admired him, I was mortally intimidated, he said "I will not eat stewed prunes by electric light."'

Why shouldn't she enjoy this atmosphere? A girl goes to a restaurant to be treated like a princess. There aren't that many of these moments, now. You look at the Lotto advert, on the screen. They'll tell you that breakfast is overlooking the beach, sea creaming on that golden strand and the kindly black man in his starched white jacket, with the passion-fruit. You know damn well it's the dressing-gown needing a wash; toasting yesterday's bread; this bit of ham is going dry round the edges. Look out at the barrack-blocks. And by electric light. Wouldn't one say – 'Come on; let's run away.' One of Bert's sadnesses is that having sold landscape gardening in Rio de Janeiro he has had breakfast on the balcony overlooking the beach of Copacabana, and a very sad moment it was.

He knew a man, perfectly decent boy, been a student along with Henk and myself. 'Boy, I'm going out to South Africa. Son, that's the lush life. And all those black men to do your bidding.'

Whatever ails myself it's paltry; a few pains, a couple of trivial humiliations. We make a few dramas. This cancer, happens to half the men my age. A bourgeois setback.

Whereas this girl, setting out, trying so hard to push her boat free of this muddy creek, no, she's not too good to be true. Stuck in that terribly deep-grooved tramline, still so very

Dutch, of petty respectability. Thinks herself a sort of leper. At least it's doing her good to spit it out, to feel confidence enough not to worry about boring me dreadfully. When I think of my own crises of confidence. When I think of losing my head over that cheap Lalage. When I think of my own nothingness, now putting on airs taking a young girl out to dinner, pretending she's my daughter ... That's the Côtes de Nuit getting to her now, best drug there is; best medicine there is.

'Clean-your-teeth and wipe your shoes on-the-mat. Brush-your-hair and scrub-your-bottom. Speak when you're spoken to and be polite to your elders. Why? What kind of temperament is this? Work – because if you don't, all day and every day, you're a nothing, a nix-nut. At school I was a joke. Sainte Barbara the patron of the fire brigade, she sure puts out everyone's fires. The shy one saying Ja-Mevrouw. Seventeen-the-shrinking-virgin. Now in the Fac: there at least you're anonymous but if I ever had a boyfriend he turned out to prefer boys.' Bert really couldn't help laughing and she forced herself into a grin. 'Why are you so nice to me?'

'Rhetorical question.'

'My parents are good to me. They're kind, and they take endless trouble and they make sacrifices, and I'm the only one they've got and they simply eat me up and it's awful.'

'Hell, being grateful.'

'I had to join the Guides, you know. There are more like me. Go on pilgrimages, singing cheerful songs. The Pope's coming and you have to line the route with your shirt starched, and he'll give you his Blessing. I used to be in the Children of Mary, vowed to virginity aged seven.' The waitress passed, and filled her glass.

'I can't get out, because I haven't a penny. I'm not even a good student. Not even like the Good Woman, in Brecht, who asked why are the good always shat-upon while evil always is instantly rewarded. I'm not Mutter Courage. There are girls of my age who go in the bordel, make themselves a little honey-pot to take them further; I haven't even the guts for that. I want to write poetry and I'll end up teaching grammar. My mother's a whining drip who looks at the sitcoms on television, my father's the man who gets a chiming clock after fifty years of being shat on, and I'm just the same. I've never even dared smoke a joint.'

I had to make her laugh.

'So now it's pudding time and you're going to do better than Shirley Temple, you're too young to remember her dancing on tables "On the Good Ship

     Acid Drop,

     It's a short trip

     To Candy Shop" – Arie de Beer in Zandvoort, one cent to spend.'

Very brief, very banal, very superficial. Can I say anything that won't be glib and pat and neat and useless? What did I ever do? Little artisanal growers' workshop, half of it owed to the bare-knuckle work of Jan and the other half to marrying into Willy's world. Now in Ruhestand. Took two, really pitifully unimportant black eyes. One from Professor Heinrich, Neat snip-snip, we put in these charming little drains, you won't even bleed on the sheet, forty-eight hours a bit rough but the girls will give you a shot of morphia. I'm not telling you about this, but you might have six months of hangover, plenty of desire and no performance, not to worry, it'll wear off.

The other, more trivial still, cousin Adrian wrapping up; no intention of having me under his feet any longer. Panic set in. Clutch at Irene. Lovely woman, take your clothes off, comfort me. Bert, my lad, for ten cents you'd have been telling her your wife doesn't understand you. Willy – a woman who if they sawed both her legs off, sit in a little box on wheels, row yourself along, she would never utter a word of complaint or self-pity.

Carla is nineteen. Angry and bewildered because this is a

desolate world and she wants to lift off it, straight into the blue horizon and she's frightened, of not having the nerve or the courage. Sees me as a tough and agile man, of experience, wisdom. Old! Old? Come on – Bert doesn't look that old. No way either of telling that he's a fairy from the waist down. Don't be absurd, she's not looking for a 'lover'. Bit of an unseemly twinge there; she might think that well, if he wants to take me to bed ... come off it, she has seen you with the stick, heavy going in the soft sand; poor old man, be sorry for him.

Who knows what goes on in her head? Bert may think himself sly and masterful; I know nothing about young girls. Lalage wanted to be thought experienced, worldly-wise. And knew how to flatter. This is not a hard little – no, but romantic, vulnerable ... Bert – you could very easily lose your head over this – Really! Had too much to drink, have you? That's another thing I've noticed, since that little surgical rearrangement; I no longer metabolize as I did. Don't be tempted into a cognac, here.

'I want to shout and scream,' said Carla eating her pudding.

These evenings come to an end, with a lot of waiters hoping you've had-a-pleasant-evening and hoping for a tip, while you're hoping – for what? That it's not over yet? Carla is not a beauty. She's a young, quite pretty, attractively innocent and perfectly ordinary girl. Is Bert about to try and seduce her? I had only a jacket. Carla has her goddam tote bag.

A lovely night, clear and sharp, a touch of frost. Some leaves have fallen on the windscreen of the dear-old-Mercedes; put on the wipers a-moment; put on the ventilator, the blower, the defroster.

'Of course I'll drive you home. It's only that I don't know where home *is*.'

'Zandvoort ... the Mimosastraat. That's in Plan Noord. I never told you, did I? Ashamed of it.'

'We'll get to it. We aren't there yet.' But there was an

unseemly piece of gristle she could neither cough up nor swallow.

'It's a rotten thing to say, but don't bring me all the way – stop short and I'll walk. You see ... they'll be on the watch.' Rotten thing to hear? One knew it was love that clung, much more strangling than fear or suspicion; the two good souls in the narrow bed waiting for the creak on the stairs and the chink of light to say 'Sleep well dear', the guardian-angel complex at length stilled until next morning's snuffle in the laundry basket. But lawdy, if they heard a car motor – at the window in a flash, and to inflict that upon a girl, forcing her to 'Oh, one of my professors, kindly gave me a lift, I don't know where he lives, Bentveld or somewhere.' ... How many are there, off to pig it in Paris, three in some extortionist attic and terrified of being caught without the métro ticket they can't afford, bread and stale Dutch cheese rather than 'Your nice home where you've every comfort'. How long would it take before she started living?

'Where are we going?'

'Anywhere it's properly dark. Starry night and we can't see it. The Fée-Electricity, otherwise Philips in Eindhoven, as-phyxiating poor Amsterdam. I want you to imagine moun-tains. The red glare on Skiddaw woke the burghers of Carlisle.'

'Red glare on what?' laughing.

'I've no idea, something I learned in England when I was your age.'

Who said that? Yes, it was Verity. That's right, the girl who took her knickers off in the old 'Ladies Only' (Aldgate to Watford Met via Baker Street). Starlight over Cassiobury Park. That had been a Summer night. Rich smell of wealthy suburb, rhododendrons. He'd *walked*, thinking nothing of it, back to Rickmansworth. Verity. Sharp acidy smell of lemony-blonde girl. And apart from whores (a thin – a kind – girl behind the old Windmill Theatre, Cockney accent, yes and thin blonde hair) the first.

I don't know what to say about this; it's too complicated. This isn't like 'Irene', I can't smile about poor-ol'-Bert. I wonder if it would be fair at all to say that a great big stretch of life – over fifty years – got compressed abruptly into a tight small ball. There are bombs like this, a physicist explained to me once that your fissile material is in a sphere, and you pack explosive all around to squeeze it very very severely. This is the biggest bang, for something not much larger than my heart.

A sadly superficial and over-simplified piece of rhetoric, that.

Could I quote 'Charlotte'? – that's only a few years back. Appallingly pretty girl, foxed me into her flat, I'd suspected nothing. Daughter of a colleague; I'm – no, not proud – no, not virtuous. I did say no. 'Don't be foolish' (and she was adult enough to accept that). You see, her parents were my close friends. I even mentioned it, filthy-prig, to her mother who said 'Oh dear ... the trouble is she's attracted to older men'. My fault entirely; I'd told her flirtatiously she had a pretty bottom, and that was the understatement of the year. I'm not about to claim that Carla is attracted to older men.

I am an expert on scents. This is part of my trade, to have a good nose. When you were last in a florist's shop, did you notice how good it smells? (Not those horrible scentless Mother's-Day roses.) This is not like the street outside. Plants eat up, even nourish themselves upon vile chemical exudations.

The stars on a frosty night are scentless. The countryside of Aerdenhout, a district of trees and expensive gardens, is not. Carla, who does not wear perfume and is in her own words scrubbed, is not scentless but is delicious. One must not say intoxicating. The word contains 'toxic': implying an irritant substance and in larger doses poisonous.

Bert smells. Not of dirt. Nor of cancer. As one gets old one begins to smell of disintegration. It is not very disagreeable, has some affinity with the good smell of fresh-baked bread.

There is a smell of alcohol, but that is of honest unfaked wine, which is not a repellant. Some plants smell revolting; they do so deliberately. A defence mechanism against predators.

His clothes have been to the cleaners. Willy sees to that. There might be a hint of cigars, but they are not vile.

Jan, a tremendous washer, smelt then of tough old countryman and Marseille soap. After shaving, I use a bit of Roger & Gallet which is old-fashioned of me. It is not offensive, which the things advertised on television are. Who says it's physically impossible? – the whole room reeks: open the windows...

I shouldn't want, you see, a girl to feel, physically, disgust with me. One uses a word about flowers in their perfection of freshness; we speak of the bloom being on them. Of a young girl it is equally true, if sentimental – a bit of a cliché. Whereas of a stem cut too soon, that tiniest bit gone off even if commercially perfect – no, we don't call it a Lalage.

One day at some bar, in some airport waiting-room (it was that sort of occasion) I fell into conversation: every man is worth listening to when talking his own shop, because of the love and enthusiasm he brings to it. A coin dealer, and they also do medals, for which the perfect mint condition counts heavily. If handled, even touched by the natural acidity of the human hand, they lose value fast, but of course there are borderline instances or why be a dealer? Only professional expertise can judge, since to us the two would look the same.

'We'd term it a slider,' he said grinning. Good word.

A lot of girls are sliders. If there were a quarrel, as can happen in Arab countries, who decides? They call in a gynaecologist? Ought to call the flowerseller, like me. I can tell, and without looking. More to it than technical virginity.

You might raise the question of my own sanity. Old men, say they 'fell in love'; what does that mean? Set up a panel of nine different doctors – or lawyers – or policemen – and what would they have to go on, once past my own 'technical' impotence?

So I maintain – I continue to maintain – that nothing vile, harmful, damaging, even thwarting, happened between Carla and myself. I have made play with the often foolish, often ridiculous figure of 'Bert'. Yes, a defence mechanism, but let me be quite clear; there's nothing schizophrenic about me. There's nothing 'Bert' does that I refuse to take responsibility for.

We studied stars, too, a while. Skiddaw I think is a mountain in Cumberland. I have been in the Lake District. I cannot recall much about Carlisle.

Further, I have nothing whatever to say.

*

'Well it's all fixed.'

'Well *what* is all fixed?'

'Oh come off it. It was you who wanted ein-zwei-drei and a great deal of trouble it was and I've *been* to a great deal of trouble and now if you feel hustled that's just too bad. You had better start planning your packing because you know how dreamy and dozy you get about that and if you've a shopping list then I want to have it and don't come afterwards saying it's the wrong kind of shaving cream or whatever it was the last time I couldn't get the ordinary brand and you kept complaining about it had a nasty smell.'

'Willy please, what are you talking about?'

'As you know perfectly well and this is to pester me it was you who –'

'Yes but skip that bit, I've heard that.'

'Wanted to go to Venice.'

I got a fright. It isn't habitual, nor even frequent, but things do go clear out of my mind without, apparently, leaving any trace – the knot in the handkerchief, in days when there were handkerchiefs – by which to recover them.

Yes I *had* wanted – had it originally been my idea or hers? I did still want – an excellent idea. It is distinctly Dutch to present other people's good ideas as though they were one's own. Willy often does this. If a bad idea, then unquestionably it had been mine. Also very Dutch is the habit of 'pestering' which takes forms of provocation like pretending-to-forget, pretending not-to-understand and things of the sort all quite gratuitous; a Dutch need to be tiresome. Best is to make no further ado. And here we are.

Things worth doing are worth doing well; to present a truism as Ur-wisdom is another characteristic trait.

That infernal Adrian had (naturally without saying a word) and doubtless as a sweetener to stop me pestering him, declared an extra dividend, handshake more like, arriving as a completely unexplained credit note from the bank. We live frugally as a rule. So not just Is this an extra holiday but unusually lavish, with a good hotel down at the end of the Canal, Riva della Thingy looking out at islands. And to make up to Willy, and obliterate an economical journey, we'll take a gondola from the station and float all the way down, with moreover an oarsman who kept his mouth shut sparing us all the claptrap so I gave him a good tip and got a tight wintry smile.

Wintry it is, and a wet cold. Doesn't bother the Dutch. We'd rather three raincoats to the sweaty-shirtsleeve routine, anyhow. Floods are second nature. I haven't lost the habit of putting on gumboots to go to work. Yes, work – this is a wonderful place and I'm going to do this properly. Not going to be Dutch either, telling them how much better we'd have done it. In my lifetime we have carried out two really large projects involving the sea. In the thirties, the closing of the Zuider Zee with the Afsluit Dike, and since the war the Delta Plan, cutting off much of the Scheldt estuary. Each time there were fearful jeremiads (and being Dutch these still go on). Frigging with the enormous tides and currents of the North Sea – natural seawalls would be demolished, there would be vast unwanted silting – Zandvoort would disappear altogether; and so on. There have indeed been many disagreeable and unforeseen phenomena. At least it stops us telling the Italians how much better we'd have done the job in Venice. It is indeed awful how much has gone green and water-logged and slipped, and how much above the sea-mirror has plain tumbled down, and the pollution is awful and the tour-ists worse and I am finding it an unending miracle and joy.

Weed-streaked marble, motoscafi, garbage scow or headless putti. We cheeseheaded Nederlanders are not as a rule sus-pected of getting lyrical: knock those heads on wood, see whose is the cheesiest. Stay clear of Harry's and Florian's and it isn't even dear. We walk everywhere, my stick and Willy's powerful boots in a harmony unguessed at these twenty years and a great joy and warmth she is. Arsenal, ghetto, anywhere you name. I follow into her churches and she gazes with me into pictures. We stop and eat fish, which out of the lagoon isn't up to much but with plenty of white wine to disinfect agrees very nicely with our digestions. My urine is the colour of lemon peel, is cloudy, smells peculiar: I am indifferent to – what? Fate, mortality, or whether it is going to rain?

I believe in being well briefed. Signor Teresio Pignati's admirable book is a massive block but in the large pocket of the anorak gets humped uncomplainingly. I am also nour-ished by the English Lord. He had for example a phrase, a line from an English writer, which struck home, for it is like a javelin, transfixes one, and which I brought along and it accompanies me everywhere.

'What became of love, I wonder, when the kissing had to stop?' This was marked 'Robert Browning': 'A Toccata of Galuppi'. Neither reference meant anything. What's a tocca-ta? Some sort of musical invention like minuet and sonata? Galuppi seemed equally obscure after Vivaldi and Scarlatti. As for Robert Browning – but I can now shed some light. Pretty obscure too, betimes, and on occasion not obscure at all. Like I said – javelins.

Early on, and we hadn't yet got names clear. Scuore Zis featuring Scuola Zat and we stopped a moment to shelter by a row of shops featuring terrible Murano glass and plastic figures masquerading as ivory. Willy mesmerized in front of shoes, mentally translating millions of lire into gulden ('dear *and* unwearable') and my eye fell, I suppose mechanically, on a stall of second-hand books. Art mostly, tatty, rainspotted and of no real interest. A drab dirty little thing shoved in and so much smaller that it caught the eye – *Shorter Poems by Robert Browning*. I had him mixed up with Lord Byron. Holland is not conspicuous for poets. It was cheap, yes, but I bought it because of the kissing which had to stop. I could have had *Italian Renaissance Influences upon Gerard Dou*. Odd? – I suppose it is odd that we have such floods of not-able painters but we don't go in for poets much. Willy wasn't interested. Her English is good, if not like mine, but Pignatti was quite enough to be going on her plate.

But this is amazing stuff. Javelins abound. I am like Saint Sebastian – very suitable here too.

> 'What's become of Waring
> Since he gave us all the slip?'
> 'I the Trinity illustrate
> Drinking watered orange-pulp
> In three sips the Arian frustrate'

– and turning the pages –

> 'Hamelin Town's in Brunswick,
> By famous Hanover city –'

but this I know!

> 'The medlars let fall
> Their hard fruit, and the brittle great fig trees
> Snap off, figs and all.'

Yes; and

> '. . . The blackbird's tune
> And May, and June . . .'

I still know nothing much about him. An Englishman who lived in and loved Italy. There are many such. They don't talk like this though. I couldn't be happier if I had found one of the exquisite old flower books: they no longer exist outside botanical libraries because they've all been cannibalized for the beautiful delicately-coloured engravings ... But it was my ruin too. My downfall.

After eating dinner that evening (calves' liver, if I may fix the occasion with a mundane detail, for it can be difficult to get in Holland and the butcher always says 'It's the Italians get it all') I began exploring with my feet up. For Willy and I have Dutch ways, one of which is bread-and-butter at lunchtime (she is trying to memorize the twenty sorts of local ham, which are remarkable). Time in the evening for a feast and the day's serious drinking. So I was tipsy in that pleasant manner; having earned it after a day in the open air. About to get drunker, for he's a peculiar fellow, this Browning; a buttonholing manner and one can easily suspect him of having had a few glasses:

> 'Ours is a great wild country;
> If you climb to our castle's top
> I don't see where your eye can stop.'

It doesn't do, one could say, to let the Dutch get hold of this. Or, even more abrupt:

> 'Some people hang pictures up
> In the room where they dine or sup...
> All I own is a print,
> An etching, a mezzotint...'

Could he have been Dutch, one wonders? (Brown or Braun, he could be from anywhere.) One has the impression that the English, who make rather a to-do of being complex and subtle, would sneer at this doggerel, because even I can see that it's hatchet-made as though by the local shoemaker.

Thunderbolt stuff though for a retired flowerseller.

One or two seemed peculiarly Venetian. A really gut-felt one of amazing texture is 'The Bishop orders his Tomb', instructing his sons (I love that) to make certain of a splendid monument for him. The wealth and splendour of this has much importance but the essential will be the position, over-looking the greatly inferior stone to another ecclesiastical dig-nity who pursued him with envy during life. A worldly sentiment, readily seen as very Venetian, and which culmi-nates in the virulent envy felt by 'old Gandalf' for the bishop's beautiful mistress. The Canon or whoever he was will lie there through eternity suffering torments of frustra-tion. Very Dutch, I should think, though we'd never allow it to be commented upon.

And of course I like the one about the painter – 'poor Lippo Lippi by your leave'. I'm afraid that what follows will seem anticlimax; I've been putting it off.

It's called 'Madhouse Cell'. As poetry peculiarly poor; limp rhymes and cliché sentiments. One wonders why he kept it and collected it in a volume. I can't quite make him out; an unashamed romantic, and suddenly a mid-Victorian fellow, pompous and parsonical in a frock-coat and side-whiskers, getting all solemn. I prefer him when pissed on the local plonk. This one is not a sermon of edifying nature; it's a horror story. I'm rather afraid this is me.

I have put off facing the final reality. I came here to think things out. It was a very lucky hit, because while one knows that this is a place to see on foot, and that every little street is full of marvels, I could not know that I would walk, and walk, knowing though that I must end by facing my respon-sibilities. I don't in fact think that the 'Madhouse Cell' is the place for me but I suppose it is a debatable question.

I have not described how Carla came to meet her death. I don't believe that I ever could. I don't think I even know, since I've been grappling with the meaning of this particular word. 'How little we Know' is a fair comment on most of what we go through. I find a certain satisfaction in reading much of it – most of it maybe – in this undistinguished set of verses barely over a page long.

She's called here 'Porphyria' which I find an unattractive name. She has 'long yellow hair'. The whole thing's extremely banal, the writing as the subject. I mean –

> 'She shut the cold out and the storm
> And kneeled and made the cheerless grate
> Blaze up'

– how Humdrum can one get? Most unhappily – 'That moment she was mine, mine, fair, I found a thing to do'. He strangles her with her hair. He is 'quite sure she felt no pain'.

The essential falseness of all this is contained in the punch-line at the end. A device beloved by bad short-story writers then and since was to put in a twist, supposed to knock the reader flat. A well-known phoney is Maupassant's couple who lose the borrowed jewels and ruin their entire lives scraping up the money to replace them. When at last they manage this – 'Oh my poor friend, but didn't you know that the jewels were false?' No no no, it's the story which is false. The stupidest couple in the most backward of Dutch villages would have taken the trouble to find out the insurance value . . .

And thus –

> 'And thus we sit together now,
> And all night long we have not stirred,
> And yet God has not said a word!'

Bullshit! Let's get back, please, to

> 'The River Weser deep and wide
> Washes its wall on the southern side;
> A pleasanter spot you never spied.'

The story of the Pied Piper every child in Holland knows and Willy wrote a splendid line to go with it. For when this business began to look a little bit 'political' she put on her Sunday suit, and a few jewels she has, inherited mostly (she has had little enough from me), and stormed in to the Burgomaster's private office, very much daughter of the dynasty, and gave him the rough edge of her tongue, ending with the very words of the Pied Piper diddled out of his payment. 'Dat zal je berouwen, Burgomeester; daar zal je spijt van hebben.' I must translate, with the detail which has vanished in English, the familiar use of the second person singular. This usage, kept for family, close friends, old comrades, is also that employed by the mistress of the house towards a negligent kitchen-maid, in the days when such things existed. The Piper's odd foreign accent is missing but not his anger. 'That, Burgomaster, you will live to regret, and for that you will know anguish.' The sadness also lacks. The Piper knew what would happen; Willy did not but was determined that 'the common little man' (a Dutch Mayor is a state-nominated civil servant; his council is locally elected) should be brought to face what Willy called his cowardice; really no more than the habitual shufflings and prevarication.

I should have liked to see her. She has two Victorian half-hoop rings from her granny, never reset. They have really good stones, one of sapphires and the other of alternate sapphs and diamonds. She has also an extremely fine sapphire and silver brooch, art nouveau in style, quite possibly a Macintosh or a van der Velde. I once gave her diamond earrings, quite pretty. I mention this because sapphires suit her, bring a blaze into her blue eyes. I defend her too, because on the big bony hands she feels ashamed of, the heavy gold rings show royally, so that pointing the finger at that municipal crowd-pleaser would make him cringe. She never wears them, but knows well that cattle of this sort are impressed by evidence of material prosperity. Hasn't forgotten her bourgeois upbringing.

*

We stayed a fortnight. I think we were pretty thorough. Every day mapped and planned. I was surprised to find myself coping with all the footwork but of course this is in key with the incredible place; I was daily stronger, thinner, lighter. You could say that it demands so much concentration that one makes the effort joyfully, without chagrin. Of course one can't take it all in. That would need many many voyages, and in different seasons, and in different frames of mind. I shall make no further voyages, but what I have stowed away is not bad. I make of course no pretence at knowledge of the art, or the history, or the politics; the sheer fabric of it all. That would be the study, the absorption, of a lifetime, from early childhood through to the ripest of age and mature enjoyment, and would exact an enlightened, professional focus. It is brought home to me that beyond the narrow limits of my own professional world (not, certainly, negligible in compass comprising as it does the natural sciences and the basics of art) I know nothing; a wretched ignoramus.

One has the right to be sure of expressing opinion. The simplest example might be the Lord's dictum that the Palace of the Doges is 'unquestioningly' the finest piece in existence of secular Gothic. I don't like the word. The Dutch are not unquestioning; known indeed for getting very ribby when given orders, and 'I choose not to' could be the historic slogan of a small, waterlogged and muddy-minded people. I have in my life employed workers. I have given orders. I have seen them received with folded arms and stubborn faces. We're a petty lot, but we plough our own furrow. I might have suggested to Lord Norwich that in our Hansa cities we have even today some pretty fine examples of 'secular gothic'. But he's so in love with Venice I can forgive him pretty near anything ... May he do as much for me, this so civilized man ...

The weather which in Italy had been so capricious is in the North still amazingly stable. But it's winter now: the clocks have gone back. We were home at four-thirty in the afternoon, in that deep blue light I love, breathed upon by a

silvery fog, a promise of frost glitter at dawn. We'd stopped a
day in Belgium. In Dinant where the Maas is still the Meuse
and runs through the wooded cliffs of the Ardennes, and in
the street was the smell of grilling chestnuts. Baked-potato
weather, the season for game. Wind blowing the fur of a
hare, the bright feathers of a pheasant hanging, outside poul-
terers' shops. I am not *all* Dutch. These are pleasures we do
not understand, on our bare sandy coasts. From the hotel I
rang one restaurant after another, to know whether they had
any woodcock.

In the letter-box at home was the usual junk mail, supermarket promotions. And a sealed envelope, my name hand-
written, and inside, a printed form. Please ring Sergeant
Bout. The Amsterdam number crossed out and a local one
instead, and 'urgent' underlined. Before leaving I had pulled
the plug on the phone recorder. Hm. From Willy's shopping
bag, dumped in the hallway, rose the delectable smell of two
ripe partridges, wrapped in greaseproof paper but now beginning to make their presence known. There could be nothing
so urgent that it would not do tomorrow morning. Sergeant
Bout would have gone home by now. I am alas a conscientious person. And besides, curious.

The phone answered on the first ring. Bout's voice sound-
ing irritable, sweeping aside explanations.

'I'd like you to come around straightaway. You know
where the station is, in the Hogeweg?' Of course I do; it's
two minutes.

'No – not tomorrow morning.' Willy – don't put the birds
in the fridge; I won't be long. Mm. I wonder...

There was a uniformed policeman, with that look of utter
incuriosity. But there was also Detective Dijksma, pottering.
A Dutch municipal space of grey linoleum, of tubular metal
chairs with plastic upholstery pretending to be leather, of
overbright light, of household disinfectant and stale cigar
smoke, since whoever tries to give up smoking the police
won't. And Sergeant Bout, now remembering again to be

polite. 'Good, that's very good. It's a duty, to be co-operative. But so few people are. Appreciate it.'

'Well now . . . well now.' Nervous? No, the police are never nervous. Tired? – end of the day? It doesn't always end at five. Inclining to scratch at his ear lobe, at the back of his neck. Hair needs cutting. To brush ash off his sleeve. To fidget. He didn't ask whether I'd had a nice holiday. Nor where we'd been. Perhaps he knew already. 'Carla Zomerlust . . .'

'I'm being polite too, you know. Was this all that urgent?'

'We'll see, won't we.' The eye like still water in cold weather. There might be a skin of ice forming. Dirty water, greyish, greenish. 'Mister van der Bijl,' putting on his reading glasses, which had expensive gold frames, 'you don't look too good. When you said you didn't know her, you lied.' He had a type-written statement. Also a photograph. Of myself. Taken in the street unbeknownst. Busy little Dijksma, now busy emptying ashtrays. 'Italian restaurant. Pizza joint in Overveen. You had lunch together, two days before her death. You have been formally identified but if necessary we'll ask you to come there, for confirmation.' I was of course prepared to some extent. 'You lied, right? Why?'

'You ought to know. There's no obligation to tell the truth to police. Everybody knows the trouble and irritation involved. A car accident, and the whole morning filling it forms.'

'And this is no car accident. This is a wilful homicide which is among the gravest charges under our criminal law.'

'What are you doing – charging me? In which case I have a number of rights, under the same law, of which I'll remind you.' A smile.

'I'll make up my mind about that, after you answer some questions, briefly, pertinently and without evasion.'

'Don't be silly, Bout. Of course I'm not denying I had lunch with her. What could be more innocent? I met her walking on the beach, I had my car on the Zeeweg, it was the simplest consequence that I should suggest a bite to eat there – it was lunchtime. Equally, I wasn't going to volunteer that information, which is pure coincidence, and coming under a whole heap of laborious suspicion. A pleasant acquaintanceship, a nice friendly girl. All open, unconcealed. And so what? But you of course build that into a great big thing because you've never found anything else. Any lawyer will tell you you've no grounds. I don't want to feel obliged to make complaint for unlawful persecutions.'

'Not quite so fast – mijn Heer.' A fragment of sarcasm there. 'Unsupported by any further detail the episode would not in itself be thought of any unusual weight. I recall that on the evening of her death you took a ramble – as is your habit – into the dunes where she was found. Quite reasonable in the circumstances; we didn't push you on the point. But taken together the two happenings might come to be thought significant: have you objections to being examined a little further on this?'

'If I'd had anything to add I would have told you. What have I to hide?'

'For a start, you were in hospital not long ago,' fidgeting with his papers. 'Would you like to tell me more about that?'

A lot of the phrases one uses are so worn down that they make no impact any longer. 'To feel the ground opening under one's feet' should be terrifying. I can do no better; that's what I felt. But it hasn't, has it?

'No.' Which is enough. One shouldn't be provoked by the innocent enquiring eye, the bland raised eyebrow. 'Those are personal matters. I resent the question.' Which merely sounded feeble.

'Quite so,' unfazed. Medical dossier, confidential, need a court order for that.

'I've been travelling all day, I'm tired, I'd like to get home to my supper.' I can count, I think, upon the discretion of doctors. Have I spoken to anyone else on this subject? To two old friends, Henk and Irene. How far has this snuffling little terrier dug and bored into my life?

'It may come to that,' as though he hadn't heard. 'I haven't altogether made up my mind. The Officer of Justice may well feel that the picture when viewed as a whole, while not perhaps in itself conclusive, allows him to pursue you.' And that, also, I told myself, is bluff. 'I may say that I don't feel at all satisfied. Charging you is a grave step and I should wish to consult my superior.' With a feint of looking at his watch – 'I don't want it said that I pressed you unduly at a moment when you felt fatigued. Very well, go home, by all means. I'll ask you – Ask you to come in here tomorrow morning, shall we say nine o'clock? The Commissaire will be here then. Adding the injunction: don't make me come running after you, there's a good chap.'

I don't want the little swine thinking he's going to soften me up that way.

'I'm not your good chap. And I'll ask you to mind your manners.'

The police! They've none too good a reputation nowadays. The police in France or Germany, of course, are known since always for the heavy hand. Though with 'the bourgeois' – and so I can be described – rather more careful with the hand and the feet both. Whereas in England they were always thought of as respectful of the people's liberties as well as polite in manner. This has been wearing thin in recent years. Some nasty things have come to light in court as well as rumour; bullying, intimidating, going as far as the faking of evidence. Ours have been getting worse, along similar ways. At the least, pretending to certainties they haven't got. I find myself quite Dutchly-bloodyminded enough to withstand a show of heavy menace. If they had anything concrete, I think I'd be ringing up lawyers, telling them to find somebody expert in the ways of criminal procedure.

It's obvious what I mean – material indices, scientific stuff. Blood, sperm, saliva, skin under the fingernails. It is quite clear that they haven't anything like this. Footprints or whatever in that soft sand. The only thing I can see, that they'd feel able to work upon, would be my own state of mind. Which is nobody's business save my own. I am not insane. I am not any sort of repulsive pervert. I meant Carla no harm. I did her no harm. It is a pity that she cannot speak out, to bear witness to this.

At breakfast I thought it as well to brief Willy. Who was up in arms at once, ready to reach for lawyers, magistrates – 'my old friend the cantonrechter' (a district judge, in days long gone by 'an admirer', and who indeed has taken a sentimental view ever since, sees her still as quondam girlfriend). I quietened her. Let's see first – a very Dutch phrase, this – how the cat gets out of the tree. We have here just a Kripo sergeant showing zeal; comfort his own superiors and throw a sop to public grumbling.

Commissaires of Police – in English the title, equally resounding is Superintendent – were in my younger days at least like MacNamara's Band. 'Although we're small in number we're the best in all the land.' Their chief characteristic was to be mightily pleased with themselves. It was an accepted article of faith that Holland was the most law-abiding of European countries. Apart from Amsterdam the-wicked-city, forever filled with inventive evildoing, nothing ever happened. Murders – rapes – armed robberies – gangsters were as rare as public holidays. Rife in the turbulent lands surrounding us, such things gave rise to consternation, shock horror – disbelief, in our placidly provincial microcosm. The Law, in Zandvoort, was greatly exercised about defective rear lights, bicycle licenses, and drunks pissing in the street. In larger towns like Haarlem there was a good deal of white-collar, paper crime; fraudulent bankruptcies and the like. Violence was little seen and mostly laid at the door of 'Socialist Agitators'. Police, few in number, apathetic in appearance, were armed with the 'sabre', which wasn't a sabre, more a kind of baton, unpleasant to be hit by (as were the rolled capes of Paris).

Officers were fewer still, lazier certainly, probably more corrupt. A municipal commissaire was a local notable, arrogant of manner and washing his hands thoroughly and often. I was not acquainted with this one, named quite recently to the post. Willy, a mine of information upon the local bourgeoisie, didn't know his wife – 'bridge-playing female'. He might have been competent; one wouldn't know because he sat behind a large desk bare of paper with an air of listening intelligently, didn't utter. Sergeant Bout can carry the banner; that's what he's there for. An officer will sign at the bottom of the page, when it's all nicely cleanly typed out.

I got a chair, opposite Bout. The Commissaire superintended us.

'We've been wondering,' machiavellian. 'If you had lunch with her in a public place did you perhaps have other meetings in places not quite as public? To this end – we've been looking at hotels, quite a few of whom cater for the love-nest brigade, since the bachelor flat – garconnières now a bit outdated, not to say dear.' Quite a sense of humour, our Amsterdamse sergeant. 'Surprise? – we've an identification for you. Not so many people walk now with a stick. We haven't the woman yet, but we will.'

That clutched at the heart. My poor Irene. Bout observed, doubtless with satisfaction, his hit.

'Not the Zomerlust girl. Pointer though, huh, to Walter's Secret Life. And to be sure what's possible with one is likely with another.' Lit himself a fag, causing the Commissaire to frown.

I have to put a face on this.

'First off – I'm not aware that spending time in a hotel is a criminal offence. You make much of my stick; I tire easily and often need rest. Second – whoever may be with me, anywhere, it's their affair; I might recommend a complaint for invasion of privacy. Third – as I've been given to understand, this girl, Miss Zomerlust, with whom I shared a helping of spaghetti, perfectly open and I was the first to point out that there's nothing sinister about that, was killed. I wish now to ask whether she was subjected to some sort of sexual interference; my understanding is that she wasn't.' The Commissaire appeared to have no notion what sexual interference might mean but was looking eagerly to Bout for enlightenment.

Bout, despite being the man with the Twisted Lip (see the adventure of Sherlock Holmes), wasn't discomposed.

'We needn't quibble over jargon. The phrase *criminal assault* sounds well in print. Pathology report might be more specific. Fairly frequent variation, the ones who can't get it up, impotence can be psychological, can also be mechanical. Substituted penetrating objects not unknown, in brutal terms beerbottle not unheard of. Rape just the same.' Those little eyes watching me, just praying for me to say I would never do anything like that. I felt indeed an immense anger, that these dirty-minded little people should throw filth at you, Carla.

I said nothing. I should hope my face showed only the disgust I felt.

'Remains to be seen, Commissaire,' in Bout's 'formal' voice, 'whether you find grounds enough to press charges.' Some throat-clearing going on. English friends have taught me the two classic phrases – *Definitely*, and *Up to a point, Lord Copper*.

'One would certainly feel there was a case to answer. The Offizier is enabled to order such further examination as he may see fit, psychiatric and so forth; outside our province, Sergeant.'

'You so make order?' impatient with rotundities.

'I think it undeniable that public opinion – leaving the political aspect aside for the moment – prima facie, I feel there cannot be further hesitation.'

'I'll get Dijksma to type it up.'

They put me in a cell. It was darkish. It seemed comfortably warmed. There is a sort of concrete shelf which serves I suppose as a bed in the evening when they give one a mattress. I folded my jacket to serve as a pillow and laid myself down on this. Stretched out on one's back it was not uncomfortable: I was tired and I needed to think. They did nothing denigrating like taking away one's tie or belt – even shoelaces, I have read, if they think one suicidally inclined.

They do however empty one's pockets. Watch, keys and things as well as money and papers. All perfectly polite; indifferent might be a better word. You are an entry on a form, a minor disposal problem. Around midday as I imagine, some food on a plate; meat with some unpleasantly thickened gravy, potatoes and vegetables. They've no canteen in a place like this; brought in from some neighbourhood café. There seemed to be nobody else in the row of cells; silence accompanied me but I ate with appetite. Plastic beaker with water. There is a lavatory in the cell; it's all perfectly clean. Some time in the afternoon a cop came, brought me out in the yard. 'Exercise. That's regulation. You can walk up and down. Keep the circulation moving, like. It's as you please. Want a fag?' in a perfectly friendly fashion. Seeing the sort of man I am he probably thinks I'm in for fraud, but he couldn't care less either way. When he locked me up he gave me an overnight bag packed by Willy, and a note in her large dashing writing.

'Perfectly preposterous! I'm moving everything I know. Lawyers are sending someone, say only ridiculous but legal formality, bla bla, but have you out by tomorrow, don't worry at all, stay calm and patient, not be intimidated, make no statement. See you tomorrow, all love and support, your ever-loving Mina.' Nobody's called her that since she was a young girl. Pyjamas, washing things, clean shirt. Paper, envelopes, a ballpoint. A book to read ... I am touched. Nothing and nobody alters that loyalty. I don't worry. It's not the train to Auschwitz. The State of the Netherlands is pompous but extremely conscientious.

Do some thinking. I was surprised to find myself perfectly comfortable on my concrete slab.

Banal! Meaningless! Thousands of people get picked up by the police. Appearances are against them. Coincidences,

mistaken quantities, a comma or a decimal point goes adrift
– somebody can't spell and an entire government department
has its feet in its mouth. You'll never get an apology; the
hardest thing in the world is for people to admit they were in
the wrong.

I admire their laconicism. One unlocked the door, made a
sketch of 'come on', said 'Bring the bag'.

'What's it now?' He only shrugged. Outside in the hall the
next one was collecting the envelope with 'my property',
made an equally vague gesture towards the outside. Are they
letting me go?

'In the car.' I decided to copy this energy-saving. Passivity
will suit me best. They didn't bother putting handcuffs on
me. He got in beside me; in total silence the driver brought
us to Haarlem. I was the most negligible of pickpockets.

In Haarlem two of them were subduing a little old man
who was fighting drunk. He had energy for three, kicking,
punching, cursing. They did nothing but ward off the sails of
this windmill. An astonishing huge plate of false teeth flew
out and skidded across the floor. A cop picked it up, waited
patiently to restore it to the owner.

They didn't lock me up. There was a basement where an
old grey-haired cop sat at a desk with a movie magazine, and
a haggard anaemic boy looked up smiling to see something
new, and asked 'Do you play chess?' He had a little pocket
set, put it on the bench between us. I won, twice, but he was
no sort of player either. The old man went out, came back
with two plates. Bread, some cheese, margarine. Two mugs
of something tasting of chicory. Rather later he yawned, said
'Time for bed'. The cell here was smaller, more antiquated. I
never remember sleeping better. It had, I suppose, been a
busy day.

*

More bread, in the morning, more wartime coffee. The boy
told me a long and immensely complicated story of which I
understood nothing but that he was persecuted by absolutely

everyone and his father most of all. And then a young, rather smart cop looked in, caught my eye and said 'Rightyright' in quite a wakeful voice. The old warder – or one just like him – made a note in his ledger. 'Extracted' perhaps. 'We're going to see the Officer,' to my unasked question. If I'm to go by television, in the States they put cuffs on you and leg shackles too, but this is Holland. We walked quite briskly. I didn't see much of the Palace of Justice though I'm familiar enough with the building. We whisked up stairs and straight into a large pleasantly airy office. A youngish man sat writing at a big untidy desk; off to one side a grey-haired woman – his clerk – was barricaded behind a lot of office machinery.

'Sit down then, Mr van Bijl,' polite and pleasant. 'Let's get acquainted.' Dismissing my escort with a chin movement 'I shan't need you'. He probably spent the next two hours cronying, within reach of the coffee machine. The Dutch addiction to coffee outdoes even Germany or Italy. The clerk had a smart Siemens maker parked next her computer, and the first thing she did was to give me a cup, too.

Our Dutch variation on the familiar Napoleonic system is that the 'Officer of Justice' is a state prosecutor who doubles, here, as 'judge of instruction'. In a way there's less hypocrisy than with an examining magistrate who is officially even-handed in defence as in prosecution, but as everybody knows has a bias toward pursuit. He makes no bones about it here. In the lower courts he will quite likely be presenting the case against you. But if it's the Assize Court, for grave criminal offences, there will be an Advocate-General in the prosecutor's chair. The Officer will – in most instances – have taken pains to weigh with some care the arguments on both sides. He won't – as a rule – have put you there in the dock without sifting the matter at length and with care. Unless, indeed, he is persuaded that there's a solid case to answer, he won't send the papers up to the tribunal. It is, I believe, as good a system as can exist.

Thus, this initial session was mostly formalities; factual, a very thorough personal history; stuff that isn't in dispute. A 'defender' – these detailed, meticulous explanations ... – would be called upon to sit in when there were matters 'in dispute'.

I liked him, I'm bound to say. Between two ages; dust-coloured hair with a tendency to balding; pale heavy features but sensitive sharp brown eyes with clear healthy whites. Extreme precision in his wording and phrasings. 'Read that back,' he often said to his woman (accustomed plainly to these ways). 'Scrub that, I'll rephrase it.' I have to do with a careful, an honest, an even-minded man. 'No, that's not good enough.' And once or twice 'Did I say that? Have you left out a word? Then I'll qualify that.' At this – initial – stage taking pains to be 'on my side': 'I'm not altogether satisfied that the police have done all they might.' 'We will want an opinion from an expert upon your state of mind hereabouts. You won't want to challenge my order for a psychiatric examination?' 'I don't much like this witness, sounds to me superficial and over-complaisant.' I rather think I'm in good hands.

It was to be expected that he would ask about the surgery.

'Not much point, I should think, in my refusing.' A faint smile, the barest glimmer.

'What you say to a doctor comes under professional secrets. Written records, on the other hand, can be subpoenaed.'

'Prostate.'

'They took it out? Radical?'

'They found a cancer.'

'I'm sorry if this touches a nerve.'

'I don't mind in the least: it's a commonplace at my age. I didn't see though that it was any business of the police.'

'They made a pretty good guess. True, they have their own ways of finding things out, which it doesn't do to enquire into.'

'The net result is functional impotence.'

'Quite so. I sympathize. Incidentally a fairly widespread human condition, and on the increase.'

'Just so. A banality. Hundreds. Thousands. Now that we're this far I don't in the least mind talking about it. Walk about with a stick. There is a large scar. Learn to live with it.'

'Excellent.'

'Let's have it all in the open then. A young woman was killed. Also a banality, we're afraid, also on the increase.' He said nothing at all. 'Some sort of sexual motivation would be probable. From what I gather. I don't see how this supposition would be thought applicable in my instance.'

'We're here to find out.'

'And having found out I should expect to receive your apologies.'

He put down the pen he had been playing with. Expensive pen; probably he gets them as Christmas presents. Leaned back. Smiled more broadly.

'The more old-fashioned kind of legal officer would be quite purple by now. You're lecturing me. You're asking me questions. I'm afraid you misunderstand the purpose of this office. Your surgeon examined you. Suspected, subsequently confirmed the presence of a cancer. Recommended a drastic remedy.' Drily. 'I'm in much the same position. You're an oldish man. Educated, intelligent, a man of the world. In your circles a well-known and respected figure. Mm? My manner towards you is in consequence.

'Let me in turn be open. The investigating police officer, a man of much experience, forms an opinion, sketches the outline of a theory. The purpose here will be to test this theory, before tending either to confirm or eliminate it.'

'And may I learn what this theory may be?'

'No doubt it will become apparent. I think that will be all for today. I have however one decision which I can enlarge upon. This would be whether or not to set you free or to commit you to detention. That is often thought an administrative convenience; having an individual so to speak under our hand. I believe I could rely upon you to come here freely when I ask you. I have a number of reasons for deciding to keep you under constraint. This will not be a hardship – it isn't a prison. Mevrouw, will you be kind enough to call the escort? I'm going to make this order.'

'You wouldn't care to motivate your decisions a little more clearly?'

'My motivations – like your own – will become clearer. There's a passage of time involved. Let me say this much; enlightenment, for us both, will be the quicker.' He made a hand movement towards the pile of dossiers, ungainly on his table. 'If your future were alone among my responsibilities ... Human nature, alas, is that everyone sees their own cause as unique, and of all-absorbing interest. So it is, but that is one of my more difficult tasks. Here you are,' to my guardian angel. 'I shall want to see Mijnheer tomorrow, at ten o'clock precisely – just check that, Mevrouw, would you?'

The Huis van Bewaring in Haarlem is quite a local landmark. Dates from the Belle Epoque; these star-shape or circular fortresses were thought the very last word in modern, humane prison architecture, and greatly admired. Cough, cough; the House of Keeping isn't a prison ... supposedly only for those awaiting the decision of the tribunal. But it sure looks and feels like one. True, these echoing spaces no longer resound to the roll and clatter of the sanitary bucket. We've now these dinky stainless steel WCs in every cell. Nobody, I think, can be said to have known prison who hasn't had to sit on the bucket. These places were calvinist in their domestic economy. Prayer and repentance were the mainspring of penal institutes; shit a powerful factor in the journey towards godliness.

Professionals here are brisk. A decided change from the scruffy atmosphere of the police station. I was taken in charge by a smallish, thick-set man in a blue overall, military in haircut but not in manner. Quiet in speech, unhurried in handling. Self-respect comes back. To be a detainee is not inconsistent with dignity. There are not many places where the two go together. A clean cell to myself; there was even a table and a chair. There was quiet.

I wasn't given very long to enjoy the quiet. A man with little of the guard about him but his bunch of keys said 'Parlour'. The word comes from the French I suppose; parloir, a place for talk. There are different sorts, small cubbyholes with a table and a lamp where you consult your lawyer. These are private and there's no guard, because this relation is confidential – that's a rule – and thereby privileged. Détenu gets always a body search, both before and after.

'Family' parlours too: toys for the children and a pathetic notion of being homely. I learn a lot here, listening, in the exercise yard.

'Friend of mine in France, parlour with his wife – right, lose no time; come on then, knicks down.'

'That allowed?'

'Course not. But you'd be surprised at what's Tolerated.'

'But the guard?'

'Most are bastards, mate, some are human. Reads a book.' There are civilized places where a wife, a 'concubine', can stay the night.

This one was simply 'medical'; table and chairs, examination couch. Clean sheet. Cupboard with a few necessities; lock and key to this. Moment or two alone, and a woman came in.

I would get to know her; she would be important to me. Late forties, thin and narrow. No beauty but oddly goodlooking, in the gypsy style rare in Holland; dark skin and long dark ringlets, dangly jewellery and a lot of make-up. One won't say curt, but laconic of manner. I got to liking her.

'I'm Mrs Veen.' Briefcase on the table; some long complicated forms. 'I'm a doctor in psychiatry. In general medicine too, so we'll start by taking a look at you, shall we?' Bony but attractive figure; hard, as though she were good at judo. Accustomed to giving orders but I got her to change the abrupt manner. A prison population is, I suppose in general, pretty simple of mind when not downright retarded; poor in physical health; a very high proportion on drugs of whatever sort; badly nourished. But her hands were gentle, with the blood pressure thing, the stethoscope: her touch was sensitive.

She took her time with the listening; we had plenty of it. Interested in my prostate. Sitting down then and beginning on a long printed form – 'When you're dressed come and sit, start talking, begin anywhere, oh I can listen between the lines, the tuberculosis and the arteries. Haemorrhoids, oh dear, I forgot to look.' First sign of humour; I was to learn she had more.

I'd have to say, no time for boredom. I was reminded of the schoolchild asked who the Islas Malvinas belong to. 'To England in the morning and to Argentina in the afternoon' – for between the Officer of Justice and Mrs V. I was kept at full stretch. In the evenings Willy came and we had a family parlour. I didn't tell her the French anecdote; she's puritanical in public. I was also touched, perhaps a little surprised, by visits from my daughters. Indignant, vociferous, full of ploys for making the legal authority eat it all up, every scrap, and leave the plate clean (like a lazy child, won't eat its pudding) and inclined to make much of the important people they know who could be asked to say a word in a highly placed ear. But I saw also loyalty and kindness. Better, the tie forged, which one will never entirely lose, between a man and the daughters he played with when little. The male rough games girls love: the strong hands that threw them up and caught them, the grip on a wrist and ankle to play aeroplane, the small hand digging into a pocket for treasures, arranging one's hair 'to make you beautiful', struggling to open the fist which holds a hidden sweet, wheedling for a penny, coaxing for five more minutes before bedtime. The father who is both more indulgent and more violent, who is gentler and more patient than brisk-handed mamma, who can be teased and tormented – and can suddenly explode into slapping one's bottom. A great deal of nonsense is talked about this tie.

Daily I am reminded that I belong to 'the upper class'. In Holland this scarcely exists in the terms generally understood in England (or even in 'republican' France). We have a few Counts and Barons, families with lengthy names, distinguished in history. Some may still own broadish acres, elegant houses. They play no role and nobody pays them any heed. The élite, the privileged class – strange to say, that is myself.

Willy brings goodies 'to ameliorate the ordinary'. The ordinary is fairly rough – I eat it, and with appetite; the beans and the cabbage, the small ball of mince and the square of stringy stew, the slice of cornflour sausage and the mousetrap cheese; all of it balanced and calculated for adequate nourishment and never filthy. I have night-time feasts; the tiny tin of foie gras and jar of (Swedish) caviare; the stick of beautiful dark unsweet chocolate which breaks with a sharp snap; the lemon (I must borrow a knife from the indulgent guard). I have clean underclothes daily; we are allowed a shower twice a week. Exquisite-smelling soap, and my own eau-de-cologne and *proper* lavatory-paper.

In the exercise yard I would be put with the prison aristocracy, but since I come back late from legal and psychiatric sessions I take my turn with the poor – worn-out basketball shoes and no socks. They can be deadened by hopelessness and misery. Little to look back upon and nothing to look forward to. Many are on treatment for addiction or Aids – or tuberculosis. Some few are alive and funny, but most are already dead. They would not thank me for foie gras. I have nothing to give them.

My lawyer comes, the 'eminent criminal pleader' who sniffs at the Officer's plodding hairsplitting ways. 'We'd knock them silly in court': yes but we aren't in court and one wonders whether we'll ever get there.

I have my neurologist, my 'Court Jew'. For Dr Rubinstein (a crony of the lawyer's, hired at immense expense – 'but we'll get it all back in damages') is our expert, the counterblast when the need may arise, to Mrs Veen and her works ('wouldn't trust that woman further than she can throw me'). Dr R. says nothing like this; one does not comment on colleagues. He is very courtly, a thoroughly eighteenth-century figure satined and brocaded, a Riesener or Oeben desk of the most delicate marquetry and exquisite workmanship, full to the brim of secret papers and the most confidential of diplomatic coded telegram. He is ready to blast Professor Heinrich out of the skies. 'A radical prostatectomy can indeed give rise to the most radical neuro-psychiatric consequences.' We think, increasingly, that this will never come to court, but if it should 'we'll astonish their weak nerves'. The phrase could have been better chosen. I look at the pleader's heavy, handsome face. He is laughing at his own jokes.

Two chins, fleshy folds, silver hair better than any periwig, a mouth whose many subtle tucks and curves advertise scepticism; I must not say cynicism.

'Even assuming what they cannot prove, that we met, stumbled upon, or had some sort of assignation with this girl – what then? All that follows is untenable and the question of sanity/insanity is legally nonexistent. This theory of our impotence being merely technical due to our inability to attain erection –' One could enjoy this. I could feel that with an effort it would again be Bert planted here, and that I were the spectator, amused by this gluttonous manner – 'Totally beside the point. This comic fabulation of Veen's – I'd have some fun in court with her erectile tissues – whereby we are tormented by frustrations and make a sacrifice of Zomerlust's virginity; grand stuff but I'd be the cold spoon in her soufflé.' I would suspect him of being vain of his own outstandingly erectile set of cavities.

I was – I am – profoundly grateful to Professor Heinrich for making a good job. Many men, after this surgery, cannot contain their urine. Forced to wear a nappy. My own trouble was perhaps a small price to pay for avoiding that. It was, true, agonizing to feel desire, the more acute knowing that I could never again – should gather the courage to ask whether this is 'normal' and whether it will die down. My own feeling is that it has, to some extent. I wonder whether that is psychological, or only physio.

'Veen – we're not sawing her off for incompetence or sentimentality; would be seen as an anti-feminist attitude and a court might well take a dim view. But that she falls in love with her own theory, no sex-prejudice nonsense then applies.'

It seems I have to ask an obvious question.

'To your mind – who killed her?' And triumphant –

'That's for THEM to find. The police, for the quietening and reassurance of the populace, for their own lazy comfort and convenience, for their nice neat paperwork, for the kudos of claiming to solve an obnoxious affair, settle upon us. Vulnerable, simple, unpremeditating. Haven't we the proof! That absolutely openly we took the wretched girl out for a pizza. Feeling sorry for her!' I'm ready to believe it myself.

'All the rest is bullshit. So you had a rough time with sexy Irene. As she CONFIRMS. A very natural, human, demonstrably innocent passage with a friend you trust and for whom you feel a real and deep affection of many years standing.'

Which is all true, after all. Confirm, confirm, whatever that may mean. Irene was a pathetically human figure in front of the judge of instruction.

'Now this morning,' said the Officer, 'I'm proceeding to a confrontation between yourself and an essential witness. My examination may appear harsh. In the presence of your advocate, you are entitled to raise objection – of which I am the sole judge – or to put further questions. Freely, to make further statement. Unforced, be it understood. Untainted by imputation.' He is given to 'formulating suggestions' hedged by legal jargon.

Irene was produced. She was self-possessed, dignified. Under strain garrulous – so am I. She hadn't tried to fake anything. Slightly overdressed, as she always is, and neither more nor less than usually made up. She looked straight at me and said, 'Henk has understood everything. He told me to say so.'

'You will not speak to anyone,' sharp. 'You are here to answer my questions. When you have anything to add, you address your word to myself. Is that clear? Then let's have no utterances, if you please. For the record, you are not represented by counsel, you are ready to answer me without fear or hindrance, you are not under oath but you will speak the truth as you know it, open and spontaneous, you understand and agree?' Her expression was *amiable*. She had even a very faint smile, not such as could be called sarcastic, and certainly not insolent.

Well, of course, the Dutch ... yell at them and they'll just go mulish. A life's experience has taught me contempt for national clichés and we're no more law-abiding than anyone else; nor I suppose less. We do have a dislike for being hectored, and we always have to have the last word in any argument. Which is why an argument among the Dutch always goes on for a very long time.

Respect for 'The Law'? My generation did. Religious belief was still very strong, and that has a lot to do with it. And being respectable in small-town communities having the police on your doorstep, or the bailiff, which is worse, serving you a summons, is a disgrace – has even today much weight. To be 'in trouble with the law' will always fluster Willy, and our daughters more so, for they are fearfully concerned about 'their good name'.

The young, of course, of today's generation have no respect and jeer openly, in court or out. For someone like myself – I think one must draw a distinction. The civil law, the commercial codes in particular and especially on an international scale is such a jungle that in the Trade it is a built-in hazard to get rights respected, your patents protected, your royalties paid, your contracts registered. One is forever suing and being sued, though most of it is bluff, and 'one's man' in Venezuela or Djakarta has always to be a lawyer...

At home I suppose one could very often be in trouble with social legislation. One was in arrears with alimony to the divorced wife or the social security contributions concerning an undeclared part-time employee – what a blameless life I have always led.

But the real law is the criminal code; am I right? Anyone, I think, who lived even a childhood during the Third Reich's occupation years, when so many infractions were offences against their 'criminal' mass of ukase and you could be hanged, shot, or sent to Neuengamme for saying oh, fuck-the-Führer, feels still the bite of those times. I was a little boy. I didn't take my life in my hands. I didn't jam the railway points or fill in the manifest all wrong for a truckload of nuts-and-bolts. And I grew up with a healthy sense of moral right and wrong. People got into the paper for burglary or blackmail, armed robbery and causing bodily harm, even rape or homicide. What had got them into that? What weird motives, distorted impulses, led to it? The police came and got them. Before the court – of Assize, the Schwurgericht – the judges and a jury of men and women like them ('the folk on the Clapham omnibus') listened to their complicated and unconvincing – and sad – explanations, and sent them off to prison, often for many years. It possesses a hell of a crunch, the criminal law. Sometimes there are crimes of passion, and a court can understand, can feel sympathy, can and does say 'You've had a very hard time. We take that in account. You may also have had months and even years of stewing and sweating in jail while a complicated instruction went on and on. We believe you have suffered punishment enough.' They may sentence you to a year or so; make that suspended; even free you altogether, forthwith. They can also say that in all honesty they cannot find extenuating circumstances. A life in prison with the recommendation that this should not be less than a total of twenty-five years.

At my age a year is short. But nobody, certainly not Professor Heinrich or any other expert witness, would care to prognosticate and promise me 'so many' years. I would never see Venice again.

I am in two minds. One says that there are holes in the criminal as in the civil code. A lawyer will always get you off; that's what they're paid for. Another voice is distinctly Old-Testament. Eye for an eye, boy; tooth for tooth. I vary; one would almost say it's according to whether or not I have slept well.

But I'm rambling; aren't I. The point here at issue is that Irene is an Amsterdammer. We've always loathed and envied them. This was the town that wouldn't have any Romans. Wouldn't have the Spanish – drove indeed Philip out of his neat, careful, conscientious bureaucratic mind. Wouldn't be bullied by the English. It's lucky they thought, that all our precious far-Eastern trade has to pass the Channel. That sailing ships are at the mercy of the wind, and the prevalent wind hereabouts is always south-west. Which puts one at such a disadvantage; as children say, *so unfair*. Typically Dutch to say, Well, if you want a war that badly you can have it, and conduct several battles exactly like Jutland, which nobody will win and the losses are appalling. But it's the English who start hastily to prate about Peace.

Saw off the French the same way: they swallowed Amsterdam but found it so full of fish bones they soon sicked it up again. Napoleon, who said he'd be an Attila to Venice (was, too) steered well clear of these frightful pigs. And Hitler of course had the brilliant idea of sweeping the place right out; dump them all in Poland. Thought better of that.

To this day the place is full of inventive ideas, leading everybody else to sputter furiously; hippies, squatters, cafés selling cannabis. The Queen herself, aware they'd dislike her marrying a German, faced them down by doing it right in their midst. Hardheaded woman; they were less trouble than expected.

I was proud of Irene. She saved me, I think, from being intimidated. I should think that most people in my situation would be. Just like me, hereabout. Becoming overloquacious, losing countenance, gabbling.

Sure, the experienced, the guilty, the crafty, tell their lies brazen and unperturbed by disbelief. Or threat. Or mockery. The judge is used to both attitudes. He has so much on his side, and he knows how to search hearts.

She told it all and with no hesitation. That was absolutely right. She did not fear humiliation and she did not humiliate me. The truth has a bare simplicity which is telling. To these veteran listeners the more striking: the woman who, colourless, consigns it all to print. To the magistrate, who has a private life of his own, and some of it he would not like to see made public. And the advocate, who hears, knows as much dirt as the Provincial of the Jesuits and keeps the same bland inscrutable face, of the experience and wisdom so reassuring to his client.

'It does not in the slightest harm us,' he would say at the next 'parlour'. That I knew already. 'A human thing, and bravely told. Nothing, you know, in Dostoevsky or any other fella, comes anywhere near reality. No no, quite the contrary, created an excellent impression. If she had been evasive, taken refuge in prudent euphemism, you could have looked a sad mess.'

'What I had feared,' I said, 'was that this would add fuel to Veen's contention that I might have killed that girl in the storm of feeling unable to rape her.'

'Let me tell you, I'm now virtually certain you'll never be called to face a courtroom. But if – an eventuality I'd have welcomed for myself though naturally not for you – I'd have socked it to them. Zomerlust too, she's dead and one is sorry about that, but it makes her you see a sort of martyr. That pathologist who did the post-mortem, saying she was intacta. I'd have challenged that. These girls today, menstruating they use a tampon, you can't tell what they might have been up to.'

Carla, you have more than I thought, to forgive us.

*

It is late at night. They put the light out early, after shovel-
ling in the mattress and the rest and giving you just enough
time to make the bed up. Then it's quiet. Light filters in
through the window, it's floodlit out there in the courtyards.
But it's not enough to read by. Stillness. Every second hour
you hear the click as they let fall the little shutter on the
'judas' after they've taken their routine peek to be sure you
continue to be a good boy. You sleep. Mostly I do. But it can
take an hour or two.

*

'And of course, someone is in my parking slot so I must
walk across just when it's at its worst.' It is lashing down
outside, with a high wind; I can taste it, loving it. The wonderful smell comes in with Veen, with the smell of wet um-
brella, of Burberry, of her dark pungent perfume. Her voice
is level and controlled as usual. She hangs up her wet things,
produces indoor shoes from her carrier bag. Lithe neat move-
ments. Sits at the table with her writing pad. She doesn't
scribble; regular, Greek-looking script. Straight on from the
day before.

'A stable, secure boyhood you called it. Only child. For
your parents, can you find a single word which seems to
sum up the character and your relation to it? Your father?'

'Abrupt. Sharp. Kind. Quick-tempered, but soon over. Fair.'

'Yes, that's good. And for your mother?'

'Patience, warmth, love, occasionally sentimental – even
silly.'

'Protective?'

'Yes I think so, but if you mean possessive, then no.
Unselfish.'

'Showing love for each other?'

'Yes but not demonstrative. Respect might be the better
word.'

'Any idea why you were the only child? Accident would
you think, or deliberate choice?'

'I never thought about it.' I'm ready to cut this woman off upon occasion. She starts on, about did they make love and was I aware of it, I'm not having any of that.

'We're nowhere near as interested in sex as legend has it, but that's still a prominent, vital fact of existence.'

'I don't have to be reticent all the time.'

'Poverty, chastity, and obedience, early Christian preoccupations – very Dutch preoccupations, up to the war obsessively so. Prevalence of sex in daily intercourse.' She's only doing her job, I suppose; mustn't show irritation.

'Children play games, explore, and inform themselves. I was in no way over-protected.'

'A normal boyhood?'

'No quarrel with that expression.'

'Exploration would include village girls?'

'First I ever had was an Amsterdam prostitute.'

'Leentje uit de Lange Niesel.' An old music-hall song.

'Exactly. Efficient, good-hearted, and matter-of-fact.'

'So no troubles? Fine. Suppose now we skip a bit, come to your wife.'

'No we won't. That's a subject I don't discuss.'

'I take your point. Put it as an abstract question. I like your being detached; you're good at that. Find a word, can you, to describe marital relations. Satisfying? Enjoyable?'

'You could say we don't get bored.'

'Your reticence doesn't fash me at all. Would you feel upset if I were to describe you as stiff? Rigid, even? On this subject prudish?'

'You used the word; I wouldn't feel fazed about it.'

'You do realize that the report I make goes to the Officer of Justice, for a specific judicial purpose? The position you take might alter his view.'

'You're trying to put pressure on me.'

'We'll not pursue it; it's his worry and not mine. But you won't mind my asking whether you have been tempted into adventures.'

'There are species of animal true to one mate. I don't think they go in for these notions of chastity and obedience. Do geese have a concept of fidelity? I'm not a biologist.'

'We live in a world, however, where the other's wife appears desirable, simply because she's the other's.'

'I have occasionally slipped. When on trips for instance. With professionals. Underline – neither men nor boys. You'll have to be satisfied with that.'

'Oh, I am.' Let me just try, to see whether she can laugh.

'You don't ask whether I find you attractive.'

'And do you? See me in an unprofessional light? How flattering. I'd fail to be human if I made faces.'

'But I dare say, in the present circumstances, I'd be ill advised to ask you to take your clothes off.' Yes, she laughed. A good ringing one.

'I can bring objections and hindrances to mind.'

Not bad. Leave it at that. Was there 'a test'? Did she 'pass it'? But do I pass? Do I reach the requisite level of balanced and well-compensated sanity? Or do I slip from time to time?

*

Late at night. Curfew here comes early. Outside, the night has hardly begun but we are abed and asleep, like good children. And like conscientious parents the guardians come to look, to make sure. One does not hear them coming; there is only the minute click of the metal cover of the 'judas'. Everything is quiet and they pass on. By some trick of sound, even the noise of the city does not reach in here. The moveable pane in my little window is hygienically open but no murmur that I can identify arrives.

At night I imagine the house as a castle. Not with round towers and battlements like a child's toy; nor is it gothic. Of later date, a smooth-walled fortress with sharp-angled entrants and recessions, on some crag high above the city, bathed in moonlight – it would be floodlit nowadays to accentuate the picturesque, and a narrow shaft of this hard bluish-white brilliance spears in at my window-slot. In here

145

are men, I wonder how many men, men without women. Some lie still, others turn restlessly. Some dream, and some snore. Some think, I suppose. I try not to think. A book I have read – what, and where? – recommended not-thinking. Shut off the interior dialogue. Good advice, no doubt.

Why, somebody once asked me, does the strelitzia flower open, always, at that same odd angle to the stalk? Why indeed, but it is a childish question. Watching any flower unfold, one will see the shapes and colours of a daisy as the most extraordinary of biological phenomena. But there, the man who has spent his life among spiders will say the same.

We know that we are losing species both animal and vegetable at a frenzied pace; irreplaceable and irrecoverable. Just as we know that upon this small planet, which we bestride with such arrogance , there are species still undiscovered. We know, further, that no oddity in the natural world can rival the realities of human behaviour. To any observer of the human species, even to someone like Veen, I am a banality.

Justice; we talk about it. Like any businessman I have some experience of tribunals. The paraphernalia of judges and clerks and advocates – tomes and masses of paper. Customers being what they are, litigation is a commonplace. Jan – he used to say *pay* – pay the skin off your arse, rather than trust a court. But one can get dragged into court, and then one must defend oneself. Jan suffered much from feelings of humiliation at not being 'educated'. I had to be educated. Jan, I hated you often, I don't think I failed in respect for you. 'Justice! that's the trap for flies. Only the spiders come out of that fatter.' Not a profound judgement, for Jan was no shining light. No humour either, much. Some sense of irony, of the ridiculous. A man to be proud of, still. A man who couldn't steal and couldn't tell a lie; a man incapable of hypocrisy, of being devious, and of being obsequious.

I've no experience of criminal law. It's not quite as funny; people still get hanged, electrocuted, imprisoned for many weary, sad and senseless years while the criminals are rich and respected. But it's about human beings; there's that to be said for it.

*

I don't go always at the same hour, nor even every day, to get 'instructed'. The Officer of Justice has a wide clientele of the disgruntled, and of obvious villains against whom he finds it hard to get convictions: not enough evidence. I wasn't flustered to be called for earlier than is his habit – they'll leave the library books on my table, fit me in this afternoon for a shower. I've shaved, and with a new blade. Specifically male pleasure. Can't find a female equivalent – finishing with the curse maybe? Things we can't experience, though I'm learning, these days, much that is new.

He seemed rather more than usually acid this morning. When in this frame of mind he sees me as a rapist of long standing. He looks to Veen for support of his notion that surgery curdled me into an impotent old satyr. He is lighting a longish, thinnish cigar, definitely not Cuban.

'The police do their work, Mr van Bijl. They have interested themselves in a recent past. They profit from informers. Window-peeping old women appear merely pitiable. To myself they are untrustworthy sources, often malicious. So that they must be verified.' What can he have thought up now?

'We do verify. What do we come up with? A young woman more probably describable as a vulnerable young girl.' Signalled with his cigar: his clerk got up, went out, returned ushering in Veronica Lake.

This name will mean nothing to those of less than my age. To us in youth she meant a great deal. An incompetent movie actress, the despair of directors or writers who had to do with her. 'Can't learn her lines and when she does they're delivered like solid lead': I was greatly disillusioned. They had to make do with her because she was very popular. Indeed she caused much trouble, for during the war the thousands of women working in munitions factories had to be dissuaded from copying her: she became in fact a public danger.

147

Her stock in trade was very simple; she had long fair hair. (For the rest, model for a Barbie doll.) To be sure, our northern European women very often have long fair hair, and it's poker-straight – a source of despair until they learned to be feminist and to worry no longer. But occasionally this hair has a natural wave in it. Part it, comb it across and it will fall over the forehead and a much deeper wave at eye level, turning inward to mask the line of the jaw and even the eye itself. With this very beautiful natural feature (forgive me for talking like a plant biologist) Miss Lake was quite content. Indeed she was known to journalists as 'the one-eyed bird-brain'. You will ask me whether aged sixteen or thereabouts I had masturbatory fantasies about this doll which moved and even spoke, in a dulled mechanical voice. The answer is no: we romanticized it. She was a Virgin Mary and our adolescent sexual desires were concentrated upon other equally mythical figures of the times. I have to say that I had not forgotten that Lalage possessed this striking attribute. Indeed I'd have to say that it had mightily caught my eye, and contributed perhaps essentially to my – will we call it an obsession – that so intensely vigorous and striking picture, of Lalage riding her bicycle? As a schoolgirl her hair was shorter; as I remember no lower than her chin. She has grown it out to shoulder length. Washed it and brushed it to get the Lake-effect. To be honest I was fairly stunned. Thoughts of hand-grenades crossed my mind. To say shattered would be as banal as everything else about me. What does the grenade feel after flying into a thousand fragments? Satisfaction at a job well done? That this is a short life but merry? As it arches through the air a moment of intense enjoyment?

For that moment is also violently emetic. I should have thrown up but for pride, which is all one has: the don't-let-them see that they've got you down.

The judge was impressed but not I think for long. Miss Lake's lines (rewritten for her; 'Are you going to buy me a cup of coffee?') would now make one reach for that handy button which zaps the sound out. Judges have to listen.

'Tell me simply in your own words.'

'Well I met him in the library you see, that was perfectly polite. He found a book for me I needed, and I was grateful, you know.'

'I'll ask you not to interrupt, Mr van Bijl, you'll have plenty of opportunity in due course.'

'Well I was in the dunes looking for these flowers you know and he was there.'

'You suggest that he followed you?'

'It looks like it.'

'You don't suggest that he lured you into the dunes on this pretext?'

'He did say that I was likely to find what I was looking for. A school exercise you know, photograph and make a drawing because one mustn't pick them.'

'Yes – continue.'

'I didn't think, I said something like oh I found it. He found what he was looking for, more like.'

'You didn't think to scream, to run away?'

'Out there in the dunes all alone – some hope.'

'Later, Mr van Bijl; let's have this clear, first. You were saying? – that he used force on you? Tear your clothes?'

'Well it was very hot, I wasn't wearing much.'

'Yes I see.' Taking his glasses off to polish them. They can get foggy – this is known as getting steamed up. His weren't, though. 'I should like you to describe this rape, in as exact terms as you can find. As you would to a doctor.'

'I can't, not with him there. Well, I'll try.' Quite a good job she made of it. Not that I'm a judge. The phrase is ambiguous but can stand. She must have realized she could be called on to repeat all this in a courtroom, and saw the opportunity to polish the rehearsals. I was there too after all; have indeed a clear recollection of the episode.

'Do you wish at present to question the witness?' he asked me.

'Not at this moment, I think. The clerk can at any time read bits back?'

'It is an exact transcript of the verbal process, and you can reserve your right if you prefer. Very well, let's come to this second occasion when as you tell it the man came to your house.'

This was interesting. A laconic police note (I recognize the hand of Sergeant Flapear) said they'd been approached by an old woman who said she recognized a photo of me and claimed she'd seen me enter Lalage's house.

I'm not going to waste energies calling her little bitch, tra la, that would cut no ice with the magistrate. She'd made a smooth job of this, piecing together a thought-I'd-come-to-apologize, don't you know, hadn't wanted to make a fuss at the doorstep because one didn't like to create a scandal the neighbours might make a story of (since it's handed you on a plate); she'd been washing her hair and was wearing a dressing-gown. She decided I'd really come to beg – well, to urge – her to keep quiet about it all. She didn't wish to embarrass my wife.

Willy, I have the impression, would make short work of Miss Lake. Like any adult woman, takes a sceptical view of excitable teenage girls. But I have a man to deal with.

'Very well Miss, I'll ask you to wait outside for a little. I may call you back. In any case a few formalities; the transcript will be read back to you.'

Which can have formidable teeth. They hear these phrases read in the monotonous uninflected stenographer's voice, and think they can improve upon that.

'Well, what have you to say? Of course, you don't have to say anything. If you wish to sketch a generalized outline I shall be pleased to give you hearing.'

'As you can't fail to have noticed any advocate would cut down her long grass and make hay.'

'It would be improper for me to comment.'

'Yes but you stopped me questioning her. Glib, fabricated

whitewash and you let her dig herself in deeper. It's all perfectly understandable.'

'Possibly. I can agree that she doesn't make the best of impressions. That is not in contention. In any such matter, an advocate can make any young woman appear foolish, imprudent, point to evasion, even putative falsehood. That is not the point. Are you contesting the essential truth, of a liaison with this young woman?'

'No.'

'Think well. The admission would be damaging. Your age and responsibilities, and a silly schoolgirl.'

'Look – I absolutely contest the use of the slightest force or even persuasion. You can write me down a gormless – elderly – open-mouthed provincial. You can call me a lecherous old – you know perfectly that plenty of schoolgirls are vicious enough to think it funny and that there are some who boast about it afterward – I let the sugar daddy have a feel and I can do anything with the imbecile?'

'I am aware,' primly. 'A court might find your viewpoint as open to criticism as is, conceivably, hers.'

*

Carla: this is unbearable.

I can remember writing that down, as soon as I was back; once left to myself: the rule is always that one is searched. I am not made to undress. I am seen here as a harmless old man and they think it enough to go through the superficial routine of patting me down.

The phrase as written is all wrong; as though I found it unbearable to think of her. Not a bit. Her understanding I have; it was her help I needed.

Oh, I can see the patterns of these small minds. They take me for a Plouc – good word, the country cousin with cow shit on the boots. As though I weren't an Ur-Amsterdammer and rather more sophisticated than some little petit-bourgeois Haarlemmer law student. As though I knew nothing of the civilized world, of which I have seen a good deal. And the good Mrs Veen! Bright enough, I make no doubt, a kindly disposition, well up in all the very latest forms of psychiatric theory, and what shall she know of life? What could she make of that simple everyday fact, a million examples all about one; a life shared over forty years with the woman of one's life? She has spent an hour or so – I know – talking to Willy. She will have seen a woman strong in purpose and character, strong too in convention and tradition, of good and generous instincts, stubborn in belief and morally upright. Slow, and of no more than average intelligence. Shrewd, within her small and unexciting life. Apart from the fact that these people always overestimate their own intelligence, of which they have a great deal (Willy is slow, but will see through a brick wall in time, which is more than they will), the Veens of this world know nothing whatever about the Spirit. I don't think they know much about love, either: they see little enough of it, beyond sex.

I have a good understanding of flowers; a fair knowledge of biology. From this I have learned something about love, but all that I really know I have learned from my wife.

My judgement is poor; that's obvious. I had little talent for business practise, and less at the human heart. How else would I have come to make such an abject fool of myself over a pretty schoolgirl?

With hindsight of course, I have worked this out. Physiologically, men of my age are pushovers for the brilliance of the young female body; 'la jeune fille en fleur' – for the metaphor of bud, of incipient florescence, is never absent from the mind of a man of my training. I'm pretty safe, I think, in saying that the irritable prostate of a man nearing seventy (I had not of course known that mine was in the claws of the crab) makes him vulnerable. Recalling Miss Lake's appeal to a boy of fifteen – prostate at that age, also very greedy – I've no call to be surprised. Upon which conclusion I fell asleep.

A restful morning, into the bargain. No judges called for

my presence, no Veens appeared upon the scene. I was kept busy with housekeeping, in jails as everywhere else at the forefront of the Dutch mind, and a lengthy business, being issued in turn with the broom, with the dustpan and brush, with scrubbing materials, with disinfectant for the sanitary arrangements; these treasures are entrusted to one for a brief space, after which the warder comes and inspects, with a pretty critical eye, and lazybones along the passage gets told to do it all over again and look-a-bit-sharpish this time. After which it was fresh-air period, with my friends the fraudulent-conversion-chaps, as ever voluble about their symptoms of digestive disorder and coming down severely upon the negligences of the Medical Officer. Not raining this morning, so that one can venture into the great open spaces of the exercise yard. Out at sea, so to speak, instead of hugging the coastline: a narrowish area along the buildings is roofed over, to allow of stumping to and fro when the weather is bad. Back for the midday meal where cabbage follows beans, and beans the cabbage, with some regularity. Carrots and peas on Sundays. Hard to see how the intellectuals can still manage to be constipated; it must be endemic to their system. I was settling down to a library book when the door was flung open and 'Parlour'.

The legal advisor. Lawyers are all fussy about their right to see clients at any time, are given indeed to appearing late at night. He was in a high state of entertainment over poor Lalage (whose name also came in for derision.) Miss Fluffytail, Miss Flibbertygibbet. And a fine old Dutch word, Miss Hittapettit. To my father's generation any young girl of frivolous demeanour and careless ways would often be referred to as a hittapetit. A tonic accent is given to the first and the last syllables. It isn't even really pejorative, but in the mouth of an advocate it's practically open whoredom.

'They'd never dare produce her in court. In fact the Officer as good as admits the dossier is empty. You'll be taking your stroll in the dunes again any day now, an eye out for rare flowers ho ho ho. Nice young girl too,' with altogether over-much relish.

'You look out for your own prostate,' I said a bit tartly. 'In forensic terms, my penis was of respectable port, reach, dimension and capacity. Aesthetically speaking, as acceptable as the silly thing ever is. All still there but shrunk as badly as a cheap shirt in the wash. Hold on to yours while you can.' But one can never shut them up for long.

'You won't be asked to produce yours in court.'

Barely had I got back to Miss Daphne du Maurier (library books being what they are) when it started again.

'You're in much demand today,' said the warder pleasantly. And it was my old mate Henk.

'My dear boy . . . you're looking rather well. A bit thinner I'd say.'

'Yes, this is quite a good place for losing weight. A good deal of raw carrot salad and of course the haricots of the administration work wonders. Very little meat so one won't get the horn, not that the detail is likely to trouble me. Not much fish, prisoners won't eat fish, complain about bones even when there aren't any. A hard-boiled egg now and again.' I was talking too much. A strange feeling, to be ill at ease with Henk. He saw it. For a businessman he's unusually sensitive. That's why I like him.

'Would have come before but I had a job getting in.' This is like Henk, who enjoys levelling the obstacles in his path, and telling one at some length of his skill at doing so. 'Special permission you need, they said, from The Man. Off I went, told him I was Irene's husband, got rather a *look*. They went over me at the door here, case I had a knife or something. Make a good headline – WRONGED HUSBAND EXACTS – no, perhaps WREAKS? You're better at words than I am. I'm still using that slogan you wrote for me.'

'"Of the world's flowers ours are the Flower" – should have kept that for myself.'

'Eating cherrystone clams underneath Grand Central

Station. Good. Well. What I came to say. She told me, you know, I didn't get it from any judge. You know that marvellous phrase of theirs? – the girl with round heels?'

'Where we'd say she's bow-legged from catching pigs between them?' Henk was relieved, at his nervous jokes finding an echo. I wasn't about to burst into tears, ask my old friend for his forgiveness.

'Exactly. Irene's as straight as her legs. You're the only one who ever got to see her bare bottom. So I say, I regret nothing and she has nothing to regret. So came along to say Don't, you know, go looking for things to regret. I've told that judge his four home truths. Nothing of this will come out. I have his word. The police know nothing, only that you were overtired, tried to do a day's work too soon after surgery, she told you to rest up, take a siesta. None of these people will dare let out a peep, I threatened an action for slander. It stays between us.' I know Henk well enough to know there's more to come.

'Here, you bloody old fraud, have a cigar. This girl they're on about, pretending you met her in the dunes, you didn't, did you?'

'Did what?'

'No, of course you didn't, I know you too well. You're too open, that's your trouble. I told them so. Just like you, to be walking about there at night. No, I mean, what about Willy?' He isn't talking about Carla, he's talking about Irene. To say that there's no love lost between Henk and Willy would be a gross exaggeration. They respect each other. She comes from a family that he, like myself, has known all his life. Perhaps they've known one another too long, and too well. 'Listen, I know about no secrets between you and all that, but do me a favour and say nothing to Willy. That would only be to humiliate Irene unnecessarily, donchaknow.'

'I quite agree. Count on me. Now come on, tell me the gossip in the club.'

'Yes, right, you can guess, lot of jokes about teenage

schoolgirls. Every bloody one of them has got a juicy crunchy anecdote. All secretly blessing their lucky stars it wasn't them got caught in what's called the compromising circumstances with a secretary.'

I know, of course. They're all good husbands and fathers. They're all assiduous at the local bordels. Now Zandvoort is too small a place and too open to neighbours' eyes (as I ought to have known). But in the suburbs of Haarlem there are houses advertised every day in the small print, between the second-hand cars and the plumber you can rely on. 'Day and Night Service; Estimates Free'. In the club 'Huize Astrid' is well spoken of. ('New girls wanted. Accommodation assured. Excellent earnings guaranteed.') Here they've done well with the ragamuffins from Eastern Europe. Somebody has good contacts, pays efficient bribes to get working permits.

My own guess is that – hospitals are notoriously short of nurses – these Czech and Polish girls who come to seek their fortune in the opulent West come disguised as nursing aids. They're often sadly thin; childhood undernourishment. Hair in a plait. Ankle-socks. Dressed as schoolgirls they'll do very well. The mythical Astrid is I should hope a kind woman, and business apart perhaps a better mother than the one they knew. If they had none – here a least there is warmth and a square meal.

Yes, I suppose I am transparent. Henk was following the thought unspoken easily enough.

'The real schoolgirls all fuck like rattlesnakes.' This well-worn phrase has always appeared to me libellous towards these shy and harmless animals. 'Grand job, for all the spotty boys. When I think of the agonies we suffered at that age, the unmerciful palaver there was before you could get a bra strap undone.' I think he must have heard, about Lalage. 'The real death-trap there is the odd one that isn't content with those lumping adolescents. It's quite a commonplace to come across one that's attracted to older men.' To avoid a

possible smear on one of his beautiful suits he tapped his
ash off on the floor. In this house there are plenty of trusties
who are given their own broom and told to keep the place
looking nice.

'Have you met them like that?'

'One or two.' The laugh lines crinkling round his healthy
blue eyes. 'And so I told the Officer of Justice. We're not
going to let you get trapped by something that blatant. Some
of these middle-aged legalizing moralizers, you wonder
whether they ever got told the facts of life, and how they
managed to *find out*.' Yes, in our student days, Henk was the
adventurous one. Age seventeen, he and I together discovered 'Leentje'.

No doubt this is to do an Injustice to the Officer. Like any
Dutch businessman Henk is a bargainer, a great discoverer
of imagined drawbacks in any proposition made him, an immense feigner of grief and disappointment. ('Yes that's a
lovely flower; what a pity that it should be so liable to mil-
dew.' First we have ever heard of it . . .) They go well together,
Irene and himself. Her preposterous clothes, the blonde hair
which is never twice the same colour, the exaggerations of
décolleté, the outrageous jewellery, all are natural to her
style, and to Henk they are valuable business assets. A simple and an honest woman. He can make vulgar allusion to
the sexy underclothes which one knows are there, and will
remain guessed at. They understand each other very well. In
passing, it strikes me that in common parlance the phrase
'an honest woman' should have a sex connotation whereas
'honest man' confines itself to the commercial resonance.

Wives – there isn't much stays hidden from them. What
they don't know about their men is mostly what they prefer
not to know.

'Have a cigar,' said Henk all lordly and expansive to the
guard on his way out, who was drinking coffee as the Dutch
do at every hour of the day and night.

And was still loitering over the empty cup a half hour

later, when again I was summoned to a parlour. Willy this time of course. Now why – for instance – the tracksuit? True, she spends a lot of time in these sub-athletic get-ups; has at least three blouse-&-baggytrouser coveralls (always much washed and neatly pressed). Says they're 'warm and comfortable'; so they are, fleecy on the inside and sovereign against draughts, to which Willy is sensitive. They are unfeminine, dowdy? – both traits she has streaks of. In truth they are not unbecoming on this tall, rangy, bony woman. The sportive look goes well with the short windswept hair, the high-coloured weatherbeaten features, the soft expensive running shoes (they're all bloody expensive). Perhaps she has come straight on from one of her gymnastic or basketball sessions. Perhaps she wished to leave this impression of having jogged the whole way. Not that Willy would ever smell of sweat; a shower before *and* a shower after is her rule. Perhaps she's being democratic – though not being judged, none of us here wear prison uniform. You would think that this extremely conventional bourgeois woman would not sally out at night (even on this errand) without putting on a skirt, court shoes, some make-up. All this only goes to show that well though I know my wife there is always, deliberate or not, a lot that is mysterious. The girls are forever urging her to be youthful, smart, modern. One never knows how seriously she takes all this (a great reader of the 'young' women's magazines...) At one moment in the forefront of aggressive feminist dogma; at the next, restating shibboleths of nineteenth-century behaviour instilled by her granny (remembered by me as a formidable figure in the family and felt by them all as intimidating: there are flower-grannies in the dynasties, much like the celebrated champagne-grannies in Reims and Epernay).

Willy is plainly in excellent form, sparkly-eyed and triumphalist.

'Bart tells me that the Man is going to make an order for your release.' Willy comes every evening to show solidarity as well as to hand over the plastic bag of clean (and pressed) underthings. But today Bart is the advocate, an old family friend, known to Willy as 'Bartje Bier-buik' because as well as the theatrical silver hair shaken intimidatingly at witnesses he has a distinct paunch – though to suggest this is due to beer would certainly be deemed libellous.

Why is one annoyed by this kind of remark? Why, when irritated, does 'the imp of perversity' force a disagreeable answer?

'If he's making an order of course I'll be the last to hear of it. I'd keep quiet if I were you.'

'Why should I keep quiet? I see no reason to be silent at good news.'

'Better not to mention it until it's official, that's all.' Furious at cold water on the little flame.

'Do you realize how I've worked for this? You don't know that I spend my entire day listening to nasty hints and insinuations? That I go to the gym to limber up and have to put up with some spiteful woman saying oh dear I'm so sorry to hear about it? That I go shopping and get the looks of tactful sympathy from my butcher?'

'Willy, this is a tirade. There's no need for that.' Now she's crying ... 'It's only prudent, that's all. I haven't been given much reason for optimism. You know how these people are. Have to be zealous, to quiet public opinion. Always better to pull in the wrong fellow, than no fellow at all. I've told you a hundred times my usual bloody bad luck to have been out for a walk that night.'

The pale eyes watery now and pink-rimmed but very steady, and penetrating, and the face clenched in determination. Never going to ask, Did you meet that girl? Never going to say, I can't bear the not knowing. Everyone who knows me – my own daughters – could be utterly convinced of my being the one. Found guilty by an assize court, condemned. But not by Willy. 'It's only sensible to hope for the best while expecting the worst.'

'I've been under some strain too, you know.' Not going to say she's sorry. She never does.

I can see that she's quite convinced that if the judge accepts, however grudgingly, the idea of release (no way would that be a disavowal of his own settled opinion), it would be due entirely to her efforts. How she has stormed about, I know, and have been told; not only by her. 'That bloody Burgomaster' has been given no peace at all, but as well as writing letters, telephoning, talking to everyone she can think of who might remotely be thought 'influential' in political or legal circles, she has gone herself – knowing her – to knock on doors. That family has for two generations drawn a lot of water in the neighbourhood. She will have demanded, and got introductions, to newspaper editors, past and present civic dignitaries, as well as cronies at the riding school or the golf club. She may even have pushed open the door of a legal luminary, someone steps above a mere Office of Justice in the hierarchy; even an Advocate General.

For myself I know that any such order is not much more than a question of an empty dossier; no solidly conclusive evidence to put before a tribunal. Holland is not like France. Our public opinion, as well as the liberal tradition, holds strongly that it is wrong and indeed wicked to leave people stewing in jail for the one, two, even three years it can take for a Judge of Instruction to dicker with the papers. The International Court has even told the Republic, and quite abruptly, to free one or two such people forthwith, and to pay them a massive sum in compensation. Not that this will cause the Republic to change its ways.

'There now. How is it that I have always lots of hankies and you never have any? Blow your nose. Listen, if Bart says any such thing he will have good grounds. He has his ear in the conclaves. He hinted as much to me. But it doesn't do to float it prematurely; that would be just what they need to make them obstinate. Keep your patience just a day or so longer.'

Curfew has sounded in the House of Keeping when I got back, and I had to make my bed up in the dark, with the gleam from the little window of the lights which stay on all night, outside. I am weary, because a prospect of release is a greater nervous strain than the little refrain of oh well, another day swallowed.

Thought mills. Do not talk to yourself, says a good and a wise man of my acquaintance. When one reads, authors become acquaintances and now-and-again friends. Learn, he said, to shut off the interior dialogue. Easier said than done. I remember England, I remember my serious, solemn work at 'learning English'. The 'student' Dutchly ploughing through not-always-very-rewarding 'Literature' texts. Poetry, even; a sixpenny copy of some standard collection thought suitable; the 'Oxford Book' or the 'Golden Treasury'. Tagends, now and then, which stuck, embedded themselves in my mind. Did even this help civilize the boy?

One such now trots in my recollection. Nothing to do with any relevant matter. Just that nothing has changed since then, nigh on two centuries ago, because I think it's Lord Byron. Talking about banks. But maybe one is thinking that the law doesn't evolve much either. I persecute myself, the way one does when one cannot sleep, chasing the elusive rhyme. Something or other synonym for Daring? Wearing? Fairing? Smack of anti-Semitism, this century as that and the one before – 'Tra La La, Jew Rothschild and his Christian cousin Baring.' If they broke their neck there with the speculating johnny in Singapore or wherever, shows only that the Jews are cleverer: as far as I know the House of Rothschild flourishes nicely. Not perhaps quite so many prolonged lunches over the family silver and the outstanding vintage-claret, but nothing to complain of. True, Lord Byron was not a good judge of wives. They don't alter, either.

Break a routine, be it only a day – two – it's as though one had been a month away. A new policeman on duty, I looked at him almost as though he had no right to be there. Waiting in the familiar passage, I studied things like door handles, electric light fittings, as though I'd never seen them before, instead of being 'an old hand at this'.

Rather formal too this morning, the Officer of Justice. In his manner, that is. Something about his clothes too; that Tattersall check shirt is just what I like myself. Not perhaps what I would have chosen to wear with a brown suit but he conveys a smart, even an elegant impression. At this time of the morning he is in general easy, looking as though he'd slept well. A smile will come quite readily. It's at the end of the day that he looks marked, the face as though clawed by too many hours of crime. But this morning a little stiff; encompassed. Shuffled a lot of papers together, tapped with them to get the edges straight. Where is the habitual polite, even pleasant 'Good Morning'?

'I have reviewed this matter with some care.' An orderly exposition, point by point. This man is entitled – he doesn't use my name, he doesn't say 'You', he speaks of some third person, who is not present; is it 'I', or is it perhaps Bert? – to the consideration normally accorded, to persons moreover of some standing in the community. A measure of disbelief; a certain scepticism in the face of grave imputations. Hesitation is a duty. Prudence. For a man in this position, an accusation would have serious consequences.

A settled, regular life. A stable, loyal, supportive marriage. It had been felt necessary, the charge – the putative charge – being of much gravity – to place the subject under detention. Detenu had behaved with noticeable balance and restraint, showing no hostility or aggressivity in this context. Detenu is also commended for a co-operative manner by guardians and by examiners.

'I pass to the results of medical and psychiatric study ... I abbreviate: subject is attracted by young girls, a familiar feature in men of this age-group. The word "senile" is not appropriate; the tendency is well controlled and compensated. Subject is in good health, both mental and physical – I can sum up these reports in lay terms: no suggestion of insanity is anywhere put forward. Rational, lucid. Higher than average intelligence; some degree of rigidity, numerous inhibitions and blockages – we can skip that – felt to be of no lasting consequence.

'Surgical intervention, mm yes, radical prostatectomy, inevitably traumatic – with some natural reluctance Professor Heinrich concurs – a frustration; mm, directed towards the wife, an old friend, of a – yes, yes ... both of whom refuse to feel aggrieved by this outburst.

'Now we come to the central point of this enquiry: subject's acquaintance with the girl Zomerlust. Straightforwardly – there's no direct evidence beyond the openly admitted fact of the meal shared; that's an open friendly relationship. I think this must be seen as unprejudicial. An unhappy coincidence but one must read no more into it: subject showed no unusually cramped nor excessive reticence in face of police interrogation. Mm, that's something of a compliment; it's not all that frequent. Further ... the theory of the psychopath who just happened to be wandering about just then. This is extremely thin. However, subject has the well-established habit of walking in the dunes at all hours and has made no secret of being out and thereabouts within the parameters of time – la la la, probable death as indicated following autopsy; that's all highly technical and it's too easy to follow a slippery – I might call it rather too flowery a slope; brief and a bit bleak, subject's highly active and vigorous advocate makes the point, and it's a telling point, I must not obscure it, that the police settled upon this likely and even obtrusive suspect quite largely because they were under considerable pressure to satisfy inflamed opinion; any comment would border upon improper view.

'I thus conclude. I am far from satisfied. There is no better argument in favour of release than there is of continuing to hold detenu under restraint.

'Since, after review, a strong argument has been made that

continued detention will be incompatible with natural justice, I hereby make an order for conditional release.

'I demand that subject should hereby consider himself bound to reply to the needs of justice at all moments. In the light of enquiries continued and pursued, if and when duly mandated, the ministry-public may apply for a detention order. I do not ask subject to surrender his passport. In view of suspect's position and situation I demand that he should not quit nor take any prolonged leave of absence from his place of residence without duly notifying the local police authority of his motivation and purpose. In short, subject is bound to hold himself at the disposal of all constituted authority until further notice is conveyed to him – *is that clear?*'

'Altogether.' Bravo, Willy. Thus to be prised loose is due to your hard work. The Man is not letting me go on account of my great personal charm. Just that he's as conscientious as he is meticulous. He stood up, because his code of manners is as exacting as his code of law, and we shook hands in protocolaire style, like a President with the foreign ambassadors on New Year's Day. The hand is not limp; it is dry, hard, and chilly. No paternal look deep into the eye. *Good luck with your perilous mission, Oh Oh Seven, and don't forget your cyanide capsule.*

Guards make their little jokes, which are always the same and long emptied of any sarcasm.

'So you're leaving us, then? Didn't you like it here? Do our best to make you feel welcome.' Being signed out at the 'greffe' and collecting one's personal property, struck by this quantity of rubbish which lives in one's pockets. The extraordinary feel of great luxury at being met by Willy with the car and being chauffeured home like a Minister after a hard day spent Defending the Department, except that I am in the front seat where the Security man sits.

In the hallway of the flats a neighbour, retired, like me, was emptying his mailbox; turned and gave me a long look of careful blankness before managing a 'Good Morning' with some disbelief in it, as though it had been but no longer was.

'As you see,' said Willy. 'Miscarriages of justice also occur.'

'Glad to hear it,' pious. 'Glad to hear it,' scuttling for the stairs.

'Churchgoing bastard,' muttered Willy, scrabbling for her latchkey.

Bert was greeted by a noisy show of jollity. The Dutch on peoples' birthdays are hideously given to a triumphal chant of 'Lang zal hij leven' which goes to a childish Rule-Britannia sort of tune. Bert didn't feel much cheered by the Long Shall He Flourish; had been looking forward to a bit of peace, but couldn't be cross with his own daughters come to say Welcome Home. There were two large bunches of flowers and two bottles of champagne. He was annoyed to see that they'd laid hands on his best glasses.

'How nice,' he managed. 'How very nice of you both.' Willy hadn't said anything, reserving this doubtless as a surprise. She can be alarmingly obtuse. If later he were to mutter, she would be defensive but genuinely shocked: how could he possibly complain of his own family showing solidarity?

Two middle-aged women, now greedily attacking the salt bikkies after a generous gulp at the juice and talking over his head, the way they did. Two very Dutch-looking women; you would take them for sisters but both belong to a commonplace physical type: tallish and big in the bone, blonde-haired and ample in build. Steff's hair is the fairer and Nat has the better legs. Modishly dressed and modishly unbecoming hairstyles; both strident, with scratchy penetrating voices. Good wives and good mothers, good housekeepers and both with good, steady, prosperous men. Both good at their work, reliable and valued. How will one tell them apart? One is richer than the other; a bigger car and a bigger diamond on her finger. One wears a Chanel perfume and the other a Dior; he knows because of giving them presents. You would be wrong in suspecting either of adulteries or stealing from supermarkets. Christian Democrat voters, socially concerned, generous to good causes, worrying about the Third World. Ten million of them and the backbone of the country. Ten million homes largely indistinguishable, with brightly shining windows, neatly polished furniture and plenty of fresh flowers. The curtains not drawn at twilight, and conspicuous consumption of electricity, for they are houseproud and have nothing to hide.

Or have they? One will not and one cannot know. Could they bully their husbands or use a cutting silence with the children? Many, still, do not go out to work, or have small part-time occupations undeclared to the tax man or the social security office. They spend inordinate hours reading the medical and psychological health columns in magazines, planning their holidays (and sorting out the photos into albums), drinking coffee with the neighbours and saying Isn't-it-awful about earthquakes in Anatolia, learning Spanish because We're thinking of Miami, next year, or how to bake that Turkish bread but I don't know, the oven seems wrong, somehow.

It is impossible to imagine their private lives. Do they have lesbian relationships? – very fashionable nowadays and they all take with enthusiasm to a fashion. Could they possibly like being tied up in the bedroom and whipped? – surely not? Not in accordance with the Dutch character, and since in all the bordels there's plenty of this fakery one can believe that back at home it'll all be very blameless and indeed very dull. The naughty nighties and the sexy lingerie are draughty and uncomfortable.

But how can you tell? Knowledge, and even experience, have taught Bert this much: nothing in fiction, nothing in a (limited?) Dutch imagination, nothing in (nowadays quite surprisingly mixed-blooded) this populace comes within nightmare distance of the day-and-night facts of their superficially obvious lives. If Steff were suddenly to say 'I'm joining Mother Teresa in Calcutta'; if Nat were to announce that she was setting up house with the neighbours' daughter and they were looking for a child to adopt – one would hardly blink. Willy won't – like his, hers is the pre-war generation – but they might. They seem very boring and aren't. Do my daughters smoke cannabis at parties? I must ask Sergeant Boa and Policeman Vos. And what do they do, when they're at home? What did Bert ever do, which wasn't appallingly banal, trite, worth nobody's notice?

The girls have begun to quarrel, as in this house they always do.

'Once an accusation of *that* sort gets made one can never get rid of it entirely, that's all I meant.'

'By paying attention to it or imagining you do – you're simply watering the root, that's all.'

'Nee, hoor.' I have commented before on this conversational leitmotif: flat contradiction is the nourishment of a Dutch argument. 'Scrub as you may you never quite get rid of it, even after people have long forgotten why it was made.'

'Or that it was false in the first place,' put in Willy quietly.

'It would be better to move, and that way it dies out. Some people would *want* to move.'

'If you're talking about Pa, in the first place he's as stubborn as the next and in the second place he was born here and why the hell should he move? One will just know who one's friends are, that's all.' The trouble with saying 'that's all' is that it never is. The one will never let the other have the last word.

'You'd get a good price for this flat. It isn't as though one was *forced* to sell. Now I know a man in a house agency who's honest which few enough of them are, I'm not suggesting you put up a notice outside the door, but handled discreetly –'

'You sell up, any way at all, and it's simply tantamount to admitting people have got you down, it's a surrender.'

'Nee, hoor.' Bert poured himself another glass and lit a small cigar. They both rounded on him, glaring.

'Have you *still* not stopped smoking?' The fact of the matter is that the two of them believe him guilty, though both no doubt have been angered by their husbands saying so. Bert cannot say Oh get out of here the pair of you. He'd like to, but he can't.

*

Bert hasn't the least intention of moving. Nor of changing any of his habits. Or as the English say 'Well, hardly any'. People are not as bad as they seem. In Zandvoort, which is just like anywhere else, the people who know him behave as though nothing had happened whatever they may have thought earlier, and if this is just good manners then so much the worse for those who think that good manners prove hypocrisy. The people who don't know him, and that's the vast majority, have other things to bother their heads about. As for the police, they don't care one way or another. Sergeant Bout in Amsterdam has probably some phrase about things getting put on the back burner. Life goes on . . . if this is a remark of shattering triteness at least nobody is going to say 'Nee hoor' to that.

In this small town – 'the dorp' – there will always be a few to say that the 'Mr N.' mentioned in the paper was certainly guilty and got out of it being 'a bourgeois' and doubtless enjoying 'protection where it matters'. Bert thought it possible (seeing that Willy looked at the post with dread) that there might be nasty anonymous letters. Which he would take to the police, with a formal complaint. It wouldn't come to graffiti aerosoled on the wall outside. 'A Murderer Lives Here'. Don't let imagination run away with you. He has always walked in the dunes. He has loved them since childhood.

It was only the second day when the doorbell rang, quite early in the evening (the evening meal in Holland is early and Zandvoort will have cleared away – done the washing-up? – and settled down to the television). Willy whose nerves are visibly on edge went to answer; there was a bit of palaver in the hallway. She came in and said 'You've a visitor. I think this has nothing to do with me and that I'd prefer to look at the television, so would you mind talking in your own room, if you're going to talk.' This isn't so much 'tact', of which she hasn't much more than her daughters, as a clear message that this is something 'she doesn't want to know'. So Bert agrees; tact he's had to learn. 'Please come in,' she said, in her 'social' voice.

A man came in, whom I do not know. Tall, thin, sallow-faced, late forties or maybe fifty, it doesn't matter; an unaggressive manner. But a businessman, believes in being blunt and coming straight to the point.

'Reemtsma. Engineer Reemtsma.' Seeing that Bert was not quite sure whether he'd recognized this, for it's quite a common name – 'Lalage's father.'

'Do please sit down. A drink, perhaps? Drop of cognac? You know, it oils the wheels.'

'Thanks very much. Yes, I will. You're right. I have something don't you know, that I want to get off my chest. Not too much – whoa. I don't smoke, thank you.' Knees, elbows, get in his way.

'It's quite straightforward really. There are those who'd think you a dirty dog. There was this story about a girl killed in the dunes. As I understand the matter there wasn't any evidence. I'm a factual sort of man, I programme computers for a living. What isn't there, isn't. They don't think for themselves, only what's put in them. Come the year 2000 I'm going to find myself putting in one hell of overtime on New Year's Day. No time for fireworks.

'So okay, there's my daughter. Hell of a pretty girl, huh? Want to say straight out there's a big crowd thinks so. I think so myself. You got any daughters?'

'I have two. Not the easiest in the world to cope with.'

'That's true. That's a relief. Do you know that I've even had accusations put to me of wishing, myself, to...' He searched for a word.

'Fancy her? If you'll forgive the filthy phrase.'

'It is. But I like to look things straight in the eye.'

'Not – as it happens –' said Bert 'one of my, we go about talking of problems. But as you may perhaps know I've had labels stuck to me. I've problems of my own.'

'I rather thought you had. Like people saying something they can't prove, but which you can't disprove.'

'That about sums it up.'

'But you did have a turn-up with my girl, I mean my daughter.'

'I'm afraid that's true.'

'Look, I didn't come here to yell at you. She's a harlot.'

'I don't think that's true.'

'I'm the one who hasn't slept with her.'

'I mentioned it, I've two daughters. One is a harpy and the other a harridan. That's equally true.'

'Been in bed with every boy in the class. I suppose that's a commonplace, they all do that, it means no more to them than sharing a joint of grass. But when it comes to...'

'What you need is another drink.'

'I'm trying to say I don't think you took advantage of her. She led you on. Right?'

'I've spent a lot of effort on being honest with myself. I'm in no position to whitewash my own behaviour, towards her.'

'But there's something in what I say.'

'Yes.'

'That's all I came for. Thanks for the drink. You got pegged by the police and that wasn't very funny. Let you go with a not proven and that's not funny either. They didn't come on at me with an accusation of abusing my own daughter. But you know who did? My wife, that's who. How do I disprove it?'

'You'd tell her what you'd tell the police. Abused children don't behave the way she does.' A thought struck me. 'Does she say this? Lallie?'

'No. Says she's leaving the house. She's uncontrollable anyhow.'

'Maybe that's the right thing.'

'You tell me you've trouble with yours?'

'I'm a lot older than you. Married women. Children of their own. Anxieties of their own. I see little of them, now.'

'Is it better to think back? To when they were little. You could sit them on your knee, then. Play with them. Innocence.' He offered his hand. Conventional remark. But no hard feelings.

'How many of us can tell the truth, and be believed?'

Willy was looking at a gangster movie, without taking much of it in.

'Was that troublesome?'

'No. Decent man. Like we're all decent men.'

'Except on the screen,' turning it out. 'Where they're all simply foul. D'you want some cocoa?'

The final touch came only a day later.

This was much earlier in the evening. They hadn't even had supper: in fact Bert was in the kitchen, wearing Willy's apron. He likes cooking, in a small-scale way; an evening meal for two. Some soup – or even simpler; grill a couple of bratwurst sausages with a sweet red pepper maybe, a banana. Scrambled eggs with asparagus, that sort of thing. Really only to lift the cooking chore off Willy, take some small share of the housekeeping routines and be responsible. Likes to do a bit of ironing, of an afternoon. In the summer, grow vegetables in their garden plot. Sea-kale you know, something a bit out of the way. Salads, herbs. Just for the two of them, you understand. Round the edges, a few simple flowers, to cut for a vase, Willy's living-room. Compost heap. Simple bio-chemistry. Often, a fresh vegetable is enough. Who needs sausage? Two eggs a week is as much as is good for one anyhow.

I thought afterwards; this man hasn't even had his own supper. Is it any different to the most dismally uniform of Dutch conventions? One piece of bread-and-butter with ham, one with cheese, one with jam. Peanut-butter, maybe, or what the English still call 'German sausage'? Or something laughably Dutch, like chocolate sprinkle instead of jam? He'd felt he couldn't eat until he'd gone through with this job which had to be done. Been thinking about it these days until his stomach got in a knot, and made up his mind to come here, straight from work. No point in upsetting his wife. Go home then and say to her 'Sorry, a bit of work came in, kept me late at the office. I'd have rung you but it took longer than I'd counted on. Haven't made the tea yet, have you?'

Most men are cowardly about answering the doorbell because too often it's something bothersome. Bert was closest but Willy went. Busy, he said; apron. Wives understand this. But she came back with a lengthened lip and a business card.

'Whatever it is we don't want it.' She didn't say anything. Bert stared at the card. The usual ordinary printed thing.

GERARD ZOMERLUST
BUSINESS MANAGER

Below, a professional address in Spaarndam and a personal address in Zandvoort.

'Do you want me to tell him to go away? . . . Or make a proper appointment? . . . Or what?'

As Engineer Reemtsma says, look it straight in the eye. What is the rest of my life going to be – afraid of meeting people?

'I'll see him.' She made no protest.

'I'll finish this for you?'

'It's done. Only some cream to be added. You might chop a bit of parsley. I'll try not to be long,' taking off the apron, which she put on.

One repeats oneself.

'Do please come in. Won't you sit down. Can I offer you a drink perhaps?' Business as usual. After the newspaper office was bombed, in Colombia, the editor walked in, looked about him, said 'Seguimos adelante' – business as usual. Nothing else was needed. 'Je maintiendrai' but we don't need it on a coat-of-arms.

'Thank you, no. I won't be but a minute...

'You killed her, didn't you.' Not put as a question.

Throat; clear.

'I can understand that you should feel convinced that I did.'

'I am trying to say – speak – forgiveness.'

'We all need forgiveness.'

'Yes, myself also. I wished to kill you.'

'What gives you the right, either to forgive or to condemn?'

'I have no right. I need none.'

'But I have a right. No tribunal has judged me. So you may not.'

'Human judgements, at best, are only rational.'

'Possibly,' says Bert, mighty dry. 'Often. Also based upon prejudice, anger, fear, revenge – envy, and spite. Every irrational, and ignoble sentiment.'

'That is true. Also true is that you know, in your heart. What is in your heart? That is not known to me. It is not hidden from God. I have no more to say.'

'Then I must thank you. I must say – that I feel the sincerest sorrow. The sincerest sympathy. What's this word sincere? Everyone signs it to letters. But since you mention God, God will be my witness.'

'Thank you. I accept that. Asking your forgiveness. Will you then pardon me, for adding a word more?'

'Neither God nor humanity could forbid.'

'I am a small man. An employee; it would be true to say a slave. I could be nothing else. My wife dreamed – of having money. Of winning the Lotto. I know better. My life long, I have subordinated every instinct to the caprice of superiors. I am valued only for being a faithful and conscientious slave.

'I have two points to make. One was that I had a bright, an

able daughter. So that in her I put my hopes. Now, I have no daughter.

'The other: losing that, in whom all my hopes were vested – now I am free. I do not expect you to understand this. I know about you. You inherited a family business. You had no slavedom.'

'That's all you know.' A childish interjection.

'No. You were never a slave. It gave you privilege, freedom, immunity from pursuit. Do not interrupt, I am almost done.

'I am now free – through her death – to state a certainty.

'I know that you killed her. I do not judge. That is not my role. I know it. That suffices. You must answer. It is your responsibility. Since you are not a slave. Mine is only to remain faithful, to all I know to be false, valueless – worthless even when not actively evil. This fidelity is also the truth I owe and bear towards myself. Please make my excuses to your wife for this vulgar interruption upon your evening.'

This dignity shakes me. Bert – Willy – Mutti, Hilfe!

The man has gone as quietly as he came.

I stood there like the Stocking Post. A mythical baulk of wood, planted upright on the beach where the barelegged shrimp-fisher could hold on to it while getting his boots back on. I was still clutching that damn business card.

Men in three-piece suits. Clean white shirt. In France they often have 'Fondé de Pouvoir' printed under their name. Means literally 'empowered to act'. To reach decisions; it impresses the simple. You can be a manager, lording it over fifty thousand square metres of factory space, and you can't spend half a crown without ringing up head office for permission. One goes into the bank, there's an hour of laborious chitchat with a type like this and then he gets up saying he has to consult a colleague.

When they're young they're full of hope. They've diplomas and university degrees, come well recommended, are well thought-of. They put in the hours. Eager, loyal, reliable.

Never take a day off, rather be ill than thought half-hearted. At thirty-five they've a future and at forty everyone but themselves knows they've none.

There's nothing Dutch about this; all over the world you count them by the trainload – bundled indeed into cattle trucks on their way to the final solution; Untermenschen on their way to dusty death. When that famous word 'restructuring' heaves in sight so does the sack. They clung on in the old days but the computer now is ruthless. Sales figures have replaced human kindness. Everyone likes Joe but our duty is to the shareholders.

What is it, asked the black man, that white men write at their desks all day? A good question. What do the Dutch do, after supper, after the curtains have been drawn?

'Are you ready for supper?' asked Willy. Soup won't take but a second to reheat. Eaten in silence; she has nothing to say and there's no way of saying it.

Don't I belong, in those dusty ranks? Am I any better? – certainly no less banal a figure. My cousin Adrian ejected me from my own business. More or less politely. Among the growers, in the Club, there would be many to see me as an amiable but erratic figure, not very competent. Old Hubert – likeable chap. Bit of an anachronism.

How do I dare to sneer at a man like Zomerlust? He is so plainly the better man. What has changed me? The girl Lalage? That would be seen in these days as a harmless, even amusing adventure. I did her no damage. Why do I see this as a smear, ineradicable, inexpugnable? I cannot rub it out, scratch or dig it away. The boughs of resinous trees leave smears that will not yield to soap and water. In the old days we used pumice stone.

I made a fool of myself. If it were only that – I think I could forgive myself (I cannot answer for Willy) some putative, hypothetical adultery with Irene.

Willy says nothing whatever. She must know – but she has decided not-to-know. Undoubtedly the best way of handling these episodes. She is not injured, diminished or humiliated; they never happened.

Lalage belongs in the realm of odious but inoffensive fantasy, like the so-called 'erotic' movies on late-night television. When after losing my prostate I was perturbed to find that I still had strong erotic instincts, wishes, the more pathetic when one can no longer get an erection. I have watched these things sometimes; they are for the impotent old men rather than the spotty schoolboys. Technically they aren't porn, which is forbidden on the national open networks. A number of ludicrous hypocrite conventions apply. Very dull indeed, too woefully and unlaughably bland even to be mocked. They mime sexual intercourse but the man has to keep his underpants on. Fellation behind draperies. Or the girl's hair. The indispensable lesbians are limited to un-enthralling strokings of stomach. Before being overcome by this mechanical dreariness I found some amusement in national characteristics. Italians like a dash of decoration, a stutter never quite suppressed of taste, a plasticity in composing the cheesiest of naked limbs for a camera. Maybe, a beautiful bottom. The French believe that nothing must happen but if it happens in Paris it *must* be exciting. Americans think it erotic in squalid places – their rest-room complex. German and Brits rely upon a noisy vulgarity, hopefully facetious. Schoolgirls and policewomen lose their knickers in the most monotonous foreseeability. This I suppose is where Willy would envisage Lalage; if she did at all.

Henk – and Irene – have blown in. Unannounced and unwanted. Henk on these occasions is one of the immortal Tintin characters; the salesman. In the original 'Seraphim Lampion'. In the English translation, cruder but stronger, 'Jolyon Wagg'.

'Don't tell me you haven't some good stuff hidden away, Bert. Come on up with the magnum of Krug.' He is convinced that my release is entirely his doing. 'You know, I had a word with the Advocate-General. Good customer of mine and I've made him a price often enough he owed me a favour.' Willy, who doesn't drink, takes a bleak view of Irene (who does). These two women who never have held the other really hugged to their heart.

Bert does have a few 'good bottles' stowed away. Single malt mostly (to which he is partial). An unusually good cognac (being French, invariably much too expensive). Not, bless us, the 'magnum of Krug'. Doesn't matter, Henk has one in the back of the car. 'Bert, you are impossibly *austere*. You only believe it had done you good when you've gone without.'

I mean, who *wants* a magnum of Krug? Of furthermore a fine vintage, ten years ago? I suppose that if one has never drunk such a thing (hardly anyone on the earth's surface has ever been near one) it would be one of those glittering prizes, next door to winning the Lotto. So that people like Henk who have made a success of their lives – what else does this word 'success' mean? They want you to know it, they insist on underlining it. Drink it quick before the Ayatollah comes and takes it away.

Oh well, I enjoyed it. Even Willy, persuaded into taking a glass which in Henk's book *has* to be a Baccarat tulip (they have no longer the fragile perfection of a real tulip; too easily broken), tasted gingerly and said 'Delicious. Wasted on me.' The champagne growers, like ourselves an exclusive and close-knit corporation, have better still in their private cellars, but keep it for themselves.

Of such small things decisions are born. The very next day I wrote (can't blame it on Bert) a 'formal' letter to Henk's great pal. Since this is supposed to be the supreme legal authority, under God, upon the administration of law governing the State of the Netherlands, I am presuming that he of all people can cut through these ties which bind me. Gordian knot, in mythology so famous a cliché it has come down to our days. Challenged to undo this abominable complication Alexander drew his sword. Or that other famous example, the man who knew how to make an egg stand on its end. Simple when you know how, so that we all say 'now why didn't I think of that?'

Mark it 'Personal'. Write it by hand. We had of course a printer in the office on our computer. At home, a pen given me by Willy many birthdays ago. Solid silver but I never used it much.

'Sir'. Jan in the old days would have used the antique form of address. 'Edelachtbar'. 'Noble and respected'.

'I was accused of the crime, than which few are thought graver, of murder upon a young innocent girl. I was arrested and imprisoned. The Officer of Justice in charge of this case, after thorough examination found himself obliged to conclude that there was insufficient evidence to place before a tribunal, and ordered my release. I am thus neither guilty nor innocent, since no court of law has pronounced.

'In the unhappy state of society such occurrences are frequent. They attract no great publicity and opinion remains limited to a local circle of acquaintance, which is quite enough to make my position intolerable. I remain unheard, because there is no explanation I can give.

'I beg, thus, since you alone can take the necessary steps in furtherance, that you will move the machinery either to place me before the Court or to issue the public statement that no presumption against me is held viable, since a non-proven of this sort is neither fish nor flesh but leaves a permanent cloud of suspicion.

'In good faith and trust yours truly.'

Bert wrote this letter, knowing of course that from a member of the general public it would be ill-advised and could be thought foolish. He tells himself that when all is said he is a member in good standing of the Club. This circle is important to Holland. In economic terms it is an important source of revenue, in the hardest of currencies. But in advertising terms, much the more power. Without us Holland would be of small weight: shipping, cheese, oil-refining. Skills with dykes and waterworks, and huge milk-factory cows. Do not think of us as a potty tourist attraction, a barrel-organ tingel-tangel about Tulips-from-Amsterdam. Busloads of fatties in baseball caps and Hawaiian shirts and sailcloth shorts gawking at the bulb fields in Lisse. That is a mistake many make.

The truth is rather that we are the motor of the future, which – many hold that it is too late – may preserve our planet a while longer. We are Green Power. Commerce being what it is we do not make noisy and disruptive manifestations about the Environment. But we are the sharp point, the hard edge. We have led, indeed, the war against the chemical firms. Look for the brains, the research, and the money too, behind the struggle to put a stop to pesticides and insecticides, to find biological balances: plants, insects, animals which will be predators upon the devouring weed, beetle or caterpillar. If something is done to combat entrophied waterways or the loss of toads – or cholera and malaria – do you know that this is very largely due to ourselves? And even myself? And Henk, too? He doesn't spend his whole life boasting, drinking beer when there's no champagne. Did much indeed to throw beer money behind biological research, when the big money which controls United States Presidents – and elects the Houses of Congress – was the big cock crowing on the top of the poisoned toxic dust heap.

A legal officer with some weight in the councils of government isn't going to disregard this altogether. But he may not be the big personal pal Henk says he is.

We may just rescue Holland. We might – just – help to rescue the Everglades. An Advocate-General ought to be aware enough, and civilized enough, to know this.

Bert sent that letter, and the result was nothing at all. A dead silence. Oh well, I thought; letters from dotty people. Do they even get past some sub-secretary in The Hague? Here – or in Amsterdam – we have the utmost detestation and contempt for the little bureaucrats in the administrative 'capital'. Jokes about them have proliferated – and have grown sourer – ever since the Seven Provinces decided they were going to do without Philip of Spain. Jan – my father – was fond of repeating a piece of old corn about the wooden ham displayed on the dining-room table. Going to work carrying a violin case, which contains the sandwiches. That is bad-tempered; recalls too closely Thomas Bernhard's phrase about Austrians playing the fiddle on the first floor while gassing Jews in the basement, but it's true that the administration didn't come out too well from the Occupation during the last war.

Amsterdammers are fond of mimicking the precise and slightly affected Hague accent. The place was always saturated with paperwork like nitrates in the soil. Jan would grumble that one took a shit and rang up The Hague to ask how many pieces of lav paper one was allowed to use. A pity that all Dutch jokes are scatological. We have to fall back (like the French; they have so few of their own) upon Belgian jokes. Henk, who was just back from Paris, in hopes of one of those incredibly wasteful government contracts ('I'm going to Carpet the forest of Fontainebleau with flowers') brought a good one. A man parachuting, off a high hill, with a sail. On the ground, two Belgians. 'Look look, a very big eagle. I'm going to shoot it.' 'You've missed.' 'Maybe, but I've made it drop its prey.' Forgive me; this sort of joke has become highly pertinent. One has to remember that in Belgium all the jokes are about the Dutch.

When they came, the gentlemen from the Hague, they were very well-mannered; quiet and polite, nowise brutal or impatient. (A French woman Minister with a cutting peremptory manner is known as 'la Mère Emptoire' – now that is a French joke.) They didn't have blue coats, nor white ones, nor even suits; were dressed like you and me.

Willy didn't want to let them in. Politely they showed a paper, which she studied: then she called me. Letterhead, Ministry of Binnenlandse Zaken; that's the Interior, in

English the Home Office. Typewritten heading 'Custodial Order'. One neat paragraph – 'Order to take into administrative custody for the purpose of examination De Heer van der Bijl, Hubert', and the usual guff about place and date of birth, 'at present residing'. The usual illegible signature, a tampon in bas-relief and three rubber stamps. 'For and pp. the Chef of Legal Affairs Section.'

'Now I want to see your own, personal, authority. Very sorry but somebody with a cap, says he's from the Gas Board...' Quite good-humouredly they produced identity cards. Light dawned.

'Marechaussée.' The name is given to the State Police of Holland. The difference is that they have authority over the entire territory and aren't just municipal dogsbodies.

'This is perfectly arbitrary.'

'Ach, it's purely administrative.' Still good-natured. 'We aren't gestapo-men. Not even the FBI.' No doubt they always say this, with the same well-worn grin. 'These things sound very haughty. Office language. Custodial only means preventive. Protective.'

'Purely administrative,' the other added helpfully.

'In case I run away?'

'That's about the size of it.'

'But you're arresting me.'

'Look, we're given an order, we know nothing about it. Some misunderstanding no doubt, you'll clear it up quickly enough. These bureaucrats are always heavy-handed.'

'Look, we don't want to hurry you but we have to account for our time. Suppose you get a few things together, overnight bag, just in case it takes longer than foreseen.'

'Here we go again,' said Willy bitterly. 'Huub, I think you ought to ring the advocate.'

'Wouldn't do any good, missus, even if we had the time, he can't contest an administrative order.'

'It'll all be explained, Mevrouw, you'll know all about it, you'll have time to see a judge and everything. Ring him by all means, he'll tell you the same, only right now we better get a move on, don't want any panic.'

'Where are we going?' I put in. They just shrugged.

'With the overnight bag you're comfortable, see? Then you can ring Mevrouw here, sort it all out.'

''Tisn't the train to Auschwitz.' They both laughed heartily. They had a grey station-wagon, something quite grand, Volvo or Mercedes.

'Sure. Not like getting taken off in handcuffs between two patrolmen. If you'd just get in the back with Willem, plenty of room for us all.' I gave Willy a kiss. 'Won't be long.' She stood desolate, before flinging back inside. The car had venetian blinds. Willem pulled the string. Discreet donchaknow. Not a lot of gossip among the neighbours. Klaas-or-Piet drove fast and well; we were on the autoroute in no time. I could only see peering forward, through the windscreen. Utrecht road but then we branched off going east.

'Which way are we going?'

'Who said we're going to The Hague?' Willem sat back peaceful, offered me a cigarette. 'Sorry we've no coffee.' There wasn't any point in further questions; they knew no more than they'd told me. The car sped. Holland is small. Peeking, I started to see signs saying Enschede, Hengelo, places like that. Dutch as I am I still never know which comes first. Almelo? It was puzzling, this is the eastern border of Holland. The Rhine comes out of Germany, reaches Holland at the placid, peaceful towns of Nijmegen and Arnhem: places famous in history for 'the bridge too far' where General Montgomery thought himself very clever and wasn't. Inside Holland the Rhine splits into a number of waterways and potters on down to the estuary – a whole bundle of estuaries. I wished I had a map. But we were already north of this heavily populated and much built-up area; somewhere closing on the border with East Friesland, even in Germany a largely forgotten 'backward' part of the world; there are jokes about Ost-Friesland the way there are jokes in France about southern Belgium. We had left the autoroute and were driving through woodland country. Few people, those mostly on bicycles and around villages. Countryside patchy, sometimes scrubby moorland and betimes richer, fertile farming land. Frankly, I hadn't a clue. They had, but they weren't saying. There are weird 'military areas' forbidden to the public; like the 'forbidden dunes' now far away in my homeland. Here there was a close belt of conifer shelter-planting. And a high discouraging gate saying, No Admission. We got admitted, because Piet-Klaas showed some kind of pass to the electronic eye on the doorpost. A park, pretty with some quite good professional landscaping. A glimpse of a group of low-lying military sort of blocks; but we drew up at the foot of steps leading to a respectable, large and pretty country house, which had belonged to some broad-acred count or baron in less hassled times. Eighteenth, with nineteenth-century additions? – I am not that strong on architecture and hadn't time to look: we bustled in with Willem worrying, 'We're a bit behind time.'

Such a country house, peaceable and forgotten, the Dutch gave as asylum – I think it was civilized of us and I'm proud of it – to the Kaiser after 1918, and in the woods round Doorn he lived on (they say he liked to chop firewood) until '42, forgotten by the world. Probably he never really grasped what Hitler was on about. Maybe the Occupiers were tactful for once. One can imagine some officer, of fairly low rank, a major perhaps, giving a stiffish salute. 'Majesty, the Führer has given instructions'. Queen Victoria's nephew saying a courteous word.

I had a moment, on the steps outside, to look about me. Piet had got a rag out to clean his headlamps, and Willem had forgotten his briefcase, before taking my elbow to bustle me in. It has the look of a prison all right. A prison farm, perhaps.

The hallway had still faded remnants of past grandeur; large blotched mirrors in ornate frames and stiff heavy chairs covered in velvet that had been red, against a panelled wall. An ante-room remodelled with office furniture, wood veneer and steel legs, where a middle-aged secretary looked up incurious from behind grey IBM machines. A private office beyond had once been a library perhaps, to judge from glass-fronted bookcases, tall windows giving a lovely light, a big – and good – mahogany desk. 'God,' muttered Willem 'dying for a slash. Just wait here one second.' On the desk were boxes, the usual, with papers for disposal, a few on the blotter awaiting signature. I had time for a quick look. A printed letterhead. 'Doornbos' and in discreetly small lettering below; 'Psychiatric Institute for the Criminally Insane'. Below that, rather larger 'Director: Dr M. Metzger'.

Bert hadn't time for more. He had, surely, guessed from the start, but one hadn't known, and there had been, too, an instant apathy, even a kind of paralysis. A big man had come bustling in. I say bustle because he moved quickly, but softly, light on his feet. The carpet helps, and thick soft soles. He had a big winning smile. Armour plate, all right, but lots of honey spread on it.

I will know them always and forever as the three Ms. I wouldn't want to be thought libellous towards a firm – Minnesota something – who make office equipment; sticky tape, felt markers, that sort. But so they became at once and so remained.

'Do sit down and make yourself comfortable. Yes?' impatient as Willem pelted in, bladder mercifully empty but still clutching the briefcase. 'Please excuse me for one second.'

'Sorry, Doctor – the signature...' What do they call that form – a Body Receipt?

'Thank you – there you are – and do thank your colleague for me – that's most satisfactory – off you go now, you've quite a drive ... where were we?'

'Asylum. "Thornwood". Rather like the Kaiser.' Took him aback for a moment.

'I never thought of that. Before my time. Now that you

mention it, there is some resemblance. Asylum, yes, but in the true sense of refuge, we would say.'

'But I'm not criminally insane. Never been declared such, never been even thought such. Neither of course was the Kaiser, though I believe the viewpoint has been advanced. Interned. Administrative measure. Not free to wander about. Brits, French, wanting to hang him. Public example. We had a more civilized idea.'

'One thing you plainly are and that's intelligent. So, my dear fellow, do allow me to explain. You wish me to make myself clear.'

*

An orderly, white coat but polite, anyhow while the Director's around, has shown me to my room. I have been allowed to phone Willy. Reassurance, quoi? She's a tough woman and she comes of tough stock. She's blitzed but she'll cope. I can rely upon her. For the present, the postcard, which the Jews of Bordeaux wrote home from the transit camp at Drancy. 'All well. Keep up your spirits. Look after the children. Don't worry. Back soon. Love.' That was all they wrote, but with God's help, and Willy's, I will arrange to do better. Dutch or no Dutch. They also had a 'transit camp' – up in the north: Westerbork. 'Je Maintiendrai.'

Time to take stock. This is a well-organized place. A lot of money has been spent. Indeed, at a guess, the germ of the idea might have been a hidey-hole for something governmental, in Cold War times, in case even of Atomic Attack; there are underground passages, and a few of these concrete emplacements resemble bunkers. That scare once past – we are good at not getting overpanicked – somebody got the bright notion that this would do very well as a loony-bin. The criminally insane how are you? I wonder how many of us there are.

Back of the old country house, which has been left much as it was, is a courtyard. The stable block behind has been redesigned with kitchen, refectory, gymnasium, 'therapy'.

From here passages lead to the housing, inmates, staff. Barred window stuff but made comfortable the way a middle-class country hotel would be. I have a pleasant, quite large room and even a little bathroom. A proper table and chair. An armchair. A wardrobe and a chest of drawers. We're all set for a long stay. Not a prison; I haven't been bolted-in. They could do so if they thought fit. An 'open' prison? I don't suppose one escapes much. But first things first. I have a pen, paper. One will be encouraged to write; that's therapeutic. The first thing I think of is a quotation, or like most of my slogans a half-remembered paraphrase, more like.

Immanuel Kant the Weltburger, the old boy from Königsburg, had three questions to ask:

> What can I know?
> What ought I to do?
> What may I hope?

These will do to be going on with.

I felt tired and lay down to rest, was called by a young orderly saying 'Supper time' in a jokey way. I wasn't quick enough to please him. 'Come on Pops. Slow, aren't you.' I'm not having any of that.

'I'm not your Pop and you'll behave properly.' Stung, he said 'Sounds like you need a bit of sedation.'

'Listen, son, I'm aware your job isn't always easy. Perhaps you'd like to look for another, or shall we settle for being polite to one another.'

The dining-room isn't bad at all; tables for two and flowers. Self-service food, remarkably good. I ate by myself. There might have been thirty men, of all ages. Nobody seemed really eccentric, let alone violent, or are they separate? An orderly was on duty to see that things were tidily cleared away. An impression of a quiet, efficient routine. I went back to my room, cleaned my teeth, and took to the book I had brought. Nobody pestered me.

*

The Head M explains that he is a Doctor (always the capital letter here) of General Medicine, puts Bert through a pretty complete physical. Thereafter we all sit while he makes notes, and a dialogue develops.

'This is a perfectly arbitrary proceeding, as you must know.'

'May seem so, but is altogether proper and legally correct.'

'Am I to understand that this is of indefinite duration?'

'My colleague in psychiatry will be seeing you this afternoon.'

'I must ask for clear answers.'

'I am not at liberty to discuss your legal status. Have patience,' quite kindly 'and questions answer themselves. You will find that good advice. By the way, your wife telephoned. She'll be here today. In this building upstairs we have rooms where she can upon occasion and by arrangement stay the night. Not perhaps this early; get yourself settled is the priority.'

'I see. At least, I think I do. I'll have to talk with her.'

'Your health is good for your age. Plenty of exercise. The park is large, and pleasant. Noticing your lifelong interests, you might envisage some gardening. But don't neglect the gym, it's well equipped.'

'I'm here for good, is that what you're telling me?'

Smiling faintly. 'As circumstances may determine.'

'Being neither criminal, nor insane, appears to me the chief circumstance, as already determined.'

'You've made a good recovery from losing the prostate. We'll run a blood test for your PSA level – the local pharmacy fills our prescriptions and we get a lab girl up here as needed. I think I'll hand you on to our Administrator, I know he's anxious to have a word. I'm pleased about your health. I'm always here of course, and any time you wish to consult me you've only to mention it to an orderly. You'll find them a nice crowd. They're hand-picked to be sure. Let me show you the way to Mr Moerdijk's office.'

The second M is a thin, dry, accountancy sort of chap, imbued with his own importance: a very Dutch sort of bureaucrat but maintaining the generally high level of formal politeness.

'Glad to know you. Glad to say, we have very few complaints, but any little initial hitches, we're here to smooth them out. Myself, my most admirable assistant, Mevrouw Maximowitsch, our housekeeper.' I'll get to know this busy lady. To the inmates and the staff she likes to be known as Maxie. She is also often called the Maxiburger, a harmless sort of joke. On occasion, 'interfering nosy old bitch'; inevitable in a place where a hundred people have their being, sealed totally from the outside world. A widow one gathers, lives on the premises, devoted to her calling...

From the financial – and fiscally-minded Mr Moerdijk, I learn that the State of the Netherlands subsidizes 'most generously' the criminally insane. But one must watch the pennies. Quite: I learn that my pension is diverted to this good end; that my private resources are subject-to-deduction by various fiscal bloodsuckers; that 'we live very well' upon condition of balancing our budget. Quite a number of thisses-and-thats, like food, clothing, laundry soap-&-toothpaste stuff, is 'Maxie's' province. Number-two-M, I learn, is also consultable on demand should difficulties arise, but that I am told is seldom.

Lunch; a good lunch. Bert has made Maxie's acquaintance. She is also a dietician and is justifiably proud of the very good food – for Holland – provided. We buy the best raw materials and we make war upon waste. Salads are our speciality. The kitchen staff is 'quite admirable' as well as 'highly trained.' Mr van der Bijl – that's Bert – is a great acquisition. We're going to be proud of him...

After lunch, the third M, Dr Maartens, is the 'Chef' – are there others? – psychiatric wonder-worker. The Grand Vizier, quoi. He's roundish, fattish, more like the Chief Eunuch. Apart from a couple of cleaning-women, strapping souls one is told 'come in by the day', I've seen no women. Are there women? Among the criminally insane there should by rights be a few. Unseen. So is every sign or hint of the black side.

One may guess. Paedophile child-stranglers, axe-murderers and chain-saw dismemberers, runners-amok. The term 'mother-fucker', now worn down to the level of playground scuffle, is here to be taken literally.

In our pre-war childhood the loony-bin was a place of terror. To the adult also. A profound disturbance, a horrified shrinking, an appalling reek of urine and paraldehyde. Modern chemistry, the tiny pill, the colourless prick, the easy level voice, the search for understanding and yes, affection; we are grateful but are we humble? We'd rather see the comic side, telling each other Jewish jokes. Bert teased Dr Maartens (circles round his eyes give him a panda look) with an uproarious happening of only a few weeks back. Selected inmates – 'internees'? – got ferried, one presumes with discretion and security, to the local bordel, since the head psychotherapist had decided that sex would do them all a lot of good. Arranging, frugally, for a discount. One didn't hear what the girls made of these experiments, but all went well until the bill went for settlement to the local social security office, when a monstrous outcry went up about public funds getting diverted for immoral purposes. A very Dutch story. Maartens smiled blandly and said, 'Well, it won't affect you, will it,' which Bert thought rather nasty of him. But as in all the best prisons we have an elegant suite upstairs for wives and companions. 'Have a word with Maxie.' He only needs a cotton-wool beard to be Santa Claus. In Holland the good saint comes from Spain for the festive season, accompanied by a little Moorish page called Zwarte Piet. Black Peter distributes sweeties among good children and had (before the war) a stick for whacking bad ones; threat often made by harassed mums. Maxie is plainly 'Zwarte Piet'. She whizzes about everywhere, popping suddenly out of linen cupboards, with black horn-rims and a black, false and greasy-looking fringe, terrorizing the cleaners. She's nosy, on the whole harmless, even kindly, but I do wish she wouldn't appear so suddenly on such soundless feet.

'Has anyone ever got out of here?' asked Bert, innocent.

'Oh we do have our successes.' Maartens has a lazy pleasant smile. I'll be seeing quite a lot of him, I think. Bert is just recovering from the initial debate as to whether anybody of sound mind could ever seriously view him as criminally insane (who *does* have a sound mind? whatever that is) when an orderly knocked politely and said I was wanted in the parlour. They call it that here too. Some 'morning room' with much of the original chairs and sofa, brocade; that pretty, faded strawberry pink. But one has suspicions about microphones and possible two-way mirrors.

Willy has brought suitcases; clothes, books, various cherished objects to make a longish stay more comfortable. Remind one of home? Above all she's brought her blessed self; pale, gaunt, steely-solid with common sense and clear mind. And her precious gift of undaunted, unwavering loyalty. We will quarrel violently. Hard words will be hurled. But with her there is nothing I will fear. She has talked with lawyers. I was right; there is nothing to be done. I dissuade her, no easy job, from going to argue with an Advocate-General. Arbitrary commitments of this sort are (say the lawyers) infrequent. But legally unattackable.

Said she, 'Well I'm not going to stay home knitting like the sailor's wife.'

Sailor's wife?

'Oh you know; so good and virtuous. While the man is out getting drunk in the bordel in Buenos Aires. People being sorry for her because she's so *courageous*.'

'Is that what I'm doing?' Was one of those sudden frightful rows about to happen?

'A woman's place is with her man. I had a word with this house agent the girls know. I'm quite confident I can find a good flat – housing is easier over this end of Holland – and a lot cheaper. Not in this awful village – the town's only twenty kilometres.' I might not, then, have been able to stop a tear. Welling, as the English put it. Because – but just then the door opened and Maxie came floating in. No knock, no Oh, please forgive me. As though Madam owned the bloody place.

An Englishwoman might have said 'Do you mind awfully?' They are never short of some polite acid formula. Willy's Dutch and despises phrases. Shot to her feet.

'So nice of you to come,' said honeybum. 'I'm delighted to meet you.'

'You're invading my privacy. Get Out.' For two pins she'd have marched to the door and held it open.

'Now you've made me an enemy.'

'Not at all. Put them in their place. You'll never hear a peep out of her. Who is it anyhow?' I told her about 'Zwarte Piet'.

'She might have disappeared up the chimney.' Willy gave a loud crude Dutch laugh, clutched me suddenly and welled.

*

When I was left to myself I welled too. 'I'd better be going,' she'd said. 'I don't much like driving at night as you know. I'll be across tomorrow – no, the day after. We'll work out a routine until I get things organized.' Laughing a lot and crying rather. 'Till then, schat.' 'Schat' means treasure. A frequent term of endearment in this country. Not a word of Willy's as a rule.

I have plenty of time before supper. I have decided to keep a sort of diary. We have, so Anton tells me (I'll come to Anton in a minute) a sort of shop for handy little necessities and here I found an exercise book (writing is encouraged). But I didn't want anyone reading this. Willy is good at thinking things out, and has brought a largish steel lock-box 'for your personal papers and things'. Brows were knitted but my position here is a little bit special. I keep the key attached to

my belt with a shoelace. (They aren't afraid I'll hang myself.)
I gave Willy the second key.

I have deserved all I get. My behaviour was silly, false, and
worse than irresponsible; a breach of faith.

I can't sort out the different sorts of love. The thing is,
they must be true. I loved Carla. At that moment I truly
loved Irene. In a silly, but none the less real on account of
that, compelling if ignoble sense of the word, I even loved
Lalage. Just as when I was a schoolboy I loved – yes –
Veronica. As, a few years on, I would love Verity. It is all
fashioned and twisted together. How do they fix a rope into
place? They don't just twist the fibre together; left to itself
that would slacken and unwind. Willy is the last as she was
first, but both before and after – I don't understand love,
except that it all goes together.

Women – the subject of a couple of lively passages with
Frau Veen and certainly will be again with this man
Maartens, who finds 'the case' a 'fascinating study'. Begins,
like any sound psychologist, with the 'physio' aspect. 'Good,
we don't know a lot about the prostate, beyond the obvious
mechanical role. The whole genito-urinary apparatus; I'd like
to do a bit of work on this. Losing it has the obvious result,
that you no longer get erections. Plainly that so tickled up
your entire nervous system that even months after – as you
tell me this is now dying down – you had these powerfully
male sexual impulses, and then we start crossing this tricky
borderline between neurology and psychology. If I write
down some meaningless piece of jargon like residual psycho-
neurotic symptoms and start looking for a – there are some
well-described if little-understood syndromes – nobody can
say (and this was at the bottom of whatsername, Veen's con-
clusions), that any of this could be called a pointer to clinical
insanity. You've been brought up on this crude rule of
thumb, that a neurosis can be crippling but is basically con-
trollable, whereas a psychotic condition will be overmaster-
ing without appropriate treatment: I'm putting it to you in

simple layman's terms.' Oh, quite! I wasn't legally insane, meaning Veen didn't think so and neither does Maartens. Neither did the Officer of Justice, but legally they were all at sea. Legally they can shut me up in a dump like this: it's a handy bureaucratic way of getting shot of the problem. There is also 'public opinion to consider' – never far from any politician's mind.

I am left with my unshakeable love for my wife. In today's world thought suspect: eccentric enough to be judged unbalanced. A pack of little quackers tell us that the nuclear family is a Bad Idea. I'd certainly call myself feminist enough to agree that subjugation and enslavement go with being human. But don't start telling me that all traditional moral values are a pious fraud because I'll catch you a smartish kick in the goolies before telling you to stop looking in the mirror and loving what you see there. Want to learn, do you, something about life? Stay clear of the intellectuals. Upon which I put the pen down and burst out laughing. Look where it has got me! Even Bert – rather a pompous fellow – can't stop laughing. Look at us writing it all down! Maartens doing his damnedest to find some insanity, since that's what he's paid for. I'd do better writing it all with my finger. Intellectual reasoning, rational argument – these are exactly what we need to discard. God forgive me – scribbling away with a Bic ballpoint bought in the loony-bin's little shop.

I know of a man who defeated the world, and the first of his gift is laughter. Mexican Indian – did well, by god, not to show his face in Holland: they'd have had him in here. His chronicler (remarkable example of the imperfect narrator) always gives him the title of respect in a Spanish-speaking country; Don Juan. It's the first of the jokes: we define donjuanism as collecting, seducing, subjecting, despising, discarding a great many women, compulsively, out of fear and loathing. Not all that rare; one wonders whether there are any in here.

This one is a sorcerer; again, lacking a better word. In

trying to describe his thinking and doing, vocabulary is a perpetual problem. We just don't *have* words, since all ours have been designed for logical intellectual processes. Willy is quite a good example. She certainly does not lack intelligence. But her instinct for things that we know of, but understand hardly at all, is strong, and she suffers from the lack of means of expressing thought. To illustrate, her green fingers, born in her, very likely hereditary in her blood. Why does a plant grow for her which would sulk in other hands? Does it listen to her? Is it happy in her company? I am a trained, diploma'd, experienced plantsman and she can make a fool of me.

Don Juan is no necromancer. He does astonishing, incomprehensible things but black arts do not enter into design or execution. He speaks of power – a villainous, a nefarious word since it connotes ignoble purpose. He does manipulate people but that is his rule. His knowledge is an unbroken chain, which must be handed on.

I am going a little too fast. Don Juan can be in two places at once; I cannot. I am rooted, corporeally, in a village in Holland, situate in a cold and acid moorland; I must see what I can do with the acid-loving plants. Rhododendron has been planted here, and azalea; a good start in the past may give shelter enough from wind to allow of more ambitious effort. My imagination can range but I am landlocked. I have travelled in Arizona and New Mexico but Don Juan's world is difficult for me to enter: I am, too, a European. His world ranges far back of the Spanish Conquest in the New World, but enslavement of his people by the Conquistador has most profoundly modified his being. We Dutch managed to fight, to resist, eventually to throw off the power of Spain. But we had modern, European weapons, and we understood the Spanish; were they not our brothers? As Indians could not. I have much in common with them, but my present duty is to understand the Dutch. As for instance Anton.

He is an orderly; perhaps a little older, quieter, greyer

than the run of them. They have all some psychiatric formation – are we not the criminally insane? The State of the
Netherlands is highly conscientious. Two at least have mas-
seurs' training. All have something extra; the gym instructor,
the swimming monitor have their diplomas. They are, I suppose, fairly well paid. They are expected to take on some
extra responsibility. One is in charge of the library, which
isn't bad at all, if a bit heavy with the exotic travel, while the
'reading room' is respectably equipped with weeklies – and
to be sure the *National Geographic.* Welcome; I can easily get
addicted to butterflies and polar bears.

Anton's thing is music: we have even a piano. Nobody
plays on it but him, and surprisingly Mr Moerdijk (rather
well), but it's there, to show that we are after all civilized
people. The fact of – nearly – all these folk being very nice;
of much pains being taken (Maxie giving herself trouble to
be helpful though I notice she keeps well out of Willy's way),
doesn't alter matters. It was decided that I should be put out
of society. 'Out of harm's way'. That is a basic injustice, isn't
it? But there's nothing I can do. Or there is, perhaps, but it
will be very slow, and extremely difficult.

The companion of my first meal has taken a fancy for
sharing my table. He seems to enjoy my company, laughs
heartily at any scrap of talk. He seems quite normal except
that his eyes blink continually. I can never make out what he
did in his former existence; some sort of small shopkeeper?
There is something precise, as it were prim, about his
speech; vaguely ecclesiastical? An unfrocked priest?

'What did they get you for?' he asked suddenly.

'I'm supposed to have killed a girl.'

'Ah.' Plainly pleased; the eyes did not 'light up' because
they always are lit up, in an odd mechanical sparkle. 'I've
killed several. Women...' Women what? Shouldn't be allowed? Are the curse of existence? Have been my downfall?
I had better not ask, and do not pursue the subject.

'We have a little club,' said Anton. 'Just for listening to

records. Sometimes jazz, might be eight or ten of us. Others less. Tonight we're going to do some Schubert songs, not so many there.'

The most that can be said for my fellow-travellers is that they put up with me. Tolerance is a key word around here. Mark, they'd better, because any aggressive discontent meets with a standard chemical response: sedation. Some of these worthy people are up to here in the feel-good pills.

I walk about, a good deal in the park, which is large. The vast majority here prefer to sit. Television is their great stand-by. Not a moment without the jolly song and dance. 'Tingel-tangel' – a good Dutch word. Authority allows Anton some real music.

Sometimes he and I are alone and we choose themes to-gether; polite of him since I know nothing and he knows a lot. I have been perhaps three times in the Concertgebouw; hideous but marvellous acoustic. It is among the world's very best and I went like most people out of snobbery. I am begin-ning to learn what I have missed.

Singing Schubert – I like the women better than the men. I said as much: Anton smiled. 'You love women. We must have an opera season.' Anton likes this. With much naïve astonishment I remarked that these operas are all about the gallantry and fidelity of cheated, betrayed, abandoned women. He smiles a bit at my innocence.

'But yes – opera is about Love. Not just Mozart and Verdi – Berg too, Janáček. Just so,' in his dry way.

Schubert – one does wish he hadn't liked so many trashy verses; spring greenery, maidens praying. 'Ständchen' is wonderful 'Leise, leise.' Moving...

Has Anton been looking at my legal dossier? I asked about 'the Dwarf'. This song – he kills the Queen and she accepts it. I suppose naturally, this has a particular message for me. He tells her that only her death can give him peace and she says 'May you never feel pain from my death'. He kisses her and ties a red ribbon round her neck.

'But why,' I asked, 'are they in a boat?'

'Listen to the last line,' said Anton. 'He will never again land on any shore.'

'Litanei' I love but my favourite is from – of all people – Sir Walter Scott, and a 'maiden's prayer' at that...

We're close to the German border, here. Lot of German words in the spoken Dutch; just as you will hear Dutch expressions in their language, as far down as Köln; our slice of the Rheinland world. Oh well, I'm half German myself.

In Amsterdam we tend to jeer. Much as do the English, about German sentimentality. Ro-man-tic. Forever shedding tears about the woods and the water. Not sure I don't prefer myself, the early nineteenth century to the world of today. I don't have any shares in Daimler-Benz. Poor old Bert, a century out of date.

I struggle with the metaphysics. The demon's magic bullet, in *Freischütz*, strikes Agathe down; she is the dove which her lover is told to shoot. She is saved, and he is redeemed, and the demon defeated, by her innocence, her purity. I ought to understand, if anyone ever did, this antique legend of the German forest. These women's voices call me out of myself.

Anton understands. But he is concerned with the sheer musicianship, of which I know little. I dramatize. Maria Callas driving home the knife, hissing 'Here is the kiss of Tosca' – ridiculous; it's a paper-knife from the writing-desk. The moment becomes stupendous when she places the candles round Scarpia's body, and prays for his wicked soul. Still more, that moment when Leonora stops the assassin, saying so simply 'I am his wife'...

'Comes handy, that trumpet call from the tower,' said Anton drily. 'Which does not diminish its sheer magnificence. And busty sopranos dressed in boys' clothes – familiar convention of the period. It's the music which gets us.' I suppose so. 'Octavian making love to the Marschallin would be just two lesbians playing with each other if it wasn't for

Dr Strauss.' He is being kindly; he saw my tears pouring down.

I am working at these books Willy has brought me, tatty old paperbacks dug out of second-hand shops; a remarkable effort to have found them and still more to have imagined the idea. They too are remarkable. The first three are pretty easy; designed to sell, to appeal to a wide public. The first is all about psychedelic plants, hot news in the sixties in California, but they do not play large role in this metaphysical system, and while expert in their use Juan employs them essentially to jolt his apprentice loose from his mistakenly rational and intellectual standpoint. One cannot blame Carlos; he is a highly intelligent and trained graduate student in anthropology; a typical 'university-formed' taker of the most scrupulous field notes; a procedure which makes Don Juan laugh, mercilessly if never uncontrollably. In the two next books many basic dogmas appear. Obliterate personal history. Abandon self-importance. Combat all self-indulgence. Lessons for myself. But there is still a considerable showmanship element. Jugglery, thinks poor Carlitos, when his car refuses to start – disappears altogether – and when sorcerers can defy gravity, can fly, can turn the entire physical world into illusion which the battered boy imagines to be delusion.

But with the next three books layers of infolded, intricate, abstract thought begin – petal by petal – to become apparent. Carlos must learn, through pain and sorrow, most bitter, that he has himself unknown and unmastered powers; that he is part of an age-old continuing pattern. That he was not alone; that he had without knowing it nine teachers and that without realizing it he is one of nine apprenticed learners. I must abbreviate here, because these patterns are extremely intricate: they are indeed a fundamental challenge to everything we have ever thought of, ever believed, a negation of our every concept.

Indeed it becomes, as one digs deeper, pretty esoteric, and

I wouldn't know whether I would ever have the patience and the strength of purpose to tussle with it. Carlos says that his apprenticeship lasted fourteen years. It has too the disadvantage of all written instructions – like learning how to be a motor mechanic out of a handbook: nothing can ever replace the man who stands behind you saying 'Look, try it this way' ... Also, Juan has an Indian mind. To survive in the desert needed delicate skills of hunting, stalking; stillness, invisibility. These Indian peoples (one catches glimpses of times hundreds of years before the Conquest, of the Maya and Toltec civilizations) were mercilessly pursued and exterminated. Replaced in our European context the closest parallel might be that of the tziganes, the gypsies hunted down by the Hitler regime. One will not easily enter into the separateness, the apartness, of such a man.

The basic outline is simple: the first step towards becoming a warrior is that nothing we view as essential – no possession, no attitude – is held to have the slightest importance. And that learning laughter we will fear no hardship, no setback, no defeat, no humiliation.

Juan is full of surprises. How come that he speaks a beautiful articulate Spanish, expressive of the most complex abstract thought, and has a sophisticated taste in poetry? How does this old starveling (he must be close to eighty) have the physique and endurance of youth, and in the hardest condition? How does this primitive peasant have hand-made suits, and appear at ease in urban conditions of wealth and comfort? It is certain that he is no juggler or charlatan, and that his world is of incomparable richness; a knowledge and a wisdom perfectly controlled.

We learn that he has friends and helpers, both men and women, nine in all, sorcerers like himself. Carlos learns, bewildered, that he is regarded as Don Juan's successor, that he too must assemble a similar group, and that after his teachers have left this earth (they do not die but disappear) his duty will be to pursue the path of knowledge, and come eventually to form a further group of apprentices. In his band are three boys he knows and is friendly with; three young girls whom he can barely remember meeting. Primitive, ignorant villagers but having strange powers, surprising him. Mysteriously he is responsible for them. More enigmatic are three further figures who seem to know more than he does.

Hereabout, I have struck upon a major obstacle to my own efforts at understanding.

One of these figures is familiar to him. A fat stupid slut who picked up a living doing washing, whose bulimia was such she'd eat the throwaways from garbage; smelly and horrible, known to all as 'La Gorda', which is Fatso. Astoundingly she is now a slim, muscular and beautiful young woman, further in knowledge than himself, calm and in perfect possession of herself. 'Don Juan healed me,' she says laconically. Vaguely he grasps that she will be a companion, a helper, a comforter. Nowise a sexual relation. 'But, but,' he stammers (the fat girl, casually abused, had two children). 'They no longer exist,' Maria Elena tells him calmly. 'I have effaced them.' She surprises him, and me. Standing, she cocks a leg up on a chair, pulls up her skirt. She has no knickers on. 'Look at my vagina,' she tells him. 'I have never born children.' Suspension of belief here is pretty breathtaking. Don Juan's powers are great, but this . . .

Her explanation is of great interest. Sorcerers perceive human beings as an egg shaped luminosity. Sexual relations dull and diminish the light. To have born – to have fathered, as Carlos has, a child, to which he is most profoundly attached – creates as she tells him calmly, an ugly and crippling black hole in the luminosity, a great and possibly permanent handicap. Juan has patched her, says Maria Elena. She is as good as new, now. But he is not.

I have the greatest possible difficulty in assimilating this. I have, to be sure, two children by my legally-married and most ineradicably-beloved wife. Every bodily, sexual relation I have ever had is of the greatest importance: scarcely ever have I had a useless, a meaningless, a worthless physical union with a woman I have known, as who hasn't, prostitutes. And even then it isn't, it just isn't, a throwaway. But to bear a child and then to say it no longer exists, it has no importance – can even Juan do this? Often enough, during apprenticeship, the boy Carlitos stuck fast on something of the sort. He managed? To a man of my age, I beg leave to call it impossible.

I suppose that this will forever rule me out of Don Juan's world. Me – am I quite simply too Dutch? We are called a hardheaded crowd, not like these simpleminded Germans. I hesitate always to use the word 'race' (source of too many ugly confrontations). True it is that when Angles, Saxons, invaded England (were they fortunate to have been spared Goths and Huns, the Vandals and the rest, who have so vivified Europe?) we stayed obstinate in our sour soggy corner. 'My name is little Jock Elliott and who dares meddle with me?'

I cannot follow this path. To reject my children, as though they had never been? I am perfectly at liberty to be annoyed by them; to be indeed ashamed of them as they are of myself. My personal history – most of it would be Bert's, and to lose that I feel would cost me little. My wife: the question does not arise; the decision is not mine to take, any more than it would be hers. A good example of a fact well known in metaphysics: the whole is greater than the sum of the parts.

The women I have known ... and the first, in time, of course my own mother. Of whom I know so little; Jan, by nature silent on personal subjects, was most so on the subject of his own wife. That she came out of the East: was she even German? In history a great many people have come out of the East. The Germans themselves have a good deal of difficulty with the question. In most places the matter of nationality is settled by a tenet going back to Roman law.

Who after all were Romans? – the phrase *Civis Romanus sum* applied to some remarkable oddities, like Etruscans. This, the *droit de sol*, has the merit of being beautifully simple. Born on Roman ground you're Roman. If through your parents you laid claim to some other nationality, well and good, we take a generous view. Most people get on well enough with this rule of thumb and if you happen to have two passports so much the better; you never know when they might come in handy.

But not Germans. Here the *droit de sang* applies: blood; they want you to have German blood, and to prove it. Which has given the Bundesrepublik a lot of trouble in recent years. I don't know how far back it goes. Around what time did people like the Quadi and the Marcomani start saying they were German?

I don't think my mother knew herself. In my own early childhood the question didn't interest me. I believe she might have had one of those refugee 'Nansen' passports. She had been wandering ever since she could remember, and escaped from Germany in the Kaiser's time: he wasn't the only one to settle down in places like Doorn. Jan picked her up. She knew her name, which was Tatiana, commonplace enough. Since the Dutch clip everything back to the minimum she was always known as Tiana. A quiet, pretty name for a quiet and secretive woman. I have a very early memory – of what exactly, and how early? Of camellia petals floating upon water. What is buried here? What is glimpsed? But that is what 'Tiana' means to me; camellias. I have loved them ever since.

She died of pneumonia; I was still a boy; 1944, the Hunger Winter we have always called it in Holland. Hardship and malnutrition; eroded resistance; there were very many such. I have a photograph, in faded sepia, of a young, grave, wise face.

In the village she was called 'the Moffin', the German-woman; no especial cruelty. The usual mix of coarse peasant humour and the crude xenophobia of little provincials. Odd word: German officers were supposed to look like Erich von Stroheim, to wear monocles, and to warm their hands in fur muffs. To this day the tourists (many come holidaying to our Nordsee beaches) are always known as the Moffen. But a young girl, called the Moffinetje – as though our milkmaids were of a superior race – will feel the snub, the disdain.

Well, I'll understand it all one day. Soon. Often I feel I'm on the verge – that I'll understand tomorrow.

Around the time that Carlitos finds companionship with Maria Elena he discovers that much of his memory has been obliterated; it is another of Don Juan's powers. There has been another world in which he had his being, and in this he has known a woman truly – truly what? Not 'his'. But with her he has shared immeasurable joy and peace. She was not old; she had no age. Wisdom made her seem older. For some while, for how long he does not know, they were together; she taught him, she loved him; he understood. But she has gone. The rule is that she leaves this world, together with the older group of teachers. But one day he will find her again.

Surely there is some echo here in *The Magic Flute* which Anton has been explaining to me. Tamino – Pamina – they must pass through fearful ordeals. The sorcerer, Sarastro, has imposed this upon them. And there is a woman, the Queen of the Night, a very beautiful and very terrible woman. I have not got it very clear yet. The clownings of Papageno the bird-catcher are of metaphysical nature; yes. These rituals are in some sense parallelled in the Indian world of the Mexican desert. Juan was known to the apprentices as the Nagual, a rare and precious kind of luminous being. Carlos learns that he too is a nagual, and that for a brief moment he has known his other half, the nagual-woman, source of every delight the spirit encompasses. But she has gone away, and he must stay behind. In a bleak world; so much to learn and now no guidance.

He does have a companion, a wise girl, true and good. But they remain apart. Is this going to be the harshest of his tests, that he is – for how long? – apart; alone?

I found a magazine in the reading-room. There was a brief explanatory text, for the lummox-readers like myself, about an exhibition of pictures, by a little-known seventeenth-century painter called Georges de la Tour. There are also good colour reproductions of some of his subjects. For example, one of those fairground scenes, familiar I think in Brueghel and other Flamand painters, in which travelling charlatans, spot-the lady men, pea-under-the-cup men, plucked innocent country gulls like myself.

This one is a Fortune-Teller. A young girl, pretty and demure with the most wonderful sly eyes, is picking the pocket of some provincial gull while he listens entranced to the glittering tale of his Fortune. It caught my eye; it struck me that she had more than a passing resemblance to Lalage. I am wrong, I hope, as well as unfair. I do not believe Lalage to be a bad girl, though she may well be a thief of men's fortunes.

But there is more important. The text explains poorly; one would hardly expect anything better in a popular magazine. Reduced to basic vocabulary, Monsieur de la Tour like other painters of the time (Caravaggio gets mentioned) was much interested in light and especially in shadows. Thus, quite a lot of his subjects are lit by a single source. One – I've seen it before, it is certainly famous – shows a man in prison, humble, emaciated; one would say resigned. But a woman bends over him, to console. She carries a candle, symbol of hope and of faith; she herself is charity. Is she his wife? She is dressed as a woman; it cannot be Leonora.

I think I know who it is. One day – quite soon – I'll know, for sure.

This year, the spring is taking a long time to come. I am looking forward to making a garden.